HAVE YOU EVER had a friend turn on you? Just totally transform from someone you thought you knew into someone . . . else? I'm not talking about your boyfriend from nursery school who grows up and gets gawky and zitty, or your friend from camp who you've got nothing to say to when she comes to visit you over Christmas break. No. I'm talking about your soul mate. The girl you know everything about. Who knows everything about you. One day she turns around and is a completely different person.

Well, it happens. It happened in Rosewood.

ALSO BY SARA SHEPARD

Perfect

PRETTY LITTLE LIARS

Sara Shepard

HARPER TEEN
An Imprint of HarperCollins Publishers

HarperTeen is an imprint of HarperCollins Publishers.

Perfect
Copyright © 2007 by Alloy Entertainment and Sara Shepard

Library of Congress Cataloging-in-Publication Data
Shepard, Sara, 1977–
   Perfect : a pretty little liars novel / Sara Shepard. – 1st ed.
      p. cm.
   Summary: After their missing friend's body is found and another of
their friends commits suicide, four former best friends live in fear of
their secrets being exposed by someone who is stalking them via their
cell phones.
   ISBN 978-0-06-314461-3
   [1. Secrets–Fiction. 2. Conduct of life–Fiction. 3. Friendship–
Fiction. 4. High schools–Fiction. 5. Schools–Fiction. 6. Mystery and
detective stories.] I. Title.
PZ7.S54324Pe 2007   2007020830
[Fic]–dc22   CIP
         AC
                  Typography by Andrea C. Uva

     22 23 24 25 26   PC/LSCH   10 9 8 7 6 5 4 3 2 1
                         ❖
            Revised paperback edition, 2022

To ALI

Look and you will find it—what is unsought will go undetected.

—SOPHOCLES

PERFECT

KEEP YOUR FRIENDS CLOSE. . . .

Have you ever had a friend turn on you? Just totally transform from someone you thought you knew into someone . . . else? I'm not talking about your boyfriend from nursery school who grows up and gets gawky and ugly and zitty, or your friend from camp whom you've got nothing to say to when she comes to visit you over Christmas break, or even a girl in your clique who suddenly breaks away and turns goth or into one of those granola Outward Bound kids. No. I'm talking about your soul mate. The girl you know everything about. Who knows everything about you. One day she turns around and is a completely different person.

Well, it happens. It happened in Rosewood.

"Watch it, Aria. Your face is going to freeze like that." Spencer Hastings unwrapped an orange Popsicle and slid it into her mouth. She was referring to the drunk-pirate face her best friend, Aria Montgomery, was making as she tried to get her phone's video function to focus.

"You sound like my mom, Spence." Emily Fields laughed, adjusting her T-shirt, which had a picture of a baby chicken in goggles on it and said INSTANT SWIM CHICK! JUST ADD WATER! Her friends had forbidden Emily from wearing her goofy swimming T-shirts—"Instant Swim Dork! Just add loser!" Alison DiLaurentis had joked when Emily walked in.

"Your mom says that too?" Hanna Marin asked, throwing away her green-stained Popsicle stick. Hanna always ate faster than anyone else. *"Your face will freeze that way,"* she mimicked.

Alison looked Hanna up and down and cackled. "Your mom should've warned you that your *butt* would freeze that way."

Hanna's face fell as she pulled down her pink-and-white striped T-shirt—she'd borrowed it from Ali, and it kept riding up, revealing a white strip of her stomach. Alison tapped Hanna's shin with her flip-flop. "Just joking."

It was a Friday night in May near the end of seventh grade, and best friends Alison, Hanna, Spencer, Aria, and Emily were gathered in Spencer's family's plushly deco-rated family room, with the Popsicle box, a big bottle of cherry vanilla Diet Dr Pepper, and their cell phones splayed out on the coffee table. A month ago, Ali had come to school with the latest iPhone model, and the others had rushed out to buy their own that very day. They all had pink leather cases to match Ali's, too—well, all except for Aria, whose case was made of pink mohair. She'd knitted it herself.

Aria fiddled with the phone to zoom in and out. "And anyway, my face isn't going to freeze like this. I'm concentrating on setting up this shot. This is for posterity. For when we become famous."

"Well, we all know *I'm* going to get famous." Alison thrust back her shoulders and turned her head to the side, revealing her swanlike neck.

"Why are you going to be famous?" Spencer challenged, sounding bitchier than she probably meant to.

"I'm going to have my own show. I'll be a smarter, cuter Kendall Jenner."

Spencer snorted. But Emily pursed her pale lips, considering, and Hanna nodded, truly believing. This was *Ali*. She wouldn't stay here in Rosewood, Pennsylvania, for long. Sure, Rosewood was glamorous by most standards—all its residents looked like walk-on models for a *Town & Country* photo shoot—but they all knew Ali was destined for greater things.

She'd plucked them out of oblivion a year and a half ago to be her best friends. With Ali by their sides, they had become *the* girls of Rosewood Day, the private school they attended. They had such power now—to deem who was cool and who wasn't, to throw the best parties, to nab the best seats in study hall, to run for student office and win by an overwhelming number of votes. Well, that last one only applied to Spencer. Aside from a few twists and turns—and accidentally blinding Jenna Cavanaugh, which they tried their hardest not to think about—their lives had transformed from passable to perfect.

"How about we film a talk show?" Aria suggested. She considered herself the friends' official filmmaker—one of the many things she wanted to be when she grew up was the next Jean-Luc Godard, some abstract French director. "Ali, you're famous. And Spencer, you're the interviewer."

"I'll be the makeup girl," Hanna volunteered, rooting through her backpack to find her polka-dotted vinyl makeup bag.

"I'll do hair." Emily pushed her reddish-blond bob behind her ears and rushed to Ali's side. "You have gorgeous hair, *chérie*," she said to Ali in a faux-French accent.

Ali slid her Popsicle out of her mouth. "Doesn't *chérie* mean *girlfriend*?"

The others were quick to laugh, but Emily paled. "No, that's *petite amie*." Lately, Em was sensitive when Ali made jokes at her expense. She never used to be.

"Okay," Aria said, making sure the shot was level. "You guys ready?"

Spencer flopped on the couch and placed a rhinestone tiara left over from a New Year's party on her head. She'd been carrying the crown around all night.

"You can't wear that," Ali snapped.

"Why not?" Spencer adjusted the crown so it was straight.

"Because. If anything, *I'm* the princess."

"Why do *you* always get to be the princess?" Spencer muttered under her breath. A nervous ripple swept through the others. Spencer and Ali weren't getting along, and no one knew why.

Ali's cell phone let out a bleat. She looked down and tilted the phone the other way so no one else could see. "Sweet." Her fingers flew across the keypad as she typed a text.

"Who are you writing to?" Emily's voice sounded eggshell-thin and small.

"Can't tell. Sorry." Ali didn't look up.

"You can't tell?" Spencer was irate. "What do you mean you can't tell?"

Ali glanced up. "Sorry, *princess*. You don't have to know *everything*." Ali set her phone on the leather couch. "Don't start filming yet, Aria. I have to pee." She dashed out of Spencer's family room toward the hall bathroom, plopping her Popsicle stick in the trash as she went.

Once they heard the bathroom door close, Spencer was the first to speak. "Don't you just want to *kill* her sometimes?"

The others flinched. They never bad-mouthed Ali. It was as blasphemous as burning the Rosewood Day official flag on school property, or admitting that Chris Hemsworth really wasn't *that* cute—that he was actually kind of old and creepy.

Of course, on the inside, they felt a little differently. This spring, Ali hadn't been around as much. She'd gotten closer with the high school girls on her JV field hockey squad and never invited Aria, Emily, Spencer, or Hanna to join them at lunch or come with them to the King James Mall.

And Ali had begun to keep secrets. Secret texts, secret phone calls, secret giggles about things she wouldn't tell them. Sometimes they'd see Ali was active on Instagram just minutes before, but when they DM'd her, she didn't respond. They'd bared their souls to Ali—telling her things they hadn't told the others, things they didn't want *anyone* to know—and they expected her to reciprocate. Hadn't Ali made them all promise a year ago, after the horrible thing with Jenna happened, that they would tell one another everything, absolutely *everything,* until the end of time?

The girls hated to think of what eighth grade would be like if things kept going like this. But it didn't mean they hated *Ali*.

Aria wound a piece of long, dark hair around her fingers and laughed nervously. "Kill her because she's so cute, maybe." Her finger hovered over the red circle to start recording.

"And because she wears a size zero," Hanna added.

"That's what I meant." Spencer glanced at Ali's phone,

which was wedged between two couch cushions. "Want to read her texts?"

"I do," Hanna whispered.

Emily stood up from her perch on the couch's arm. "I don't know. . . ." She started inching away from Ali's phone, as if just being close to it incriminated her.

Spencer scooped up Ali's cell. She looked curiously at the blank screen. "C'mon. Don't you want to know who texted her?"

"It was probably just Katy," Emily whispered, referring to one of Ali's hockey friends. "You should put it down, Spence."

Aria walked toward Spencer. "Let's do it."

They gathered around. Spencer turned the phone over and pushed a button. "It's locked."

"Do you know her password?" Aria asked, still filming.

"Try her birthday," Hanna whispered. She took the phone from Spencer and punched in the digits. The screen didn't change. "What do I do now?"

They heard Ali's voice before they saw her. "What are you guys doing?"

Spencer dropped Ali's phone back onto the couch. Hanna stepped back so abruptly, she banged her shin against the coffee table.

Ali stomped through the door to the family room, her eyebrows knitted together. "Were you looking at my phone?"

"Of course not!" Hanna cried.

"We were," Emily admitted, sitting on the couch, then standing up again. Aria shot her a look and then held up the phone, which was still in video mode. She hid behind the camera lens.

But Ali was no longer paying attention. Spencer's older sister, Melissa, a senior in high school, burst into the Hastings's kitchen from the garage. A takeout bag from Otto, a restaurant near the Hastings's neighborhood, hung from her wrist. Her adorable boyfriend, Ian, was with her. Ali stood up straighter. Spencer smoothed her dirty-blond hair and straightened her tiara.

Ian stepped into the family room. "Hey, girls."

"Hi," Spencer said in a loud voice. "How are you, Ian?"

"I'm cool." Ian smiled at Spencer. "Cute crown."

"Thanks!" Spencer fluttered her coal-black eyelashes.

Ali rolled her eyes. "Be a little more obvious," she singsonged under her breath.

But it was hard not to crush on Ian. He had curly blond hair, perfect white teeth, and stunning blue eyes, and none of them could forget the recent soccer game where he'd changed his shirt midquarter and, for five glorious seconds, they'd gotten a full-on view of his naked chest. It was almost universally believed that his gorgeousness was wasted on Melissa, who was totally prudish and acted way too much like Mrs. Hastings, Spencer's mother.

Ian plopped down on the edge of the couch near Ali.

"So, what are you girls doing?"

"Oh, not much," Aria said, adjusting the focus. "Making a film."

"A film?" Ian looked amused. "Can I be in it?"

"Of course," Spencer said quickly. She plopped down on the other side of him.

Ian grinned into the phone screen. "So what are my lines?"

"It's a talk show," Spencer explained. She glanced at Ali, gauging her reaction, but Ali didn't respond. "I'm the host. You and Ali are my guests. I'll do you first."

Ali let out a sarcastic snort and Spencer's cheeks flamed as pink as her Ralph Lauren T-shirt. Ian let the reference pass by. "Okay. Interview away."

Spencer sat up straighter on the couch, crossing her muscular legs just like a talk show host. She picked up the pink microphone from Hanna's karaoke machine and held it under her chin. "Welcome to the Spencer Hastings show. For my first question—"

"Ask him who his favorite teacher at Rosewood is," Aria called out.

Ali perked up. Her blue eyes glittered. "That's a good question for you, Aria. You should ask him if he wants to *hook up* with any of his teachers. In vacant parking lots."

Aria's mouth fell open. Hanna and Emily, who were standing off to the side near the credenza, exchanged a confused glance.

"All my teachers are dogs," Ian said slowly, not getting whatever was happening.

"Ian, can you *please* help me?" Melissa made a clattering noise in the kitchen.

"One sec," Ian called out.

"*Ian.*" Melissa sounded annoyed.

"I got one." Spencer tossed her long blond hair behind her ears. She was loving that Ian was paying more attention to them than to Melissa. "What would your ultimate graduation gift be?"

"*Ian,*" Melissa called through her teeth, and Spencer glanced at her sister through the wide French doors to the kitchen. The light from the fridge cast a shadow across her face. "I. Need. Help."

"Easy," Ian answered, ignoring her. "I'd want a base-jumping lesson."

"Base-jumping?" Aria called. "What's that?"

"Parachuting from the top of a building," Ian explained.

As Ian told a story about Hunter Queenan, one of his friends who had base-jumped, the girls leaned forward eagerly. Aria focused the iPhone lens on Ian's jaw, which looked hewn out of stone. Her eyes flickered for a moment to Ali. She was sitting next to Ian, staring off into space. Was Ali *bored*? She probably had better things to do—that text was probably about plans with her glamorous older friends.

Aria glanced again at Ali's cell phone, which was resting on the cushion of the couch next to her arm. What was she hiding from them? What was she up to?

Don't you sometimes want to kill her? Spencer's question floated through Aria's brain as Ian rambled on. Deep down, she knew they all felt that way. It might be better if Ali were just . . . gone, instead of leaving them behind.

"So Hunter said he got the most amazing rush when he base-jumped," Ian concluded. "Better than anything. Including sex."

"Ian," Melissa warned.

"That sounds incredible." Spencer looked to Ali on the other side of Ian. "Doesn't it?"

"Yes." Ali looked sleepy, almost like she was in a trance. "Incredible."

The rest of the week had been a blur: final exams, planning parties, more get-togethers, and more tension. And then, on the evening of the last day of seventh grade, Ali went missing. Just like that. One minute she was there, the next . . . gone.

The police scoured Rosewood for clues. They questioned the four girls separately, asking if Ali had been acting strangely or if anything unusual had happened recently. They all thought long and hard. The night she disappeared had been strange—she'd been hypnotizing them and had run out of the barn after she and Spencer had a stupid fight about the blinds and just . . . *never came back*. But had there been other strange nights? They considered the night they tried to read Ali's texts, but not for very long—after Ian and Melissa left, Ali had snapped out of her funk. They'd had a dance contest and played with Hanna's karaoke machine. The mystery texts on Ali's phone had been forgotten.

Next, the cops asked if they thought anyone close to Ali might have wanted to hurt her. Hanna, Aria, and Emily all thought of the same thing: *Don't you sometimes want to kill her?* Spencer had snarled. But no. She'd been kidding. Hadn't she?

"Nobody wanted to hurt Ali," Emily said, pushing the worry out of her mind.

"Absolutely not," Aria answered too, in her own separate interview, darting her eyes away from the burly cop sitting next to her on the porch swing.

"I don't think so," Hanna said in her interview, fiddling with the pale blue string bracelet Ali had made for them after Jenna's accident. "Ali wasn't that close with many people. Only us. And we all loved her to death."

Sure, Spencer seemed angry with Ali. But really, deep down, weren't they all? Ali was perfect—beautiful, smart, sexy, irresistible—and she was ditching them. Maybe they did hate her for it. But that didn't mean any of them wanted her gone.

It's amazing what you don't see, though. Even when it's right in front of your eyes.

1

SPENCER'S HARD WORK PAYS OFF

Spencer Hastings should have been sleeping at six thirty on Monday morning. Instead, she was sitting in a therapist's blue-and-green waiting room, feeling a little like she was trapped inside an aquarium. Her older sister, Melissa, was sitting on an emerald-colored chair opposite her. Melissa looked up from her *Principles of Emerging Markets* textbook—she was in an MBA program at the University of Pennsylvania—and gave Spencer a motherly smile.

"I've felt so much *clearer* since I started seeing Dr. Evans," purred Melissa, whose appointment was right after Spencer's. "You're going to love her. She's incredible."

Of course she's incredible, Spencer thought nastily. Melissa would find anyone willing to listen to her for a whole uninterrupted hour amazing.

"But she might come on a little strong for you, Spence," Melissa warned, slapping her book closed. "She's going to tell you things about yourself you don't want to hear."

Spencer shifted her weight. "I'm not six. I can take criticism."

Melissa gave Spencer a tiny eyebrow raise, clearly indicating that she wasn't so sure. Spencer hid behind her *Philadelphia* magazine, wondering again why she was here. Spencer's mother, Veronica, had booked her an appointment with a therapist—*Melissa's* therapist—after Spencer's old friend Alison DiLaurentis had been found dead and Toby Cavanaugh died by suicide. Spencer suspected the appointment was also meant to sort through why Spencer had hooked up with Melissa's boyfriend, Wren. Spencer was doing fine though. Really. And wasn't going to her worst enemy's therapist like taking fashion advice from that cousin who always hated you. Spencer feared she'd probably come out of her very first shrink session with the mental-health equivalent of a hideous outfit.

Just then, the office door swung open, and a petite blond woman wearing tortoiseshell glasses, a black tunic, and black pants poked her head out.

"Spencer?" the woman said. "I'm Dr. Evans. Come in."

Spencer strode into Dr. Evans's office, which was spare and bright and thankfully nothing like the waiting room. It contained a black leather couch and a gray suede chair. A large desk held a phone, a stack of manila folders, a chrome gooseneck lamp, and one of those weighted drinking-bird toys that Mr. Craft, the earth science teacher, loved. Dr. Evans settled into the suede chair and gestured for Spencer to sit on the couch.

"So," Dr. Evans said, once they were comfy, "I've heard a lot about you."

Spencer wrinkled her nose and glanced toward the waiting room. "From Melissa, I guess?"

"From your mom." Dr. Evans opened to the first page of a red notebook. "She says that you've had some turmoil in your life, especially lately."

Spencer fixed her gaze on the end table next to the couch. It held a candy dish, a box of Kleenex—of *course*—and one of those pegboard IQ games, the kind where you jumped the pegs over one another until there was only one peg remaining. There used to be one of those in the DiLaurentis family den; she and Ali had solved it together, meaning they were both geniuses. "I think I'm coping," she muttered. "I'm not, like, suicidal."

"A close friend died. A neighbor, too. That must be hard."

Spencer let her head rest on the back of the couch and looked up. It looked like the bumpily plastered ceiling had acne. She probably needed to talk to someone—it wasn't like she could talk to her family about Ali, Toby, or the terrifying notes she'd been getting from the evil stalker who was known simply as A. And her old friends—they'd been avoiding her ever since she'd admitted that Toby had known all along that they'd blinded his stepsister, Jenna—a secret she'd kept from them for three long years.

But three weeks had gone by since Toby's suicide, and almost a month had passed since the workers unearthed Ali's body. Spencer was coping better with all of it, mostly, because A had vanished. She hadn't received a note since before Foxy, Rosewood's big charity benefit. At first, A's silence made Spencer feel edgy—perhaps it was the calm before the hurricane—but as more time passed, she began to relax. Her manicured nails dislodged themselves from the heels of her hands. She started sleeping with her desk light off again. She'd received an A+ on her latest calc test and an A on her Plato's *Republic* paper. Her breakup with Wren—who had dumped her for Melissa, who had in turn dumped him—didn't sting so much anymore, and her family had reverted back into everyday obliviousness. Even Melissa's presence—she was staying with the family while a small army renovated her town house in Philly—was mostly tolerable.

Maybe the nightmare was over.

Spencer wiggled her toes inside her knee-high buff-colored kidskin boots. Even if she felt comfortable enough with Dr. Evans to tell her about A, it was a moot point. Why bring A up if A was gone?

"It is hard, but Alison has been missing for years. I've moved on," Spencer finally said. Maybe Dr. Evans would realize Spencer wasn't going to talk and end their session early.

Dr. Evans wrote something in her notebook. Spencer

wondered what. "I've also heard you and your sister were having some boyfriend issues."

Spencer bristled. She could only imagine Melissa's extremely slanted version of the Wren debacle—it probably involved Spencer eating whipped cream off Wren's bare stomach in Melissa's bed while her sister watched helplessly from the window. "It wasn't really a big deal," she muttered.

Dr. Evans lowered her shoulders and gave Spencer the same *you're not fooling me* look her mother used. "He was your sister's boyfriend first, wasn't he? And you dated him behind her back?"

Spencer clenched her teeth. "Look, I know it was wrong, okay? I don't need another lecture."

Dr. Evans stared at her. "I'm not going to lecture you. Perhaps . . ." She put a finger to her cheek. "Perhaps you had your reasons."

Spencer's eyes widened. Were her ears working correctly—was Dr. Evans seriously suggesting that Spencer wasn't 100 percent to blame? Perhaps $175 an hour wasn't a blasphemous price to pay for therapy, after all.

"Do you and your sister ever spend time together?" Dr. Evans asked after a pause.

Spencer reached into the candy dish for a Hershey's Kiss. She pulled off the silver wrapper in one long curl, flattened the foil in her palm, and popped the kiss in her mouth. "Never. Unless we're with our parents—but it's not like Melissa talks to *me*. All she does is brag to my parents about her accomplishments and her insanely boring town house renovations." Spencer looked squarely at Dr. Evans. "I guess you know my parents bought her a town house in Old City simply because she graduated from college."

"I did." Dr. Evans stretched her arms into the air and two silver bangle bracelets slid to her elbow. "Fascinating stuff."

And then she winked.

Spencer felt like her heart was going to burst out of her chest. Apparently Dr. Evans didn't care about the merits of sisal versus jute either. *Yes.*

They talked a while longer, Spencer enjoying it more and more, and then Dr. Evans motioned to the Salvador Dalí melting-clocks clock that hung above her desk to indicate that their time was up. Spencer said goodbye and opened the office door, rubbing her head as if the therapist had cracked it open and tinkered around in her brain. That actually hadn't been as torturous as she'd thought it would be.

She shut the therapist's office door and turned around. To her surprise, her mother was sitting in a pale green wing chair next to Melissa, reading a *Main Line* style magazine.

"Mom." Spencer frowned. "What are you doing here?"

Veronica Hastings looked like she'd come straight from the family's riding stables. She was wearing a white

Petit Bateau T-shirt, skinny jeans, and her beat-up riding boots. There was even a little bit of hay in her hair. "I have news," she announced.

Both Mrs. Hastings and Melissa had very serious looks on their faces. Spencer's insides started to whirl. Someone had died. Someone—Ali's killer—had killed again. Perhaps A was back. *Please, no,* she thought.

"I got a call from Mr. McAdam," Mrs. Hastings said, standing up. Mr. McAdam was Spencer's AP Economics teacher. "He wanted to talk about some essays you wrote a few weeks ago." She took a step closer, the scent of her Chanel No. 5 perfume tickling Spencer's nose. "Spence, he wants to nominate one of them for a Golden Orchid."

Spencer stepped back. "A Golden *Orchid*?"

The Golden Orchid was *the* most prestigious essay contest in the country, the high school essay equivalent of an Oscar. If she won, *People* and *Time* would do a feature story on her. Yale, Harvard, and Stanford would beg her to enroll. Spencer had followed the successes of Golden Orchid winners the way other people followed celebrities. The Golden Orchid winner of 2017 was now managing editor of a very famous fashion magazine. The winner from 2015 had become a congressman at 28.

"That's right." Her mother broke into a dazzling smile.

"Oh my God." Spencer felt faint. But not from excitement—from dread. The essays she'd turned in hadn't been hers—they were Melissa's. Spencer had been in a rush to finish the assignment, and A had suggested she "borrow" Melissa's old work. So much had gone on in the past few weeks, it had slipped her mind.

Spencer winced. Mr. McAdam—or Squidward, as everyone called him—had loved Melissa when she was his student. How could he not remember Melissa's essays, especially if they were *that* good?

Her mother grabbed Spencer's arm and she flinched—her mother's hands were always corpse-cold. "We're so proud of you, Spence!"

Spencer couldn't control the muscles around her mouth. She had to come clean with this before she got in too deep. "Mom, I can't—"

But Mrs. Hastings wasn't listening. "I've already called Jordana at the *Philadelphia Sentinel*. Remember Jordana? She used to take riding lessons at the stables? Anyway, she's thrilled. No one from this area has ever been nominated. She wants to write an article about you!"

Spencer blinked. Everyone read the *Philadelphia Sentinel* newspaper.

"The interview and photo shoot are all scheduled," Mrs. Hastings breezed on, picking up her giant saffron-colored Tod's satchel and jingling her car keys. "Wednesday before school. They'll provide a stylist. I'm sure Uri will come to give you a blowout."

Spencer was afraid to make eye contact with her mom, so she stared at the waiting-room reading material—an assortment of *New Yorker*s and *Economist*s, and a big book of fairy tales that was teetering on top of a Dubble Bubble tub of Legos. She couldn't tell her mom about the stolen paper—not now. And it wasn't as if she was going to *win* the Golden Orchid, anyway. Hundreds of people were nominated, from the best high schools all over the country. She probably wouldn't even make it past the first cut.

"That sounds great," Spencer sputtered.

Her mom pranced out the door. Spencer lingered a moment longer, transfixed by the wolf on the cover of the fairy-tale book. She'd had the same one when she was little. The wolf was dressed up in a negligee and bonnet, leering at a blond, naïve Red Riding Hood. It used to give Spencer nightmares.

Melissa cleared her throat. When Spencer looked up, her sister was staring.

"Congrats, Spence," Melissa said evenly. "The Golden Orchid. That's huge."

"Thanks," Spencer blurted. There was an eerily familiar expression on Melissa's face. And then Spencer realized: Melissa looked exactly like the big bad wolf.

2

JUST ANOTHER SEXUALLY CHARGED DAY IN AP ENGLISH

Aria Montgomery sat down in English class on Monday morning, just as the air outside the open widow started to smell like rain. The PA crackled, and everyone in the class looked at the little speaker on the ceiling.

"Hello, students! This is Spencer Hastings, your junior class vice president!" Spencer's voice rang out clear and loud. She sounded perky and assured, as if she'd taken a course in Announcements 101. "I want to remind everyone that the Rosewood Day Hammerheads are swimming against the Drury Academy Eels tomorrow. It's the biggest meet of the season, so let's all show some spirit and come out and support the team!" There was a pause. "Yeah!"

Some of the class snickered. Aria felt an uneasy chill. Despite everything that had happened–Alison's murder, Toby's suicide, A–Spencer was the president or VP of every club around. But to Aria, Spencer's spiritedness sounded . . . fake. She had seen a side of Spencer others hadn't. Spencer had known for years that Ali had threatened Toby Cavanaugh to keep him quiet about Jenna's accident, and Aria couldn't forgive her for keeping such a dangerous secret from the rest of them.

"Okay, class," Ezra Fitz, Aria's AP English teacher, said. He resumed writing on the board, printing *The Scarlet Letter* in his angular handwriting, and then he underlined it four times.

"In Nathaniel Hawthorne's masterpiece, Hester Prynne cheats on her husband, and her town forces her to wear a big, red, shameful *A* on her chest as a reminder of what she's done." Mr. Fitz turned from the board and pushed his square glasses up the bridge of his sloped nose. "Can anyone think of other stories that have the same falling-from-grace theme? About people who are ridiculed or cast out for their mistakes?"

Noel Kahn raised his hand and his chain-link Rolex watch slid down his wrist. "How about that English baking show where people get kicked off for not making perfect cakes?" Everyone laughed. Noel looked around sheepishly. "*I* don't watch it. My mom does."

The class laughed, and Mr. Fitz looked perplexed. "Guys, this is supposed to be an AP class." Mr. Fitz turned to Aria's row. "Aria? How about you? Thoughts?"

Aria paused. Her life was a good example. Not long ago, she and her family had been living harmoniously in

Iceland, Alison hadn't been officially dead, and A hadn't existed. But then, in a horrible unraveling of events that started six weeks ago, Aria had moved back to preppy Rosewood, Ali's body had been discovered under the concrete slab behind her old house, and A had outed the Montgomery family's biggest secret: that Aria's father, Byron, had cheated on her mother, Ella, with one of his students, Meredith. The news hit Ella hard and she promptly threw Byron out. Finding out that Aria had kept Byron's secret from her for three years hadn't helped Ella much either. Mother-daughter relations hadn't been too warm and fuzzy since.

Of course, it could have been worse. Aria hadn't gotten any texts from A in the last three weeks. Although Byron was now allegedly living with Meredith, at least Ella had begun speaking to Aria again. And Rosewood hadn't been invaded by aliens yet, although after all the weird things that had happened in this town, Aria wouldn't have been surprised if that were next.

"Aria?" Mr. Fitz goaded. "Any ideas?"

Mason Byers came to Aria's rescue. "What about Adam and Eve and that snake?"

"Great," Mr. Fitz said absentmindedly. His eyes rested on Aria for another second before looking away. Aria felt a warm, prickly rush. She had hooked up with Mr. Fitz–Ezra–at Snooker's, a college bar, before either of them knew he would be her new AP English teacher. He was the one who'd ended it, and afterward, Aria had learned he had a girlfriend in New York. But she didn't hold a grudge. Things were going well with her new boyfriend, Sean Ackard, who was kind and sweet and also happened to be gorgeous.

Besides, Ezra was the best English teacher Aria had ever had. In the month since school had started, he'd assigned four amazing books and staged a skit based on Edward Albee's "The Sandbox." Soon, the class was going to do a *Real Housewives*-style interpretation of *Medea,* the Greek play where a mother murders her children. Ezra wanted them to think unconventionally, and unconventional was Aria's forte. Now, instead of calling her Finland, her classmate Noel Kahn had given Aria a new nickname, Brownnoser. It felt good to be excited about school again, though, and at times she almost forgot things with Ezra had ever been complicated.

Until Ezra threw her a crooked smile, of course. Then she couldn't help but feel fluttery. Just a little.

Hanna Marin, who sat right in front of Aria, raised her hand. "How about that book where two girls are best friends, but then, all of a sudden, one of the best friends turns *evil* and steals the other one's boyfriend?"

Ezra scratched his head. "I'm sorry . . . I don't think I've read that book."

Aria clenched her fists. *She* knew what Hanna meant. "For the last *time,* Hanna, I didn't steal Sean from you! You guys were already. Broken. Up!"

The class rippled with laughter. Hanna's shoulders

became rigid. "Someone's a little self-centered," she murmured to Aria without turning around. "Who said I was talking about *you*?"

But Aria knew she was. When Aria had returned from Iceland, she'd been stunned to see that Hanna had morphed from Ali's chubby, awkward lackey to a thin, beautiful, designer-clothes-wearing goddess. It seemed like Hanna had everything she'd ever wanted: she and her best friend, Mona Vanderwaal—also a transformed dork—ruled the school, and Hanna had even nabbed Sean Ackard, the boy she'd pined over since sixth grade. Aria had only gone for Sean after hearing that Hanna had dumped him. But she quickly found out it had been the other way around.

Aria had hoped she and her old friends might reunite, especially since they'd all received notes from A. Yet, they weren't even speaking—things were right back to where they'd been during those awkward, worried weeks after Ali's disappearance. Aria hadn't even told them about what A had done to her family. The only ex–best friend Aria was still sort of friendly with was Emily Fields—but their conversations had mostly consisted of Emily blubbering about how guilty she felt about Toby's death, until Aria had finally insisted that it wasn't her fault.

"Well, anyway," Ezra said, putting copies of *The Scarlet Letter* at the front of each row to pass back, "I want everyone to read chapters one through five this week, and you have a three-page essay on any themes you see at the beginning of the book due on Friday. Okay?"

Everyone groaned and started to talk. Aria slid her book into her faux-fur bag. Hanna reached down to pick her purse off the floor. Aria touched Hanna's thin, pale arm. "Look, I'm sorry. I really am."

Hanna yanked her arm away, pressed her lips together, and wordlessly stuffed *The Scarlet Letter* into her purse. It kept jamming, and she let out a frustrated grunt.

Classical music tinkled through the loudspeaker, indicating the period was over. Hanna shot up from her seat as if it were on fire. Aria rose slowly, shoving her pen and notebook into her purse and heading for the door.

"Aria."

She turned. Ezra was leaning against his oak desk, his tattered caramel leather briefcase pressed to his hip. "Everything okay?" he asked.

"Sorry about all that," she said. "Hanna and I have some issues. It won't happen again."

"No problem." Ezra set his mug of chai down. "Is everything *else* okay?"

Aria bit her lip and considered telling him what was going on. But why? For all she knew, Ezra was as sleazy as her father. If he really did have a girlfriend in New York, then he'd cheated on her when he'd hooked up with Aria.

"Everything's fine," she managed.

"Good. You're doing a great job in class." He smiled, showing his two adorably overlapping bottom teeth.

"Yeah, I'm enjoying myself," she said, taking a step toward the door. But as she did, she stumbled over her super-high stack-heeled boots, careening into Ezra's desk. Ezra grabbed her waist and pulled her upright . . . and into him. His body felt warm and safe, and he smelled good, like chili powder, cigarettes, and old books.

Aria moved away quickly. "Are you okay?" Ezra asked.

"Yeah." She busied herself by straightening her school blazer. "Sorry."

"It's okay," Ezra answered, jamming his hands in his jacket pockets. "So . . . see you."

"Yeah. See you."

Aria walked out of the classroom, her breathing fast and shallow. Maybe she was nuts, but she was pretty sure Ezra had held her for a second longer than he needed to. And she was certain she'd liked it.

3

THERE'S NO SUCH
THING AS BAD PRESS

During their free period Monday afternoon, Hanna
Marin and her best friend, Mona Vanderwaal, were
sitting in the corner booth of Steam, Rosewood Day's
coffee bar, doing what they did best: ripping on people
who weren't as fabulous as they were.

Mona poked Hanna with one end of her
chocolate-dipped biscotti. To Mona, food was more like
a prop, less like something to eat. "Jennifer Feldman's got
some logs, doesn't she?"

"Poor girl." Hanna mock-pouted. *Logs* was Mona's
shorthand term for tree-trunk legs: solid and unshapely
thighs and calves with no tapering from knees to ankles.

"And her feet look like overstuffed sausage casings in
those heels!" Mona cawed.

Hanna snickered, watching as Jennifer, who was on
the diving team, hung up a poster on the far wall that

read, SWIM MEET TOMORROW! ROSEWOOD DAY HAMMERHEADS VS. DRURY ACADEMY EELS! "That's what girls with fat ankles get when they try to wear Louboutins," Hanna sighed. She and Mona were the thin-ankled sylphs Christian Louboutin shoes were meant for, obviously.

Mona took a big sip of her Americano and pulled out her Gucci wallet diary from her eggplant-colored Botkier purse. Hanna nodded approvingly. They had other things to do besides criticize people today, like plan not one but two parties: one for the two of them, and the second for the rest of Rosewood Day's elite.

"First things first." Mona uncapped her pen. "The Frenniversary. What should we do tonight? Shopping? Massages? Dinner?"

"All of that," Hanna answered. "And we definitely have to hit Otter." Otter was a new high-end boutique at the mall.

"I'm *loving* Otter," Mona agreed.

"Where should we have dinner?" Hanna asked.

"Rive Gauche, of course," Mona said loudly, talking over the groaning coffee grinder.

"You're right. They'll definitely give us wine."

"Should we invite boys?" Mona's blue eyes gleamed. "Eric Kahn keeps calling me. Maybe Noel could come for you?"

Hanna frowned. Despite being cute, incredibly rich, and part of the über-sexy clan of Kahn brothers, Noel wasn't really her type. "No boys," she decided. "Although that's very cool about Eric."

"This is going to be a fabulous Frenniversary." Mona grinned so broadly that her dimples showed. "Can you believe this is our *third*?"

Hanna smiled. Their Frenniversary marked the day Hanna and Mona had talked on the phone for three and a half hours—the obvious indicator that they were best friends. Although they'd known each other since kindergarten, they'd never really spoken before cheerleading tryouts a few weeks before the first day of eighth grade. By then, Ali had been missing for two months and Hanna's old friends had become really distant, so she'd decided to give Mona a chance. It was worth it—Mona was funny, sarcastic, and, despite her thing for animal backpacks and Razor scooters, she secretly devoured *Vogue* as ravenously as Hanna did. Within weeks, they'd decided to be best friends and transform themselves into the most popular girls at school. And look: Now they had.

"Now for the bigger plans," Mona said, flipping another page of her notebook. "My sweet seventeen, baby."

"It's going to rock," Hanna gushed. Mona's birthday was this Saturday, and she had almost all the party details in place. She was going to have it at the Hollis Planetarium, where there were telescopes in every room—even the bathrooms. She'd booked a DJ, caterers, and a trapeze school—so guests could swing over the dance floor—as well as a videographer, who would film the party and simultaneously webcast it onto a Jumbotron screen. Mona had carefully instructed guests to wear formal dress only on the invites. If someone turned up in jeans or Juicy sweats, security would not-so-politely turn them away.

"So I was thinking," Mona said, stuffing a napkin into her empty paper coffee cup. "It's a little last-minute, but I'm going to have a court."

"A court?" Hanna raised a perfectly plucked eyebrow.

"It's an excuse to get that red minidress you've been eyeing at Saks—the fitting is tomorrow. And we'll wear tiaras and make the boys bow down to us."

Hanna stifled a giggle. "We're not going to do an opening dance number, are we?" She and Mona had been on Julia Rubenstein's party court last year, and Julia had made them do a dance routine with a bunch of D-list male models. Hanna's dance partner smelled like garlic and had immediately asked her if she wanted to join him in the coatroom. She'd spent the rest of the party running away from him.

Mona scoffed, breaking her biscotti into smaller pieces. "Would I do something as lame as that?"

"Of course not." Hanna rested her chin in her hands. "So I'm the only girl in the court, right?"

Mona rolled her eyes. *"Obviously."*

Hanna shrugged. "I mean, I don't know who else you could pick."

"We just need to get you a date." Mona placed the tiniest piece of biscotti in her mouth.

"I don't want to take anyone from Rosewood Day," Hanna said quickly. "Maybe I'll ask someone from Hollis. And I'll bring more than one date." Her eyes lit up. "I could have a whole load of guys carry me around all night, like Cleopatra."

Mona gave her a high five. "*Now* you're talking."

Hanna chewed on the end of her straw. "I wonder if Sean will come."

"Don't know." Mona raised an eyebrow. "You're over him, right?"

"Of course." Hanna pushed her auburn hair over her shoulder. Bitterness still flickered inside her whenever she thought about how Sean had dumped her for way-too-tall, I'm-a-kiss-ass-English-student-and-think-I'm-hot-shit-because-I-lived-in-Europe Aria Montgomery, but whatever. It was Sean's loss. Now that boys knew she was available, Hanna's phone was beeping with potential dates every few minutes.

"Good," Mona said. "Because you're *way* too hot for him, Han."

"I know," Hanna quipped, and they touched palms lightly in another high five. Hanna sat back, feeling a warm, reassuring whoosh of well-being. It was hard to believe that things had been shaky between her and Mona a month ago. Imagine, Mona thinking that Hanna wanted to be friends with Aria, Emily, and Spencer instead of her!

Okay, so Hanna *had* been keeping things from Mona, although she'd confessed most of it: her occasional purges, the trouble with her dad, her two arrests, the fact that she'd stripped for Sean at Noel Kahn's party and he'd rejected her. She'd downplayed everything, worried Mona would disown her for such horrible secrets, but Mona had taken it all in stride. She said every diva got in trouble once in a while, and Hanna decided she'd just overreacted. So what if she wasn't with Sean anymore? So what if she hadn't spoken to her father since Foxy? So what if she was still volunteering at Mr. Ackard's burn clinic to atone for wrecking his car? So what if her two worst enemies, Naomi Zeigler and Riley Wolfe, knew she had a bingeing problem and had spread rumors about her around the school? She and Mona were still tight, and A had stopped stalking her.

Kids began filtering out of the coffee bar, which meant that free period was about to end. As Hanna and Mona swaggered through the exit, Hanna realized they were approaching Naomi and Riley, who had been hiding behind the giant swirling Frappuccino machine. Hanna set her jaw and tried to hold her head high.

"*Baaaarf,*" Naomi hissed into Hanna's ear as she passed.

"*Yaaaaak,*" Riley taunted right behind her.

"Don't listen to them, Han," Mona said loudly.

"They're just pissed because you can fit into those Rich and Skinny jeans at Otter and they can't."

"It's cool," Hanna said breezily, sticking her nose into the air. "There's that, and at least I don't have inverted nipples."

Naomi's mouth got very small and tense. "That was because of the *bra* I was wearing," she said through clenched teeth. Hanna had seen Naomi's inverted nipples when they were changing for gym the week before. Maybe it *was* just from the weird bra she had on, but hey—all's fair in love and the war to be popular.

Hanna glanced over her shoulder and shot Naomi and Riley a haughty, condescending look. She felt like a queen snubbing two grubby little wenches. And it gave Hanna great satisfaction to see that Mona was giving them the exact same look. That was what best friends were for, after all.

4

NO WONDER EMILY'S
MOM IS SO STRICT

Emily Fields never had practice the day before a meet, so she came straight home after school and noticed three new items sitting on the limestone kitchen island. There were two new blue Sammy swim towels for Emily and her sister Carolyn, just in time for their big meet against Drury tomorrow . . . and there was also a paperback book titled *It's Not Fair: What to Do When You Lose Your Boyfriend*. A Post-it note was affixed to the cover: *Emily: Thought you might find this useful. I'll be back at 6. —Mom.*

Emily absentmindedly flipped through the pages. Not long after Alison's body had been found, Emily's mother had started surprising her with little cheer-me-ups, like a book called *1001 Things to Make You Smile*, a big set of Prismacolor colored pencils, and a walrus puppet, because Emily used to be obsessed with walruses when she was younger. After Toby's suicide, however, her mother had merely given Emily a bunch of self-help books. Mrs. Fields seemed to think Toby's death was harder for Emily than Ali's—probably because she thought Toby had been Emily's boyfriend.

Emily sank into a white kitchen chair and shut her eyes. Boyfriend or not, Toby's death *did* haunt her. Every night, as she was looking at herself in the mirror while brushing her teeth, she thought she saw Toby standing behind her. She couldn't stop going over that fateful night when he'd taken her to Foxy. Emily had told Toby that she'd been in love with Alison, and Toby had admitted he was glad Ali was dead. Emily had immediately assumed Toby was Ali's killer and had threatened to call the cops. But by the time she realized just how wrong she was, it was too late.

Emily listened to the small settling sounds of her empty house. She stood up, picked up the cordless phone on the counter and dialed a number. Maya answered in one ring.

"Carolyn's at Topher's," Emily said in a low voice. "My mom's at a PTA meeting. We have a whole hour."

"The creek?" Maya whispered.

"Yep."

"Six minutes," Maya declared. "Time me."

It took Emily two minutes to slip out the back door, sprint across her vast, slippery lawn, and dive into the woods to the secluded little creek. Alongside the water was a smooth, flat rock, perfect for two girls to sit on.

She and Maya had discovered the secret creek spot two weeks ago, and they'd been hiding away here as much as they possibly could.

In five minutes and forty-five seconds, Maya emerged through the trees. She looked adorable as usual, in her plain white T-shirt, pale pink miniskirt, and red suede Puma sneakers. Even though it was October, it was almost eighty degrees out. She had pulled her hair back from her face, showing off her flawless skin.

"Hey," Maya cried, a little out of breath. "Under six minutes?"

"Barely," Emily teased.

They both plopped down on the rock. For a second, neither of them spoke. It was so much quieter back here in the woods than by the street. Emily tried not to think about how she had run from Toby through these very woods a few weeks ago. Instead, she concentrated on the way the water sparkled over the rocks and how the trees were just starting to turn orange at the tips. She had a superstition about the big tree she could just make out at the edge of her backyard: if its leaves turned yellow in the fall, she would have a good school year. If they turned red, she wouldn't. But this year, the leaves were orange—did that mean so-so? Emily had all sorts of superstitions. She thought the world was fraught with signs. Nothing was random.

"I missed you," Maya whispered in Emily's ear. "I didn't see you at school today."

A shiver passed through Emily as Maya's lips grazed her earlobe. She shifted her position on the rock, moving closer to Maya. "I know. I kept looking for you."

"Did you survive your bio lab?" Maya asked, curling her pinkie around Emily's.

"Uh-huh." Emily slid her fingers up Maya's arm. "How was your history test?"

Maya wrinkled her nose and shook her head.

"Does this make it better?" Emily pecked Maya on the lips.

"You'll have to try harder than that to make it better," Maya said seductively, lowering her green-yellow catlike eyes and reaching for Emily.

They had decided to try this: sitting together, hanging out whenever they could, touching, kissing. As much as Emily tried to edit Maya from her life, she couldn't. Maya was wonderful, nothing like Em's last boyfriend, Ben—nothing, in fact, like any boy she'd ever gone out with. There was something so comforting about being here at the creek side by side. They weren't just *together*—they were also best friends. This was how coupledom should feel.

When they pulled away, Maya slid off a sneaker and dipped her toe into the creek. "So we moved back into our house yesterday."

Emily drew in her breath. After the workers had found Ali's body in Maya's new backyard, the St. Germains had moved to a hotel to escape the media. "Is it . . . weird?"

"It's okay." Maya shrugged. "Oh, but get this. There's a stalker on the loose."

"What?"

"Yeah, a neighbor was telling my mom about it this morning. Someone's running around through people's yards, peeping into windows."

Emily's stomach began to hurt. This, too, reminded her of Toby: Back when they were in sixth grade, he was the creepy kid who peeked into everyone's windows, especially Ali's. "Guy? Girl?"

Maya shook her head. "I don't know." She blew her curly bangs up into the air. "This town, I swear to God. Weirdest place on earth."

"You must miss California," Emily said softly, pausing to watch a bunch of birds lift off from a nearby oak tree.

"Not at all, actually." Maya touched Emily's wrist. "There are no Emilys in California."

Emily leaned forward and kissed Maya softly on her lips. They held their lips together for five long seconds. She kissed Maya's earlobe. Then Maya kissed her bottom lip. They pulled away and smiled, the afternoon sun making pretty patterns on their cheeks. Maya kissed Emily's nose, then her temples, then her neck. Emily shut her eyes, and Maya kissed her eyelids. She took a deep breath. Maya ran her delicate fingers along the edge of Emily's jaw; it felt like a million butterflies flapping their wings against her skin. As much as she'd been trying to convince herself that being with Maya was wrong, it was the only thing that felt right.

Maya pulled away. "So, I have a proposal for you."

Emily smirked. "A proposal. Sounds *serious*."

Maya pulled her hands into her sleeves. "How about we make things more open?"

"Open?" Emily repeated.

"Yeah." Maya ran her finger up and down the length of Emily's arm, giving her goose bumps. Emily could smell Maya's banana gum, a smell she now found intoxicating. "Meaning we hang out *inside* your house. We hang out at school. We . . . I don't know. I know you're not ready to be, like, *out* with this, Em, but it's hard spending all our time on this rock. What's going to happen when it gets cold?"

"We'll come out here in snowsuits," Emily quipped.

"I'm serious."

Emily watched as a stiff wind made the tree branches knock together. The air suddenly smelled like burning leaves. She couldn't invite Maya inside her house because her mother had already made it clear that she didn't want Emily to be friends with Maya . . . for terrible, almost-definitely racist reasons. But it wasn't like Emily was going to tell *Maya* that. And as for the other thing, coming out—no. She closed her eyes and thought of the picture A had texted her a while ago—the one of Emily and Maya kissing in the photo booth at Noel Kahn's party. She winced. She wasn't ready for people to know.

"I'm sorry I'm slow," Emily said. "But this is what I'm comfortable with right now."

Maya sighed. "Okay," she said in an Eeyore-ish voice. "I'll just have to deal."

Emily stared into the water. Two silvery fish swam tightly together. Whenever one turned, the other turned too. They were like those needy couples who made out in the hallway and practically stopped breathing when they were separated. It made her a little sad to realize she and Maya could *never* be one of those couples.

"So," Maya said, "nervous about your swim meet tomorrow?"

"Nervous?" Emily frowned.

"Everyone's going to be there."

Emily shrugged. She'd competed in much bigger swimming events than this—there had been camera crews at nationals last year. "I'm not worried."

"You're braver than I am." Maya shoved her sneaker back onto her foot.

But Emily wasn't so sure about that. Maya seemed brave about everything—she ignored the rules that said you had to wear the Rosewood Day uniform and showed up in her white denim jacket every day. She smoked pot out her bedroom window while her parents were at the store. She said hi to kids she didn't know. In that way, she was just like Ali—totally fearless. Which was probably why Emily had fallen for both of them.

And Maya was brave about this—who she was, what

she wanted, and who she wanted to be with. She didn't care if people found out. Maya wanted to be with Emily, and nothing was going to stop her. Maybe someday Emily would be as brave as Maya. But if it was up to her, that would be someday far, far away.

5

ARIA'S ALL FOR LITERARY REENACTMENTS

Aria perched on the back bumper of Sean's Audi, skimming through her favorite Jean-Paul Sartre play, *No Exit*. It was Monday after school, and Sean said he would give her a ride home after he grabbed something from the soccer coach's office . . . only he was taking an awfully long-ass time. As she flipped to Act II, a group of nearly identical blond, long-legged, Coach-bag-toting Typical Rosewood Girls strode into the student parking lot and gave Aria a suspicious once-over. Apparently Aria's platform boots and gray knitted earflap hat indicated she was *surely* up to something nefarious.

Aria sighed. She was trying her hardest to adjust to Rosewood again, but it wasn't easy. She still felt like a punked-out, faux-leather-wearing, free-thinking Funko Pop in a sea of Pretty Princess of Preppyland Barbies.

"You shouldn't sit on the bumper like that," said a

voice behind her, making Aria jump. "Bad for the suspension."

Aria swiveled around. Ezra stood a few feet away. His brown hair was standing up in messy peaks and his blazer was even more rumpled than it had been this morning. "I thought you literary types were hopeless when it came to cars," she joked.

"I'm full of surprises." Ezra shot her a seductive smile. He reached into his worn leather briefcase. "Actually, I have something for you. It's an essay about *The Scarlet Letter,* questioning whether adultery is sometimes permissible."

Aria took the photocopied pages from him. "I don't think adultery is permissible or forgivable," she said softly. *"Ever."*

"Ever is a long time," Ezra murmured. He was standing so close, Aria could see the dark blue flecks in his light blue eyes.

"Aria?" Sean was right next to her.

"Hey!" Aria cried, startled. She jumped away from Ezra as if he were loaded with electricity. "You . . . you all done?"

"Yep," Sean said.

Ezra stepped forward. "Hey, Sean is it? I'm Ez–I mean, Mr. Fitz, the new AP English teacher."

Sean shook his hand. "I just take regular English. I'm Aria's boyfriend."

A flicker of something–disappointment, maybe–passed

over Ezra's face. "Cool," he stumbled. "You play soccer, right? Congrats on your win last week."

"That's right," Sean said modestly. "We have a good team this year."

"Cool," Ezra said again. "Very cool."

Aria felt like she should explain to Ezra why she and Sean were together. Sure, he was a Typical Rosewood Boy, but he was really much deeper. Aria stopped herself. She didn't owe Ezra any explanations. He was her *teacher*.

"We should go," she said abruptly, taking Sean's arm. She wanted to get out of here before either of them embarrassed her. What if Sean made a grammatical error? What if Ezra blurted that they'd hooked up? No one at Rosewood knew about that. No one, that was, except for A.

Aria slid into the passenger seat of Sean's tidy, pine-smelling Audi, feeling itchy. She longed for a few private minutes to collect herself, but Sean slumped into the driver's seat right next to her and pecked her on the cheek. "I missed you today," he said.

"Me too," Aria answered automatically, her voice tight in her throat. As she peeked through her side window, she saw Ezra in the teachers' lot, climbing into his beat-up, old-school VW Bug. He had added a new sticker to the bumper—ECOLOGY HAPPENS—and it looked like he'd washed the car over the weekend. Not that she was obsessively checking or anything.

As Sean waited for other students to back out in front of him, he rubbed his cleanly shaven jaw and fiddled with the collar of his fitted Penguin polo. If Sean and Ezra had been types of poetry, Sean would have been a haiku—neat, simple, beautiful. Ezra would have been one of William Burroughs's messy fever dreams. "Want to hang out later?" Sean asked. "Go out to dinner? Hang with Ella?"

"Let's go out," Aria decided. It was so sweet how Sean liked to spend time with Ella and Aria. The three of them had even watched Ella's Truffaut DVD collection together—in spite of the fact that Sean said he really didn't understand French films.

"One of these days you'll have to meet my family." Sean finally pulled out of the Rosewood lot behind an Acura SUV.

"I know, I know," Aria said. She felt nervous about meeting Sean's family—she'd heard they were wildly rich and super-perfect. "Soon."

"Well, Coach wants the soccer team to go to that big swim meet tomorrow for school support. You're going to watch Emily, right?"

"Sure," Aria answered.

"Well, maybe Wednesday, then? Dinner?"

"Maybe."

As they pulled onto the wooded road that paralleled Rosewood Day, Aria's phone chimed. She pulled it out nervously—her knee-jerk response whenever she got a text was that it would be A, even though A seemed to be gone. The new text, however, was from an unfamiliar 484 number. A's notes always came up "unavailable." She tapped the message.

> Aria: We need to talk. Can we meet outside the Hollis art building today at 4:30? I'll be on campus waiting for Meredith to finish teaching. I'd love for us to chat. —Your dad, Byron

Aria stared at the screen in disgust. It was disturbing on so many levels. One, had he *changed* his number? Granted, they'd just returned to Rosewood, and maybe he wanted a new cell plan, but . . . *weird*. And two, he'd just texted her *using Bitmojis*. Which was so seven years ago. Also? The Bitmoji he'd created looked nothing like him.

And three . . . the letter itself. Especially the qualifying *Your dad* at the end. Did he think she'd forgotten who he was?

"You all right?" Sean took his eyes off the winding, narrow road for a moment.

Aria read Sean Byron's text. "Can you believe it?" she asked when she finished. "It sounds like he just needs someone to occupy him while he waits for that skank to finish teaching her class."

"What are you going to do?"

"*Not go.*" Aria shuddered, thinking of the times she'd seen Meredith and her father together. In seventh grade, she and Ali had caught them kissing in her dad's car, and then a few weeks ago, she and her younger brother,

Mike, had happened upon them at the Victory Brewery. Meredith had told Aria that she and Byron were in love, but how was that *possible*? "Meredith is a homewrecker. She's worse than Hester Prynne!"

"Who?"

"Hester Prynne. She's the main character in *The Scarlet Letter*—we're reading it for English. It's about this woman who commits adultery and the town shuns her. I think Rosewood should shun Meredith. Rosewood needs a town scaffold—to humiliate her."

"How about that pillory thing at the fairgrounds?" Sean suggested, slowing down as they passed a cyclist. "You know that wooden contraption with the holes you can stick your head and arms through? They lock you up in it and you just hang there. We always used to get our pictures taken in that thing."

"Perfect," Aria practically shouted. "And Meredith deserves to have 'husband-stealer' branded on her forehead. Just stitching a red letter *A* to her dress would be too subtle."

Sean laughed. "It sounds like you're *really* into *The Scarlet Letter*."

"I don't know. I've only read eight pages." Aria grew silent, getting an idea. "Actually, wait. Drop me off at Hollis."

Sean gave her a sidelong glance. "You're going to meet him?"

"Not exactly." She smiled devilishly.

"Ohhhhkay . . ." Sean drove a few blocks through the Hollis section of town, which was filled with brick and stone buildings, old bronze statues of the college found- ers, and tons of casually dressed students on bicycles. It seemed like it was permanently fall at Hollis—the colorful cascading leaves looked perfect here. As Sean pulled into a two-hour parking spot on campus, he looked worried. "You're not going to do anything illegal, are you?"

"Nah." Aria gave him a quick kiss. "Don't wait. I can walk home from here."

Squaring her shoulders, she marched into the Arts Building's main entrance. Her father's text flashed before her eyes. *I'll be on campus waiting for Meredith to finish teaching.* Meredith had told Aria herself that she taught studio art at Hollis. She slid by a security guard, who was supposed to be checking IDs but was instead watching a Yankees game on his portable TV. Her nerves felt jangled and snappy, as if they were ungrounded wires.

There were only three studio classrooms in the build- ing that were big enough for a painting class, which Aria knew, because she'd attended Saturday art school at Hollis for years. Today, only one room was in use, so it had to be the one. Aria burst noisily through the doors of the classroom and was immediately assaulted by the smell of turpentine and unwashed clothes. Twelve art students with easels set up in a circle swiveled around to stare at her. The only person who didn't move was the wrinkly, hairless, completely naked old drawing model in the center of the room. He stuck his bandy little chest out, kept his hands on his hips, and didn't even blink. Aria had to give him an A for effort.

She spied Meredith perched on a table by the far window. There was her long, luscious brown hair. There was the pink spiderweb tattoo on her wrist. Meredith looked strong and confident, and there was an irritating, healthy pink flush to her cheeks.

"Aria?" Meredith called across the drafty, cavernous room. "This is a surprise."

Aria looked around. All of the students had their brushes and paints within easy reach of their canvases. She marched over to the student closest to her, snatched a large, fan-shaped brush, swiped it in a puddle of red paint, and strode over to Meredith, dribbling paint as she went. Before anyone could do anything, Aria painted a large, messy *A* on the left breast of Meredith's delicate, cotton eyelet sundress.

"Now everyone will know what you've done," Aria snarled.

Giving Meredith no time to react, she whirled around and strode out of the room. When she got out onto Hollis's green lawn again, she started gleefully, crazily laughing. It wasn't a "husband-stealer" brand across her forehead, but it might as well have been. *There, Meredith. Take that.*

6

SIBLING RIVALRY'S
A HARD HABIT TO BREAK

Monday afternoon at field hockey practice, Spencer pulled ahead of her teammates on their warm-up lap around the field. It had been an unseasonably warm day and the girls were all a little slower than usual. Kirsten Cullen pumped her arms to catch up. "I heard about the Golden Orchid," Kirsten said breathlessly, readjusting her blond ponytail. "That's awesome."

"Thanks." Spencer ducked her head. It was amazing how fast the news had spread at Rosewood Day—her mother had only told her six hours ago. At least ten people had come up to talk to her about it since then.

"I heard Taylor Swift won a Golden Orchid when she was in high school," Kirsten continued. "It was, like, an essay for AP Music Theory."

"Huh." Spencer was pretty sure Taylor Swift *hadn't* won it—she knew every winner from the past fifteen years.

"I bet you'll win," Kirsten said. "And then you'll be on TV! Can I come with you for your debut on the *Today* show?"

Spencer shrugged. "It's a really cutthroat competition."

"Shut up." Kirsten slapped her on the shoulder. "You're always so modest."

Spencer clenched her teeth. As much as she'd been trying to downplay this Golden Orchid thing, everyone's reaction had been the same—*You'll definitely win it. Get ready for your close-up!*—and it was making her crazy. She had nervously organized and reorganized the money in her wallet so many times today that one of her twenties had split right down the center.

Coach McCready blew the whistle and yelled, "Crossovers!" The team immediately turned and began running sideways. They looked like dressage competitors at the Devon Horse Show. "You hear about the Rosewood Stalker?" Kirsten asked, huffing a little—crossovers were harder than they looked. "It was all over the news last night."

"Yeah," Spencer mumbled.

"He's in your neighborhood. Hanging out in the woods."

Spencer dodged a divot in the dry grass. "It's probably just some loser," she huffed. But Spencer couldn't help but think of A. How many times had A texted her about something that it seemed *no one* could have seen? Now she looked out into the trees, almost certain she'd see a shadowy figure. But there was no one.

They started running normally again, passing the Rosewood Day duck pond, the sculpture garden, and the cornfields. When they looped toward the bleachers, Kirsten squinted and pointed toward the low metal benches that held the girls' hockey equipment. "Is that your *sister*?"

Spencer flinched. Melissa was standing next to Ian Thomas, their new assistant coach. It was the very same Ian Thomas Melissa had dated when Spencer was in seventh grade—*and* the same Ian Thomas who had kissed Spencer in her driveway years ago.

They finished their loop and Spencer came to a halt in front of Melissa and Ian. Her sister had changed into an outfit that was nearly identical to what their mother had been wearing earlier: stovepipe jeans, white tee, and an expensive Dior watch. She even wore Chanel No. 5, just like Mom. *Such a good little clone,* Spencer thought. "What are you doing here?" she demanded, out of breath.

Melissa leaned her elbow on one of the Gatorade jugs resting on the bench, her antique gold charm bracelet tinkling against her wrist. "What, a big sister can't watch her little sister play?" But then her saccharine smile faded, and she snaked an arm around Ian's waist. "It also helps that my boyfriend's the coach."

Spencer wrinkled her nose. She'd always suspected

Melissa had never gotten over Ian. They'd broken up shortly after graduation. Ian was still as cute as ever, with his blond, wavy hair, beautifully proportioned body, and lazy, arrogant smile. "Well, good for you," Spencer answered, wanting out of this conversation. The less she spoke to Melissa, the better—at least until the Golden Orchid thing was over. If only the judges would hurry the hell up and knock Spencer's plagiarized paper out of the running.

She reached for her gear bag, pulled out her shin guards, and fastened one around her left shin. Then she fastened the other around her right. Then she unfastened both, refastening them much tighter. She pulled up her socks and then pulled them down again. Repeat, repeat, repeat.

"Someone's awfully OCD today," Melissa teased. She turned to Ian. "Oh, did you hear the big Spencer news? She won the Golden Orchid. The *Philadelphia Sentinel* is coming over to interview her this week."

"I didn't win," Spencer barked quickly. "I was only nominated."

"Oh, I'm sure you *will* win," Melissa simpered, in a way Spencer couldn't quite read. When her sister gave Spencer a wink, she felt a pinch of terror. *Did she know?*

Ian let out a whistle. "A Golden Orchid? Damn! You Hastings sisters—smart, beautiful, *and* athletic. You should see the way Spence tears up the field, Mel. She plays a mean center."

Melissa pursed her shiny lips, thinking. "Remember when Coach had me play center because Zoe had mono?" she chirped to Ian. "I scored two goals. In *one* quarter."

Spencer gritted her teeth. She'd known Melissa couldn't be charitable for long. Yet again, Melissa had turned something completely innocent into a competition. Spencer scrolled through the long list in her head for an appropriate fake-nice insult but then decided to screw it. This wasn't the time to pick a fight with Melissa. "I'm sure it rocked, Mel," she conceded. "I bet you're a way better center than I am."

Her sister froze. The little gremlin that Spencer was certain lived inside Melissa's head was confused. Clearly it hadn't expected Spencer to say something nice.

Spencer smiled at her sister and then at Ian. He held her gaze for a moment and then gave her a little conspiratorial wink.

Spencer's insides flipped. She *still* got gooey when Ian looked at her. Even three years later, Spencer remembered every single detail about their kiss. Ian had been wearing a soft gray Nike T-shirt, green army shorts, and brown Merrills. He smelled like cut grass and cinnamon gum. One second, Spencer was giving him a goodbye peck on his cheek—she'd gone out to flirt, nothing more. The next second, he was pressing her up against the side of his car. Spencer had been so surprised, she'd kept her eyes open.

Ian blew the whistle, breaking Spencer out of her thoughts. She jogged back to her team, and Ian followed. "All right, guys." Ian clapped his hands. The team surrounded him, taking in Ian's golden face longingly. "Please don't hate me, but we're going to do ladders, crouching drills, and hill running today. Coach's orders."

Everyone, including Spencer, groaned. "I told you not to hate me!" Ian cried.

"Can't we do something else?" Kirsten whined.

"Just think how much butt you're going to kick for our game against Pritchard Prep," Ian said. "And how about this? If we get through the entire drill, I'll take you guys to Merlin after practice tomorrow."

The hockey team whooped. Merlin was famous for its low-calorie chocolate ice cream that tasted better than the full-fat stuff.

As Spencer leaned over the bench to fasten her shin guards—*again*—she felt Ian standing above her. When she glanced up at him, he was smiling. "For the record," Ian said in a low voice, shadowing his face from her teammates, "you play center better than your sister does. No question about it."

"Thanks." Spencer smiled. Her nose tickled with the smell of cut grass and Ian's Neutrogena sunscreen. Her heart pitter-pattered. "That means a lot."

"And I meant the other stuff, too." The left corner of Ian's mouth pulled up into a half smile.

Spencer felt a faint, trembling thrill. Did he mean

the "smart" and "beautiful" stuff? She glanced across the field to where Melissa was standing. Her sister leaned over her phone, not paying a bit of attention.

Good.

7

NOTHING LIKE AN
OLD-FASHIONED INTERROGATION

Monday evening, Hanna parked her Prius in her side driveway and hopped out. All she had to do was change clothes, and then she was off to meet Mona for their dinner. Showing up in her Rosewood Day blazer and pleated skirt would be an insult to the institution of Frenniversaries. She had to get out of these long sleeves— she'd been sweating all day. Hanna had spritzed herself with her Evian mineral water spray bottle about a hundred times on the drive home, but she still felt overheated.

When she rounded the corner, she noticed her mother's champagne-colored Lexus next to the garage and stopped short. What was her mom doing home? Ms. Marin usually worked über-long hours at McManus & Tate, her Philadelphia advertising firm. She often didn't get back until after 10 p.m.

Then Hanna noticed the four other cars, stuffed one after the other against the garage: the silver Mercedes coupe was definitely Spencer's, the white Volvo Emily's, and the clunky green Subaru Aria's. The last car was a white Ford with the words ROSEWOOD POLICE DEPARTMENT emblazoned on the side.

What the hell?

"Hanna."

Hanna's mother stood on the side porch. She still had on her sleek black pantsuit and high faux-snakeskin heels.

"What's going on?" Hanna demanded, annoyed. "Why are my old friends here?"

"I tried calling you. You didn't pick up," her mother said. "Officer Wilden wanted to ask you girls some questions about Alison. They're out back."

Hanna pulled her phone out of her pocket. Sure enough, she had three missed calls, all from her mom.

Her mother turned. Hanna followed her into the house and through the kitchen. She paused by the granite-topped telephone table. "Do I have any messages?"

"Yes, one." Hanna's heart leapt, but then her mother added, "Mr. Ackard. They're doing some reorganization at the burn clinic, and they won't need your help anymore."

Hanna blinked. That was a nice surprise. "Anyone . . . else?"

The corners of Ms. Marin's eyes turned down, understanding. "No." She gently touched Hanna's arm. "I'm sorry, Han. He hasn't called."

Despite Hanna's otherwise back-to-perfect life, the silence from her father made her ache. How could he so easily cut Hanna out of his life? Didn't he realize she'd had a very good reason to ditch their dinner and go to Foxy? Didn't he know he shouldn't have invited his fiancée, Isabel, and her perfect daughter, Kate, to *their* special weekend? But then, Hanna's father would be marrying plain, squirrelly Isabel soon—and Kate would officially be his stepdaughter. Maybe he hadn't called Hanna back because Hanna was one daughter too many.

Whatever, Hanna told herself, taking off her blazer and straightening her sheer pink Rebecca Taylor camisole. Kate was a prissy bitch—if her father chose Kate over her, then they deserved each other.

When she looked through the French doors to the back porch, Spencer, Aria, and Emily were indeed sitting around the giant teak patio table, the light from the stained-glass window sparkling against their cheeks. Officer Wilden, the newest member of Rosewood's police force *and* Ms. Marin's newest boyfriend, stood near the Weber grill.

It was surreal to see her three ex–best friends here. The last time they'd sat on Hanna's back porch had been at the end of seventh grade—and Hanna had been the dorkiest and ugliest of the group. But now, Emily's shoulders had broadened and her hair had a slight greenish tint. Spencer looked stressed and constipated. And Aria was a zombie, with her black hair and pale skin. If

Hanna was a couture Proenza Schouler, then Aria was a pilly, ill-fitting sweatshirt dress from the Target line.

Hanna took a deep breath and pushed through the French doors. Wilden turned around. There was a serious look on his face. The tiniest bit of a black tattoo peeked out from under the collar of his cop uniform. It still amazed Hanna that Wilden, a former Rosewood Day badass, had gone into law enforcement. "Hanna. Have a seat."

Hanna scraped a chair back from the table and slumped down next to Spencer. "Is this going to take long?" She examined her pink diamond-encrusted Dior watch. "I'm late for something."

"Not if we get started." Wilden looked around at all of them. Spencer stared at her fingernails, Aria chomped on her gum with her eyes freakishly closed, and Emily fixated on the citronella candle in the middle of the table, like she was about to cry.

"First thing," Wilden said. "Someone has leaked a homemade video of you girls to the press." He glanced at Aria. "It was one of the videos you gave the Rosewood PD years ago. So you might see it on TV—all the news channels got it. We're looking for whoever leaked it—and they'll be punished. I wanted to let you girls know first."

"Which video is it?" Aria asked.

"Something about text messages?" he answered.

Hanna sat back, trying to remember which video it could be—there were so many. Aria used to be obsessive about videotaping them. Hanna had always tried her hardest to duck out of every shot, because for her, the camera added not ten pounds but *twenty*.

Wilden cracked his knuckles and fiddled with a phallic-looking pepper grinder that sat in the center of the table. Some pepper spilled on the tablecloth, and the air immediately smelled spicy. "The other thing I want to talk about is Alison herself. We have reason to believe that Alison's killer might be someone *from* Rosewood. Someone who possibly still lives here today . . . and that person may still be dangerous."

Everyone drew in a breath.

"We're looking at everything with a fresh eye," Wilden went on, rising from the table and strolling around with his hands clasped behind his back. He'd probably seen someone on *CSI* do that and thought it was cool. "We're trying to reconstruct Alison's life right before she went missing. We want to start with the people who knew her best."

Just then, Hanna's phone buzzed. She pulled it out of her purse. Mona.

"Mon," Hanna answered quietly, getting up from her chair and wandering to the far side of the porch by her mother's rosebushes. "I'm going to be a couple minutes late."

"Bitch," Mona teased. "That sucks. I'm already at our table at Rive Gauche."

"Hanna," Wilden called gruffly. "Can you please call whoever that is back?"

At the same time, Aria sneezed. "Bless you," Emily said.

"Where are you?" Mona sounded suspicious. "Are you with someone?"

"I'm at home," Hanna answered. "And I'm with Emily, Aria, Spencer, and Off–"

"You're with your *old friends*?" Mona interrupted.

"They were here when I got home," Hanna protested.

"Let me get this straight." Mona's voice rose higher. "You invited your old friends to your *house*. On the night of our Frenniversary."

"I didn't *invite* them." Hanna laughed. It was still hard to believe Mona could feel threatened by her old friends. "I was just–"

"You know what?" Mona cut her off. "Forget it. The Frenniversary is canceled."

"Mona, don't be–" Then she stopped. Wilden was next to her.

He plucked the phone from her hand and placed it facedown on the table. "We're discussing a murder," he said in a low voice. "Your social life can wait."

Hanna glared at him behind his back. How dare Wilden hang up her phone! Just because he was dating her mom didn't mean he could get all dadlike on her. She stormed back to the table, trying to calm down. Mona was the queen of overreacting, but she couldn't ice Hanna out for long. Most of their fights only lasted a few hours, tops.

"Okay," Wilden said when Hanna sat back down. "I received something interesting a few weeks ago that I think we should talk about." He pulled his notepad out. "Your friend, Toby Cavanaugh? He wrote a suicide note."

"W-We know," Spencer stuttered. "His sister let us read part of it."

"So you know it mentioned Alison." Wilden flipped back through his notebook. "Toby wrote, *I promised Alison DiLaurentis I'd keep a secret for her if she kept a secret for me.*" His olive-colored eyes scanned each of them. "What was Alison's secret?"

Hanna slumped down in her seat. *We were the ones who blinded Jenna.* That was the secret Toby had kept for Ali. Hanna and her friends hadn't realized Toby knew that—until Spencer spilled the beans three weeks ago.

Spencer blurted out, "We don't know. Ali didn't tell any of us."

Wilden's brow crinkled. He leaned over the patio table. "Hanna, a while ago you thought Toby *killed* Alison."

Hanna shrugged impassively. She'd gone to Wilden during the time they'd thought Toby was A and Ali's killer. "Well . . . Toby didn't like Ali."

"Actually, he *did* like Ali, but Ali didn't like him back," Spencer clarified. "He used to spy on her all the time. But I'm not sure if that had anything to do with his secret."

Emily made a small whimper. Hanna eyed her

suspiciously. All Emily talked about lately was how guilty she felt about Toby. What if she wanted to tell Wilden that they were responsible for his death—*and* Jenna's accident? Hanna might have taken the rap for The Jenna Thing weeks ago when she had nothing to live for, but there was no way in hell she would confess now. Her life was finally back to normal, and she was in no mood to be known as one of The Psycho Blinders, or whatever they'd inevitably be called on TV.

Wilden flipped a few pages on his pad. "Well, everyone think about it. Moving on . . . let's talk about the night Alison went missing. Spencer, it says here that right before she disappeared, Ali tried to hypnotize you. The two of you fought, she ran out of the barn, you ran after her, but you couldn't find her. Right?"

Spencer stiffened. "Um. Yeah. That's right."

"You have *no* idea where she went?"

Spencer shrugged. "Sorry."

Hanna tried to remember the night Ali vanished. One minute, Ali was hypnotizing them; the next, she was gone. Hanna really felt like Ali had put her in a trance: As Ali counted down from one hundred, the vanilla candle wafting pungently through the barn, Hanna had felt heavy and sleepy, the popcorn and Doritos she'd eaten earlier roiling uncomfortably in her stomach. Spooky images began to flicker in front of her eyes: Ali and the others ran through a dense jungle. Large, man-eating plants surrounded them. One plant snapped its jaws and grabbed Ali's leg. When Hanna had snapped out of it, Spencer was standing in the doorway of the barn, looking worried . . . and Ali was gone.

Wilden continued to stroll around the porch. He picked up a Southwest-style ceramic pot and turned it over, like he was checking for a price tag. Nosy bastard. "I need you girls to remember all you can. Think about what was happening around the time Alison disappeared. Did she have a boyfriend? Any new friends?"

"She had a boyfriend," Aria offered. "Matt Doolittle. He moved away." As she sat back, her T-shirt slid off her shoulder, revealing a lacy, fire engine–red bra strap. Slut.

"She was hanging out with these older field hockey girls," Emily volunteered.

Wilden looked at his notes. "Right. Katy Houghton and Violet Keyes. I got them. How about Alison's behavior. Was she acting strangely?"

They fell silent. *Yes, she was,* Hanna thought. She thought of one memory straightaway. On a blustery spring day, a few weeks before Ali disappeared, her dad had taken them both to a Phillies game. Ali was jittery the whole night, as if she'd downed packs and packs of Skittles. She kept checking her cell phone for texts and had seemed livid that her inbox was empty. During the seventh inning stretch, when they sneaked to the balcony to ogle a group of cute boys sitting in one of the skyboxes, Hanna noticed Ali's hands trembling. "Are you okay?" Hanna asked. Ali smiled at her. "I'm just cold," she explained.

But was that suspicious enough to bring up? It seemed like nothing, but it was hard to know what the police were looking for.

"She seemed okay," Spencer said slowly.

Wilden looked at Spencer dead-on. "You know, my older sister was a lot like Alison. She was the leader of her clique, too. Whatever my sister said, her friends did. *Anything*. And they kept all kinds of secrets for her. Is that how it worked for you guys?"

Hanna curled up her toes, suddenly irritated at where this conversation was going.

"I don't know," Emily mumbled. "Maybe."

Wilden glanced down at the vibrating cell phone clipped to his holster. "Excuse me." He ducked toward the garage, pulling his phone from his belt.

As soon as he was out of earshot, Emily let out a pent-up breath. "Guys, we have to tell him."

Hanna narrowed her eyes. "Tell him *what*?"

Emily held up her hands. "Jenna is blind. We did that."

Hanna shook her head. "Count me out. And anyway, Jenna's fine. Seriously. Have you noticed those Gucci sunglasses she wears? You have to get on, like, a year-long waiting list for a pair of those—they're harder to score than a Birkin bag."

Aria gaped at Hanna. "What *solar system* are you from? Who cares about Gucci sunglasses?"

"Well, obviously not someone like *you*," Hanna spat.

Aria tensed her jaw and leaned back. "What is *that* supposed to mean?"

"I think you know," Hanna snarled.

"Guys," Spencer warned.

Aria sighed and turned to face the side yard. Hanna glared at her pointy chin and ski-slope nose. Even Aria's profile wasn't as pretty as hers.

"We should tell him about Jenna," Emily goaded. "And A. The police should handle this. We're in over our heads."

"We're not telling him anything, and that's final," Hanna hissed.

"Yeah, I don't know, Emily," Spencer said slowly, poking her car keys through one of the tabletop's wide slats. "That's a big decision. It affects all our lives."

"We've talked about this before," Aria agreed. "Besides, A is gone, right?"

"I'll leave you all out of it," Emily protested, crossing her arms over her chest. "But I'm telling him. I think it's the right thing to do."

Aria's cell phone chirped and everyone jumped. Then Spencer's phone vibrated, wriggling toward the edge of the table. Hanna's device, which she'd shoved back into her purse, let out a muffled chime. And Emily's made that old-school telephone ring sound.

The last time the girls' phones all rang at once had been outside Ali's memorial service. Hanna had the same feeling she'd had the first time her father had taken her on

the Tilt-a-Whirl at the Rosewood County Fair when she
was five—that of dizzying nausea. Aria checked her phone.
Then Emily, then Spencer. "Oh God," Emily whispered.

Hanna didn't even bother reaching for her device;
instead, she leaned over Spencer's screen.

You really thought I was gone? Puh-lease. I've been
watching you this whole time. In fact, I might be watching
you right now. And girls—if you tell ANYONE about me,
you'll be sorry. —A

Hanna's heart throbbed. She heard footsteps and
turned around. Wilden was back.

He shoved his cell phone into his holster. Then he
looked at the girls and raised an eyebrow. "Did I miss
something?"

Had. He. Ever.

8

IT'S ALWAYS GOOD TO *READ* THE
BOOK BEFORE STEALING FROM IT

About a half hour later, Aria pulled up to her fifties-modern brown box of a house. She put her phone on speaker, waiting for Emily's voice mail message to finish. At the beep, she said, "Em, it's Aria. If you're really considering telling Wilden, please call me. A's capable of . . . of more than you think."

She hung up, feeling anxious. She couldn't imagine what dark secret of Emily's A might out if she talked to the police, but Aria knew from experience that A would do it.

Sighing, she unlocked her front door and clomped up the stairs, passing her parents' bedroom. The door was ajar. Inside, her parents' bed was neatly made—or was it only Ella's bed now? Ella had draped it with the bright salmon batik-print quilt that she loved and Byron despised. She'd piled all the pillows up on her side. The bed felt like a metaphor for divorce.

Aria dropped her books and aimlessly wandered back downstairs into the den, A's threat spinning around in her head like the centrifuge they'd used in today's biology lab. A was *still here*. And, according to Wilden, so was Ali's killer. *A* could be Ali's killer, worming her way into all of their lives. What if Wilden was right— what if Ali's killer wanted to hurt someone else? What if Ali's killer wasn't only Ali's enemy, but Aria's, Hanna's, Emily's, and Spencer's, too? Did that mean one of them was . . . next?

The den was dark except for the flickering TV. When Aria saw a hand curled over the edge of the tweedy love seat, she jumped. Then Mike's familiar face appeared.

"You're just in time." Mike pointed to the TV screen. *"Coming up, a never-before-seen home video of Alison DiLaurentis shot the week before she was murdered,"* he said in his best *Dateline* narrator voice.

Aria's stomach tightened. This was the leaked video Wilden had been talking about. Years ago, Aria had thrown herself into filmmaking, documenting everything she could, from snails in the backyard to her best friends. The movies were generally short, and Aria often tried to make them arty and poignant, focusing on Hanna's nostril, or the zipper on Ali's hoodie, or Spencer's fidgety fingers. When Ali went missing, Aria turned her video collection over to the police. The cops combed through them but had found no clues about where Ali could have gone. Aria still had the originals on her laptop, although she hadn't looked through them in a long, long time.

Aria flopped down on the love seat. When a Mercedes commercial ended and the news came back on, Aria and Mike sat up straighter. "Yesterday, an anonymous source sent us this clip of Alison DiLaurentis," the anchorman announced. "It offers a look at how chillingly innocent her life was just days before she was murdered. Let's watch."

The clip opened with a fumbling shot of Spencer's leather living room couch. "And because she wears a size zero," Hanna said offscreen. The camera panned to a younger-looking Spencer, who had on a pink polo and capri-length pajama pants. Her blond hair cascaded around her shoulders, and she wore a sparkly rhinestone crown on her head.

"She looks hot in that crown," Mike said enthusiastically, tearing open a large bag of Doritos.

"*Shhh,*" Aria hissed.

Spencer pointed at Ali's brand-new iPhone on the couch. "Want to read her texts?"

"I do!" Hanna whispered, ducking out of the shot. Then the camera swung to Emily, who looked nearly the same as she did today—same reddish-blond hair, same oversize swimming T-shirt, same pleasant-but-worried expression. Aria suddenly remembered this night—before they'd turned on the camera, Ali had gotten a text message and hadn't told them whom it was from. Everyone had been annoyed.

The camera showed Spencer holding Ali's phone. "It's locked." There was a blurry shot of the phone's screen.

"Do you know her password?" Aria heard her own voice ask.

"Damn! That's you!" Mike whooped.

"Try her birthday," Hanna suggested.

The camera showed Hanna's chubby hands reaching in and taking the phone from Spencer.

Mike wrinkled his nose and turned to Aria. "Is this what girls do when they're alone? I thought I was going to see pillow fights. Girls in panties. *Kissing.*"

"We were in seventh grade," Aria snapped. "That's just gross."

"There's nothing wrong with seventh-grade girls in their panties," Mike said in a small voice.

"What are you guys doing?" Ali's voice called. Then her face appeared onscreen, and Aria's eyes brimmed with tears. That heart-shaped face, those luminous dark blue eyes, that wide mouth—it was *haunting.*

"Were you looking at my phone?" Ali demanded, her hands on her hips.

"Of course not!" Hanna cried. Spencer staggered backward, clutching her head to keep her crown on.

Mike shoved a handful of Doritos into his mouth. "Can I slide into your DMs, Princess Spencer?" he said in falsetto.

"I don't think she goes out with prepubescent boys who still sleep with their blankies," Aria snapped.

"Hey!" Mike squeaked. "It's not a blankie! It's my lucky lacrosse jersey!"

"That's even worse," Aria said.

Ali floated onscreen again, looking alive and vibrant and carefree. How could Ali be dead? *Murdered?*

Then Spencer's older sister, Melissa, and her boyfriend, Ian, walked past the camera. "Hey, girls," Ian said.

"Hi," Spencer greeted him loudly.

Aria smirked at the TV. She'd forgotten how they all lusted over Ian. He was one of the people they would prank-call sometimes—along with Jenna Cavanaugh before they hurt her, Noel Kahn because he was cute, and Andrew Campbell because Spencer found him annoying. For Ian, they took turns pretending they were girls from 1-800-Sexy-Coeds.

The camera caught Ali rolling her eyes at Spencer. Then Spencer scowled at Ali behind her back. *Typical,* Aria thought. The night Ali disappeared, Aria hadn't been hypnotized, and she'd listened to Ali and Spencer fight. When they ran out of the barn, Aria waited a minute or two, then followed. Aria called their names. But she couldn't catch up with them. She went back inside, wondering if Ali and Spencer had just ditched the rest of them, staging the whole thing so they could run off to a cooler party. But eventually Spencer burst back inside. She looked so *lost,* as if she was in a trance.

Onscreen, Ian plopped down on the couch next to Ali. "So, what are you girls doing?"

"Oh, not much," Aria said from behind the phone screen, which she was using as a camera. "Making a film."

"A film?" Ian asked. "Can I be in it?"

"Of course," Spencer said, taking a seat next to him. "It's a talk show. I'm the host. You and Ali are my guests. I'll do you first."

The phone panned off the couch and focused on Ali's phone, which was next to Ali's hand on the couch. It got closer and closer until the bright screen took up the whole frame. To this day, Aria didn't know who had texted Ali that night.

"Ask him who his favorite teacher at Rosewood is," Aria's younger, slightly higher voice called out.

Ali chuckled and looked straight into Aria's phone. "That's a good question for you, Aria. You should ask him if he wants to *hook up* with any of his teachers. In vacant parking lots."

Aria gasped, and heard her younger self gasp onscreen, too. Ali had really *said* that? In front of *all* of them?

And then the clip was over.

Mike turned to her. There were neon orange Dorito crumbs around his mouth. "What did she mean about hooking up with teachers? It seemed like she was only talking to you."

A dry rasp escaped Aria's mouth. A had told Ella that Aria had known about Byron's affair all these years, but Mike still didn't know. He'd be so disappointed in her.

Mike stood up. "Whatever." Aria could tell he was trying to be all unaffected and casual, but he bumbled out of the room, knocking over a framed, signed photo of Lou Reed—Byron's rock star hero, and one of the few Byron artifacts Ella hadn't removed. She heard him stomp up to his bedroom and slam the door hard.

Aria put her head in her hands. This was the three thousandth instance she wished she were back in Reykjavík, hiking to a glacier, riding her Icelandic pony, Gilda, along a dried-up volcano bed, or even eating whale blubber, which everyone in Iceland seemed to adore.

She shut off the TV, and the house became eerily silent. When she heard a rustling at the door, she jumped. In the hall, she saw her mother, lugging in several large canvas shopping bags from Rosewood's organic market.

Ella noticed Aria and smiled wearily. "Hey, sweetie." Since she'd kicked Byron out, Ella seemed more disheveled than usual. Her black gauzy tunic was baggier than ever, her wide-leg silk pants had a tahini stain on the thigh, and her long, brownish-black hair sat in a rat's nest at the crown of her head.

"Let me help." Aria took a bunch of bags from Ella's arms. They walked into the kitchen together, hefted the bags onto the island, and started unpacking.

"How was your day?" Ella murmured.

Then Aria remembered. "Oh my God, you'll never believe what I did," she exclaimed, feeling a surge of giddiness. Ella glanced at her before putting the organic peanut butter away. "I went down to Hollis. Because I was looking for . . . you know. *Her.*" Aria didn't want to say Meredith's name. "She was teaching an art class, so I ran inside, grabbed a paintbrush, and painted a scarlet *A* across her chest. You know, like that woman in *The Scarlet Letter?* It was awesome."

Ella paused, holding a bag of whole-wheat pasta mid-air. She looked nauseated.

"She didn't know what hit her," Aria went on. "And then I said, 'Now everyone will know what you've done.'" She grinned and spread her arms out. *Taa-daa!*

Ella's eyes darted back and forth, processing this. "Do you realize that Hester Prynne is supposed to be a *sympathetic* character?"

Aria frowned. She was only on page eight. "I did it for you," Aria explained quietly. "For revenge."

"Revenge?" Ella's voice shook. "Thanks. That makes me look really sane. Like I'm really handling this well. This is hard enough for me as it is. Don't you realize you've made her look like . . . like a martyr?"

Aria took a step toward Ella. She hadn't considered that. "I'm sorry. . . ."

Then Ella crumpled against the counter and started to sob. Aria stood motionless. Her limbs felt like Sculpey clay straight out of the oven, all hardened and useless. She couldn't fathom what her mom was going through, and she'd gone and made it worse.

Outside their kitchen window, a hummingbird landed on the replica of a whale penis Mike had bought at Reykjavík's phallological museum. In any other circumstance, Aria would've pointed it out—hummingbirds were rare here, especially ones that landed on fake whale penises—but not today.

"I can't even look at you right now," Ella finally stammered.

Aria put her hand to her chest, as if her mother had speared her with one of her Wüsthof knives. "I'm *sorry*. I wanted Meredith to pay for what she's done." When Ella didn't answer, the searing, acidic feeling in Aria's stomach grew stronger. "Maybe I should get out of here for a while then, if you can't stand the sight of me."

She paused, waiting for Ella to jump in and say, *No, that's not what I want.* But Ella stayed quiet. "Yes, maybe that's a good idea," she agreed quietly.

"Oh." Aria's shoulders sank and her chin trembled. "Then I . . . I won't come home from school tomorrow." She didn't have any idea where she'd go, but that didn't matter right now. All that mattered was doing the one thing that would make her mom happy.

9

EVERYONE, A BIG ROUND OF APPLAUSE FOR SPENCER HASTINGS!

On Tuesday afternoon, while most of the Rosewood Day junior class ate lunch, Spencer sat on top of the conference table in the yearbook room. Eight gleaming MacBook Pros, a whole bunch of long-lensed Nikon cameras, six eager sophomore and freshman girls, and a slightly nerdy freshman boy surrounded her.

She tapped the covers of the past few Rosewood Day yearbooks. Each year, the books were named *The Mule* due to some apocryphal, inside joke from the 1920s that even the school's oldest teachers had long forgotten. "In this year's *Mule*, I think we should try to capture a slice of what Rosewood Day students are like."

Her yearbook staff diligently wrote down *slice of life* in their spiral-bound notebooks.

"Like . . . maybe we could do some quickie interviews with random students," Spencer went on. "Or ask people what's on their favorite Spotify playlist, and then publish it in boxes next to their photos. And how are the still lifes going?" Last meeting, they had planned to ask a couple kids to empty the contents of their bags to document what Rosewood Day students were carrying around.

"I got great photos of the stuff in Brett Weaver's soccer bag and Mona Vanderwaal's purse," said Brenna Richardson.

"Fantastic," Spencer said. "Keep up the good work."

Spencer closed her leaf-green leather-bound journal and dismissed her staff. Once they were gone, she grabbed her black fabric Kate Spade bag and pulled out her phone.

There it was. The note from A. She kept hoping it wouldn't be there.

As she slid the phone back into her bag, her fingers grazed against something in the inside pocket: Officer Wilden's business card. Wilden wasn't the first cop to ask Spencer about the night Ali went missing, but he was the only one who'd ever sounded so . . . suspicious.

The memory of that night was both crystal clear and incredibly muddled. She remembered a glut of emotions: excitement over getting the barn for their sleepover, annoyance that Melissa was there, giddiness that Ian was. Their kiss had been a couple weeks before that. But then Ali started talking about how Melissa and Ian made the cutest couple and Spencer's emotions swung again. Ali had already threatened to tell Melissa about the kiss.

Once Ian and Melissa left, Ali tried to hypnotize them, and she and Spencer got in a fight. Ali left, Spencer ran after her, and then . . . *nothing.* But what she never told the cops—or her family, or her friends—was that sometimes when she thought about that night, it felt like there was a black hole in the middle of it. That something had happened that she couldn't remember.

Suddenly, a vision flashed in front of Spencer's eyes. *Ali laughing nastily and turning away.*

Spencer stopped in the middle of the packed hallway and someone ran into her back.

"Will you move?" the girl behind her whined. "Some of us have to get to class."

Spencer took a tentative step forward. Whatever she had just remembered had quickly disappeared, but it felt like there had been an earthquake. She looked around for shattered glass and scattering students, certain the rest of the world had felt it, too, but everything looked completely normal. A few steps away, Naomi Zeigler inspected her reflection in her mini locker mirror. Two freshmen by the Teacher of the Year plaque laughed at the pointy Satan beard and horns drawn over Mr. Craft's smiling photo. The windows that faced the commons weren't the tiniest bit cracked, and none of the vases in the Pottery III display case had fallen over. What was the vision Spencer had just seen? Why did she feel so . . . slithery?

She slipped into her AP Econ classroom and slumped

down at her desk, which was right next to a very large portrait of a scowling J. P. Morgan. Once the rest of the class filed in and everyone sat down, Squidward strode to the front of the room. "Before today's video, I have an announcement." He looked at Spencer. Her stomach swirled. She didn't want everyone looking at her right now.

"For her first essay assignment, Spencer Hastings made a very eloquent, convincing argument on the invisible-hand theory," Squidward proclaimed, stroking his tie, which had Benjamin Franklin's C-note portrait stamped all over it. "And, as you may have heard, I have nominated her for a Golden Orchid award."

Squidward began to applaud, and the rest of the class followed. It lasted an intolerable fifteen seconds.

"But I have another surprise," Squidward continued. "I just got off the phone with a member of the judges' panel, and Spencer, you've made the finals."

The class burst into applause again. Someone at the back even wolf-whistled. Spencer sat very still. For a moment, she lost all vision completely. She tried to paste a smile on her face.

Andrew Campbell, who sat next to her, tapped her on the shoulder. "Nice job."

Spencer looked over. She and Andrew had hardly spoken since she'd been the world's worst Foxy date and ditched him at the dance. Mostly, he'd been giving her dirty looks. "Thanks," she croaked, once she found her voice.

"You must have really worked hard on it, huh? Did you use extra sources?"

"Uh-huh." Spencer frantically pulled out all the loose handouts from her econ folder and started straightening them. She smoothed out any bent-down corners and folds and tried to organize them by date. Melissa's paper was actually the only outside source Spencer had used. When she'd tried to do the necessary research for the essay, even Wikipedia's simple definition of *invisible hand* had completely perplexed her. The first few sentences of her sister's essay were clear enough—*The great Scottish economist Adam Smith's invisible-hand concept can be summed up very easily, whether it's describing the markets of the nineteenth century or those of the twenty-first: You might think people are doing things to help you, but in reality, everyone is only out for themselves.* But when she read the rest of the essay, her brain got as foggy as her family's eucalyptus steam room.

"What kind of sources?" Andrew continued. "Books? Magazine articles?" When she looked over again, he seemed to have a smirk on his face, and Spencer felt dizzy. Did he *know*?

"Like the . . . like the books McAdam suggested on his list," she fumbled.

"Ah. Well, congratulations. I hope you win."

"Thanks," she answered, deciding Andrew couldn't know. He was just jealous. Spencer and Andrew were ranked number one and number two, respectively, in the class and were constantly shifting positions. Andrew probably monitored Spencer's every achievement like a stockbroker watches the Dow Jones Industrial Average ticker. Spencer went back to straightening her folder, although it wasn't making her feel any better.

As Squidward dimmed the lights and the video—*Microeconomics and the Consumer*, with cheesy, upbeat music—came on, Spencer's phone vibrated in her bag. Slowly, she reached in and pulled it out. Her phone had one new text.

> Spence: I know what you did. But I won't tell if you do EXACTLY what I say. Wanna know what happens if you don't? Go to Emily's swim meet . . . and you'll see. —A

Someone next to Spencer cleared his throat. She looked over, and there was Andrew, staring right at her. His eyes glowed against the flickering light of the movie. Spencer turned to face forward, but she could still feel Andrew watching her in the darkness.

10

SOMEONE DIDN'T LISTEN

During the break at the Rosewood Day–Drury Academy swim meet, Emily opened her team locker and pulled down the straps of her Speedo Fastskin racing suit. This year, the Rosewood Day swim team had splurged on full-body, drag-free, Olympian-caliber swimsuits. They'd had to special-order them, and they'd just arrived in time for today's meet. The suits tapered to the ankles, clung to every inch of skin, and showed every bulge, reminding Emily of the photo in her bio textbook of a boa constrictor digesting a mouse. Emily grinned at Lanie Iler, her teammate. "I'm so happy to be getting out of this thing."

She was also happy she'd decided to tell Officer Wilden about A. Last night, after Emily returned home from Hanna's house, she'd called and arranged to meet Wilden at the Rosewood police station later tonight. Emily didn't care what the others said or thought about

A's threat—with the police involved, they could put this drama behind them forever.

"You're so lucky you're done," Lanie responded. Emily had already swum—and won—all of her events; now the only thing she had left to do was cheer along with the zillions of other Rosewood students who had showed up for the meet. She could hear the cheerleaders screaming from the locker room and hoped they wouldn't slip on the natatorium's wet tiled floor—Tracey Reid had taken a spill before the first event.

"Hey, girls." Coach Lauren strode down their aisle of lockers. Today, as usual, Lauren was wearing one of her inspirational swimming T-shirts: TOP TEN REASONS I SWIM. (Number five: BECAUSE I CAN EAT 5,000 CALORIES AND NOT FEEL GUILTY.) She clapped a hand on Emily's shoulder. "Great job, Em. Pulling ahead in the medley relay like that? Fantastic!"

"Thanks." Emily blushed.

Lauren leaned over the chipped red bench in the middle of the aisle. "There's a local recruiter from the University of Arizona here," she said in a low voice, only to Emily. "She asked if she could speak to you during the second half. That okay?"

Emily's eyes widened. "Of course!" The University of Arizona was one of the best swimming schools in the country.

"Great. You guys can talk in my office, if you want." Lauren gave Emily another smile. She disappeared toward the hall that led to the natatorium, and Emily followed. She passed her sister Carolyn, who was coming from the other direction.

"Carolyn, guess what!" Emily bounced up and down. "A University of Arizona recruiter wants to talk to me! If I went there and you went to Stanford, we'd be close!" Carolyn was graduating this year and had already been recruited by Stanford's swim team.

Carolyn glanced at Emily and disappeared into a bathroom stall, shutting the door behind her with a slam. Emily backed away, feeling stunned. What just happened? She and her sister weren't super-close, but she'd expected a *little* more enthusiasm than that.

As Emily walked toward the hall that led to the pool, Gemma Curran's face peeped at her from the showers. When Emily met her eyes, Gemma snapped the curtain closed. And as she walked by the sinks, Amanda Williamson was whispering to Jade Smythe. When Emily met their eyes in the mirror, their mouths made small, startled *O*'s. Emily felt goose bumps rise to the surface of her skin. What was going on?

"God, it seems like even *more* people are here now!" Lanie murmured, walking into the natatorium behind Emily. And she was right: The stands seemed more packed than during the first half. The band, set up near the diving well, was playing a fight song, and the foamy gray Hammerhead mascot had joined the cheerleaders in front of the stands. Everyone was in the stands—the popular kids, the soccer boys, the drama club girls, even her teachers. Spencer Hastings sat next to Kirsten Cullen. Maya was up there, typing furiously into her cell phone, and Hanna Marin sat near her, all alone and gazing out into the crowd. And there were Emily's parents, dressed up in their blue-and-white Rosewood Swimming sweat-shirts decorated with GO EMILY and GO CAROLYN buttons. Emily tried to wave to them, but they were too busy studying a piece of paper, probably the heat sheet. Actually, a lot of people were looking at the heat sheet. Mr. Shay, the geezerish biology teacher who always watched practice because he'd been a swimmer about a thousand years ago, held a copy about three inches from his face. The heat sheet wasn't *that* interesting—it just listed the order of events.

James Freed stepped in Emily's path. His mouth stretched into a broad grin. *"Hey*, Emily," he said leeringly. "I had no idea."

Emily frowned. "No idea . . . what?"

Aria's brother, Mike, sauntered up next to James. "Hi, Emily."

Mona Vanderwaal came up behind the two boys. "Stop bothering her, you two." She turned to Emily. "Ignore them. I want to invite you to something." She dug through her giant butterscotch suede satchel and handed Emily a white envelope. Emily turned it over in her hands. Whatever this was, Mona had scented it with something expensive. Emily glanced up, confused.

"I'm having a birthday party on Saturday," Mona explained, twisting a long piece of white-blond hair around her fingers. "Maybe I'll see you?"

"You should *totally* come," Mike agreed, widening his eyes.

"I . . ." Emily stammered. But before she could say anything more, the band struck up another fight song and Mona skipped away.

Emily looked at the invite again. What on earth was *that* all about? She wasn't the type of girl who got hand-delivered invitations from Mona Vanderwaal. And she certainly wasn't the type who got salacious looks from boys.

Suddenly, something across the pool caught her eye. It was a piece of paper taped to the wall. It hadn't been there before halftime. And it looked familiar. Like a photo.

She squinted. Her heart dropped to her knees. It *was* a photo . . . of two people kissing in a photo booth. In *Noel Kahn's* photo booth.

"Oh my God." Emily ran across the natatorium, sliding twice on the wet pool deck.

"Emily!" Aria ran toward her from the side entrance, her suede platform boots clomping against the tile and her blue-black hair flapping wildly all over her face. "I'm sorry I'm late, but can we talk?"

Emily didn't answer Aria. Someone had placed a Xerox of the kissing photo next to the big marker board that listed who was swimming in what race. Her whole team would see it. But would they know it was her?

She tore the Xerox off the wall. On the bottom, in big black letters, it said, LOOK WHAT EMILY FIELDS HAS BEEN PRACTICING WHEN SHE'S NOT IN THE POOL!

Well, that cleared *that* up.

Aria leaned over and examined the photo. "Is that . . . you?"

Emily's chin trembled. She crumpled up the paper in her hands, but when she looked around, she saw another copy sitting on top of someone's gear bag, a fold already down the center. She grabbed it and crumpled it up, too.

Then she saw another copy lying on the ground near the tub of kickboards. And another one . . . in Coach Lauren's hands. Lauren looked from the picture to Emily, from Emily to the picture. "Emily?" she said quietly.

"This can't be happening," Emily whispered, raking her hand through her wet hair. She glanced over at the wire-mesh wastebasket near Lauren's office. There were at least ten discarded pictures of her kissing Maya at the bottom. Someone had thrown a half-drunk can of Sunkist on top. The liquid had oozed out, coloring their faces orange. There were more near the water fountains. And taped up to the racing lane storage wheel. Her teammates, who were all filtering out from the locker rooms, gave her uneasy looks. Her ex-boyfriend, Ben, smirked at her, as if to say, *Your little experiment isn't so fun now, huh?*

Aria picked up a copy that had seemingly fluttered down from the ceiling. She squinted and pursed her shiny, strawberry-red lips together. "So what? You're kissing someone." Her eyes widened. *"Oh."*

Emily let out a helpless *eep*.

"Did A do this?" Aria whispered.

Emily looked around frantically. "Did you see who was giving these out?" But Aria shook her head. Emily unzipped the pouch to her swim bag and found her cell phone. There was a text. Of course there was a text.

Emily, sweetie, I know you're all about tit for tat, so when you made plans to out me, I decided to out you too. Kisses! —A

"Damn," Aria whispered, reading the text over Emily's shoulder.

A sickening thought suddenly hit Emily. Her parents. That paper they were looking at—it wasn't the heat sheet. *It was the photo.* She glanced over at the stands. Sure enough, her parents were staring at her. They looked like they were about to cry, their faces red and nostrils flared.

"I have to get out of here." Emily searched for the nearest exit.

"No way." Aria grabbed Emily's wrist and spun her around. "This is nothing to be ashamed of. If someone says something, screw 'em."

Emily sniffed. People might *call* Aria weird, but she

celebrated her weirdness. And she had a boyfriend, so presumably he celebrated her weirdness, too. She would never know what this felt like.

"Emily, this is our opportunity!" Aria protested. "A is probably *here*." She looked menacingly into the bleachers.

Emily peeked over at the stands again. Her parents still wore the same angry and hurt expressions. Maya's spot was now empty. Emily scanned the length of the stands for her, but Maya was gone.

A *was* probably up there. And Emily wished she was brave enough to climb up into the bleachers and shake everyone until someone confessed. But she couldn't.

"I . . . I'm sorry," Emily said abruptly, and ran for the locker room. She passed the hundred or so people who now knew what she was really like, trampling over copies of her and Maya on the way.

11

EVEN HIGH-TECH SECURITY DOESN'T PROTECT YOU FROM EVERYTHING

Moments later, Aria pushed through the fogged-up double doors of Rosewood Day's natatorium and joined Spencer and Hanna, who were talking quietly by the vending machines. "Poor Emily," Hanna whispered to Spencer. "Did you know about . . . this?"

Spencer shook her head. "No idea."

"Remember when we snuck into the Kahns' pool when they were on vacation and went skinny-dipping?" Hanna murmured. "Remember when we used to practice kissing pillows? Emily always *said* she was imagining kissing various members of the men's Olympic swim team. I never felt weird."

"Me neither," Aria piped up, ducking out of the way so a freshman boy could get a soda out of the Coke machine.

"Do you think she thought any of us were cute?"

Hanna widened her eyes. "But I was so fat back then," she added, sounding a little disappointed.

"A passed around those flyers," Aria said to Hanna and Spencer. She pointed toward the pool. "A might be here."

They all peered into the natatorium. Competitors stood on the blocks, waiting. The hammerhead shark mascot paraded up and down the length of the pool. The stands were still packed. "What are we supposed to do about it?" Hanna asked, narrowing her eyes. "Stop the meet?"

"We shouldn't do anything." Spencer zipped up her khaki Burberry anorak to her chin. "If we look for A, A might get mad . . . and do something worse."

"A. Is. Here!" Aria repeated. "This might be our big chance!"

Spencer looked at the crowd of kids in the lobby. "I . . . I have to go." With that, she darted through the revolving doors and sprinted across the parking lot.

Aria turned to Hanna. "Spencer ran out of here like *she* was A," she half joked.

"I heard she's a finalist in some big essay contest." Hanna pulled out her Chanel compact and began dabbing at her chin. "You know she gets manic when she's competing. She's probably going home to study."

"True," Aria said quietly. Maybe Spencer was right— maybe A *would* do something worse if they searched the stands.

Suddenly, someone whipped her hood off her head

from behind. Aria swirled around. "Mike," she gasped. *"God."*

Her brother grinned. "Did you get a photo of Emily and that new girl hooking up? Can you get me Emily's digits?"

"Absolutely not." She surveyed her brother. His STX lacrosse cap smashed down his blue-black hair, and he was wearing his blue-and-white Rosewood Day varsity lacrosse windbreaker. She hadn't seen him since last night.

"So." Mike put his hands on his hips. "I hear you got kicked out of the house."

"I wasn't kicked out," Aria said defensively. "I just thought it would be better if I stayed away for a while."

"And you're moving into Sean's?"

"Yeah," Aria answered. After Ella had told Aria to leave, Aria had called Sean in hysterics. She hadn't been fishing for an invitation—but Sean had offered, saying it wouldn't be any trouble at all.

Hanna's jaw dropped. "You're *moving* to Sean's? As in, his house?"

"Hanna, not by choice," Aria said quickly. "It's an emergency."

Hanna cut her eyes away. "Whatever. I don't care. You're going to hate it. Everybody knows that staying with your boyfriend's parents always leads to breakups." She whirled around, pushing through the crowd toward the front door.

"Hanna!" Aria protested, but Hanna didn't turn

around. She glared at Mike. "Did you *have* to mention that when she was standing here? Do you have no tact at all?"

Mike shrugged. "Sorry, I don't speak PMS." He pulled out a PowerBar from his pocket and started to eat it, not bothering to offer Aria any. "You going to Mona's party?"

Aria stuck out her lip. "Not sure. I haven't thought about it."

"Are you *depressed* or something?" Mike asked, his mouth full.

Aria didn't have to think about it too hard. "Kind of. I mean . . . Dad left. How do *you* feel?"

Mike's face changed from being open and jokey to hardened and guarded. He let the paper fall to his side. "So, last night I asked Mom some questions. She told me Dad was seeing that girl before we went to Iceland. And that you knew."

Aria put the ends of her hair in her mouth and stared at the blue recycling can in the corner. Someone had drawn a cartoonish pair of boobs on the lid. "Yeah."

"So why didn't you tell *me* about it?"

Aria glanced at him. "Byron told me not to."

Mike took a violent bite of PowerBar. "It was okay, though, to tell Alison DiLaurentis. And it's okay for her to say it in a video that's *all over the news*."

"Mike . . ." Aria started. "I didn't *tell* her. She was with me when it happened."

"Whatever," Mike grunted, colliding with the shark mascot as he pushed angrily through the natatorium's double doors. Aria considered going after him but didn't. She was reminded, suddenly, of the time in Reykjavík when she was supposed to baby-sit Mike but had gone off to the Blue Lagoon geothermal spa with her boyfriend, Hallbjorn, instead. When she returned, smelling like sulfur and covered in curative salt, she'd discovered that Mike had set half the backyard's wood trellis on fire. Aria had gotten in deep trouble for it—and really, it *had* been her fault. She'd noticed Mike eagerly eyeing the kitchen matches before she left for the lagoon. She could have stopped him. She probably could have stopped Byron, too.

"So this one's yours," Sean said, leading Aria down his mahogany-floored, immaculately clean hallway to a large, white bedroom. It had a bay window with a window seat, gauzy white curtains, and a white bouquet of flowers on the end table.

"I love it." The room looked like the Parisian boutique hotel room her family stayed in the time her father was interviewed on Parisian television for being an expert on gnomes. "You sure it's okay for me to stay?"

"Of course." Sean gave her a demure kiss on the cheek. "I'll let you get settled."

Aria looked out the window at the pinkish, late-Tuesday sky and couldn't help comparing this view to hers at home. The Ackards' estate was nestled in the deep woods and surrounded by at least ten acres of untouched land. The nearest property, a castlelike monolith with medieval-style turrets, was at least three football fields away. Aria's house was in a lovely but rickety neighborhood close to the college. The only thing she could see of her neighbors' yard was their unfortunate collection of birdbaths, stone animals, and lawn jockeys.

"Everything okay with the room?" Mrs. Ackard, Sean's stepmother, asked as Aria drifted downstairs into the kitchen.

"It's great," Aria said. "Thank you so much."

Mrs. Ackard gave her a sweet smile in return. She was blond, a bit pudgy, with inquisitive blue eyes and a mouth that looked like it was smiling even when she wasn't. When Aria closed her eyes and pictured a mom, Mrs. Ackard was pretty much what she imagined. Sean had told her that before she married his dad she'd worked as a magazine editor in Philadelphia, but now she was a full-time housewife, keeping the Ackards' monstrous house looking photo-shoot ready at all times. The apples in the wooden bowl on the island were unbruised, the magazines in the living room rack all faced the same direction, and the tassels on the giant Oriental rug were even, as if they'd just been combed.

"I'm making mushroom ravioli," Mrs. Ackard said, inviting Aria to come over and smell a pot of sauce.

"Sean said you're a vegetarian."

"I am," Aria answered softly. "But you didn't have to do that for me."

"It's no trouble," Mrs. Ackard said warmly. There were also scalloped potatoes, a tomato salad, and a loaf of the hearty, gourmet seven-grain bread from Fresh Fields that Ella always scoffed at, saying anyone who paid $10.99 for some flour and water ought to have his head examined.

Mrs. Ackard pulled the wooden spoon out of the pot and rested it on the counter. "You were good friends with Alison DiLaurentis, weren't you? I saw that video of you girls on the news."

Aria ducked her head. "That's right." A lump grew in her throat. Seeing Ali so alive in that video had brought Aria's grief to the surface all over again.

To Aria's surprise, Mrs. Ackard wrapped her arm around her shoulder and gave her a little squeeze. "I'm so sorry," she murmured. "I can't imagine what that's like."

Tears prickled at Aria's eyes. It felt good to be nestled in a mom's arms, even if she wasn't *her* mom.

Sean sat next to Aria at dinner, and *everything* was the antithesis of how it went at Aria's house. The Ackards put their napkins on their laps, there was no television news droning in the background, and Mr. Ackard, who was rangy and balding but had a charismatic smile, didn't read the newspaper at the table. The younger Ackard twins,

Colin and Aidan, kept their elbows off the table and didn't poke each other with their forks—Aria could only imagine what atrocities Mike would commit if *he* had a twin.

"Thank you," Aria said as Mrs. Ackard poured more milk in her glass, even though Byron and Ella had always said milk contained synthetic hormones and caused cancer. Aria had told Ezra about her parents' ban on milk the evening she'd spent at his apartment a few weeks ago. Ezra had laughed, saying his family had their granola moments, too.

Aria laid down her fork. How had *Ezra* crept into her peaceful dinnertime thoughts? She quickly eyed Sean, who was chewing a forkful of potatoes. She leaned over and touched his wrist. He smiled.

"Sean tells us you're taking AP classes, Aria," Mr. Ackard said, spearing a carrot.

Aria shrugged. "Just English and AP Studio Art."

"English lit was my major in college," Mrs. Ackard said enthusiastically. "What are you reading right now?"

"The Scarlet Letter."

"I love that book!" Mrs. Ackard cried, taking a small sip of red wine. "It really shows how restrictive the Puritan society used to be. Poor Hester Prynne."

Aria chewed on the inside of her cheek. If only Aria had talked to Mrs. Ackard *before* she branded Meredith.

"The Scarlet Letter." Mr. Ackard put his finger to his lips. "They made that into a movie, didn't they?"

Sean shrugged. "Did they?"

"The one where the man falls in love with a younger girl, right?" Mr. Ackard added. "So scandalous."

Aria drew in her breath. She felt like everyone was looking at her, but in reality, only Sean was. His eyes were wide and drawn down, mortified. *I'm sorry,* his expression said. "No, David," Mrs. Ackard said quietly, in a voice that indicated she had some idea of Aria's situation. "That's *Lolita.*"

"Oh. Right." Mr. Ackard shrugged, apparently not realizing his faux pas. "I get them all mixed up."

After dinner, Sean and the twins went upstairs to do their homework, and Aria followed. Her guest room was quiet and inviting. Some time between dinner and now, Mrs. Ackard had put a box of Kleenex and a vase of lavender on her nightstand. The flowers' grandmotherly smell filled the room. Aria flopped on her bed, switched on the local news for company, and opened Gmail on her laptop. There was one new note. The name of the sender was a series of garbled letters and numbers. Aria felt her heart stop as she double-clicked it open.

Aria: Don't you think Sean should know about that extra-credit work you did with a certain English teacher? Real relationships are built on truth, after all. —A

Just then, the central heating shut off, making Aria sit up straighter. Outside, a twig snapped. Then another. *Someone was watching.*

She crept to the window and peered out. The pine trees cast lumpy shadows across the tennis court. A security camera perched on the edge of the house slowly swiveled from right to left. There was a flicker of light, then nothing.

When she looked back into her room, something on the news caught her eye. *New stalker sighting,* the banner at the bottom of the screen said. "We've received news that a few people have seen the Rosewood Stalker," said a reporter, as Aria turned up the volume. "Stand by for details."

There was an image of a police car in front of a behemoth of a house with castlelike turrets. Aria turned to the window again—there they were. And sure enough, a blue police siren was now flashing against the far-off pines.

She stepped into the hall. Sean's door was shut; The Weeknd drifted out. "Sean?" She pushed his bedroom door open. His books were strewn all over his desk, but his desk chair was empty. There was an indentation on his perfectly made bed where his body had been. His window was open, and a chilly breeze blew in, making the curtains dance like ghosts.

Aria didn't know what else to do, so she went back to her computer. That's when she saw a new email.

P.S. I may be a bitch, but I'm not a murderer. Here's a clue for the clueless: Someone wanted something of Ali's. The killer is closer than you think. —A

12

AH, COURT LIFE

Tuesday evening, Hanna strolled down the main concourse at the King James Mall, puzzling over her phone. She'd sent Mona a text asking Are we still meeting for my dress fitting? but she hadn't received a response.

Mona was probably still annoyed at her because of the Frenniversary thing, but whatever. Hanna had tried to explain why her old friends had been at her house, but Mona had interrupted her before she could even start, declaring in her frostiest voice, "I saw you and your besties on the news. Congrats on your big TV debut." Then she hung up. So sure she was pissed, but Hanna knew Mona couldn't stay mad for long. If she did, who would be her BFF?

Hanna passed Rive Gauche, the mall brasserie where they were supposed to have their Frenniversary dinner yesterday. It was a copy of Balthazar in New York, which was a copy of zillions of cafés in Paris. She caught sight of a group of girls at Hanna's and Mona's favorite banquette. One of the girls was Naomi. The next was Riley. And the girl next to her was . . . Mona.

Hanna did a double take. What was Mona doing with . . . *them?*

Even though the lights in Rive Gauche were dim and romantic, Mona was wearing her pink-tinted aviators. Naomi, Riley, Kelly Hamilton, and Nicole Hudson—Naomi and Riley's bitchy sophomore toadies—surrounded her, and a big, uneaten plate of fries sat in the middle of the table. Mona appeared to be telling a story, waving her hands around animatedly and widening her big, blue eyes. She came to a punch line, and the others hooted.

Hanna squared her shoulders. She strode through the café's antique brown door. Naomi was the first to notice her. Naomi nudged Kelly, and they whispered together.

"What are you girls doing here?" she demanded, standing over Riley and Naomi.

Mona leaned forward on her elbows. "Well, isn't this a surprise? I didn't know if you still wanted to be on the court, since you're so busy with your old friends." She flicked her hair over her shoulder and took a sip of Diet Coke.

Hanna rolled her eyes and settled on the end of the dark red banquette bench. "Of course I still want to be on your court, drama whore."

Mona gave her a bland smile. "'Kay, tubbykins."

"Bitch," Hanna shot back.

"Slut," Mona said. Hanna giggled . . . and so did Naomi, Riley, and the others. Sometimes she and Mona got in mock-fights like this, although normally they didn't have an audience.

Mona twirled a piece of pale blond hair around her finger. "Anyway, I decided the more, the merrier. Small courts are boring. I want this party to be over-the-top."

"We're *so* excited," Naomi gushed. "I can't wait to try on the dress Mona picked out for us."

Hanna shot them a taut smile. This really didn't make any sense. Everyone at Rosewood knew Riley and Naomi had been talking about Hanna behind her back. And wasn't it just last year that Mona had vowed she'd despise Naomi forever after Naomi gossiped that Mona had gotten skin grafts? Hanna had fake-friended Naomi for that—she'd pretended she and Mona were in a fight, won Naomi's confidence, then pilfered a cheesy love letter Naomi had written to Mason Byers from Naomi's notebook. Hanna posted the letter anonymously on Rosewood Day's intranet the very next day, everyone laughed, and all was right again.

All at once, Hanna had an epiphany. Of course! Mona was fake-friending! It *completely* made sense. She felt a little better, realizing what was going on, but she still wanted confirmation. She eyed Mona. "Hey, Mon, can I talk to you for a sec? Alone?"

"Can't right now, Han." Mona looked at her Movado

watch. "We're late for our fitting. C'mon."

With that, Mona strolled out of the restaurant, her three-inch heels clacking against the shiny walnut floor. The others followed. Hanna reached over to grab her enormous Gucci purse, but the zipper had come undone and the entire contents spilled under the table. All her makeup, her wallet, her vitamins, the Hydroxycut she'd stolen ages ago from GNC but was a little too scared to take . . . everything. Hanna scrambled to pick it all up, her eyes on Mona and the others as they snaked away. She knelt down, feverishly trying to stuff everything into her bag as quickly as possible.

"Hanna Marin?"

Hanna jumped. Above her was a familiar, tall, floppy-haired waiter. "It's Lucas," he reminded her, fiddling with the cuff on his white button-down, the Rive Gauche uniform. "You probably don't recognize me because I look so French in this outfit."

"Oh," Hanna said wearily. "Hey." She'd known Lucas Beattie forever. In seventh grade, he'd been popular—and, bizarrely, for a second, he'd liked Hanna. Word had gotten around that Lucas was going to send Hanna a red heart-shaped box of candy on the schoolwide Candy Day. A boy sending you a heart-shaped box of candy meant *love*, so Hanna got really excited.

But then, a few days before Candy Day, something changed. Lucas was suddenly a dork. His friends started to ignore him, girls began to laugh at him, and a rampant rumor that he liked to make out with his cat swirled. Hanna couldn't believe her luck, but she secretly wondered if he'd gone from popular to a loser all because he'd decided to like her. Even if she was Ali D's friend, she was still a fat, dorky, clumsy loser. When he sent her the candy, Hanna hid it in her locker and didn't thank him.

"What's up?" Hanna asked blandly. Lucas had pretty much stayed a loser.

"Not much," Lucas responded eagerly. "What's up with you?"

Hanna rolled her eyes. She hadn't meant to start a conversation. "I have to go," she said, looking toward the courtyard. "My friends are waiting for me."

"Actually . . ." Lucas followed her toward the exit, "your friends forgot to pay the bill." He whipped out a leather booklet. "Unless, um, you were getting it this time."

"Oh." Hanna cleared her throat. Nice of Mona to mention it. "No problem."

Lucas swiped her AmEx and gave her the bill to sign, and Hanna strode out of Rive Gauche without adding a tip—or telling Lucas goodbye. The more she thought about it, she was excited that Naomi and Riley were part of Mona's court. Around Rosewood, party court girls competed over who could get the birthday girl the most glamorous gift. A day pass to the Blue Springs Spa or a Prada gift card didn't cut it, either—the winning gift had to be totally over-the-top. Julia Rubenstein's best friend had hired male strippers to perform at an after party for a select few—and they'd been *hot* strippers, not muscle-heads. And Sarah Davies had convinced her dad to hire a Dua Lipa-esque singer to sing "Happy Birthday" to the girl-of-honor. Thankfully, Naomi and Riley were about as creative as the newborn panda at the Philadelphia Zoo. Hanna could out-glam them on her worst day.

She heard her phone humming in her bag and pulled it out. There were two messages in her inbox. The first, from Mona, had come in six minutes ago.

> Where are you, bee-yotch? If you're any later, the tailor's going to get pissed. —Mon

But the second text, which had arrived two minutes later, was from a blocked number. That could only be one person.

> Dear Hanna, We may not be friends, but we have the same enemies. So here are two tips: One of your old friends is hiding something from you. Something big. And Mona? She's not your friend, either. So watch your back. —A

13

HELLO, MY NAME IS EMILY. AND I'M GAY.

That night at 7:17 Emily pulled into her driveway. After she'd run out of the natatorium, she'd walked around the Rosewood Bird Sanctuary for hours. The busily chirping sparrows, happy little ducks, and tame parakeets soothed her. It was a good place to escape from reality . . . and a certain incriminating photo.

Every light in the house was on, including the one in the bedroom that Emily and Carolyn shared. How would she explain the photo to her family? She wanted to say that kissing Maya in that picture had been a joke, that someone was playing a prank on her. *Ha ha, kissing girls is gross!*

But it wasn't true, and it made her heart ache.

The house smelled warm and inviting, like a mixture of coffee and potpourri. Her mother had turned on the hallway Hummel figurines cabinet. Little figurines of a boy milking a cow and a lederhosen-clad girl pushing a wheelbarrow slowly rotated. Emily made her way down the floral wallpapered hallway toward the living room. Both her parents were sitting on the flowered couch. An older woman sat on the love seat.

Her mother gave her a watery smile. "Well, hello, Emily."

Emily blinked a few times. "Um, hi . . ." She looked from her parents to the stranger on the love seat.

"You want to come in?" her mother asked. "We have someone here to see you."

The older woman, who was wearing high-waisted black slacks and a mint-green blazer, stood and offered her hand. "I'm Edith." She grinned. "It's so nice to meet you, Emily. Why don't you sit down?"

Emily's father bustled into the dining room and dragged another chair over for her. She sat down tentatively, feeling jumpy. It was the same feeling she used to get when her old friends played the Pillow Game—one person walked around the living room blindfolded, and, at a random moment, the others bombarded her with pillows. Emily didn't like playing—she hated those tense moments right before they started smacking her—but she always played anyway, because Ali loved it.

"I'm from a program called Tree Tops," Edith said. "Your parents told me about your problem."

The bones in Emily's butt pressed into the bare wood of the dining room chair. "Problem?" Her stomach sank. She had a feeling she knew what *problem* meant.

"Of course it's a problem." Her mother's voice was choked. "That picture—with that girl we *forbade* you to see—has it happened more than once?"

Emily nervously touched the scar on her left palm that she'd gotten when Carolyn accidentally speared her with the gardening shears. She'd grown up striving to be as obedient and well-behaved as possible, and she couldn't lie to her parents—at least not well. "It's happened more than once, I guess," she mumbled.

Her mother let out a small, pained whimper.

Edith pursed her wrinkly, fuchsia-lined lips. She had an old-lady mothball smell. "What you're feeling, it's not permanent. It's a sickness, Emily. But we at Tree Tops can cure you. We've rehabilitated many ex-gays since the program began."

Emily barked out a laugh. "Ex . . . *gays*?" The world started to spin, then recede. Emily's parents looked at her self-righteously, their hands wrapped around their coffee cups.

"Your interest in young women isn't genetic or scientific, but environmental," Edith explained. "With counseling, we'll help you dismiss your . . . urges, shall we say."

Emily gripped the arms of her chair. "That sounds . . . *weird*."

"Emily!" scolded her mother—she'd taught her children never to disrespect adults. But Emily was too bewildered to be embarrassed.

"It's not weird," Edith chirped. "Don't worry if you don't understand it all now. Many of our new recruits don't." She looked at Emily's parents. "We have a *superb* track record of rehabilitation in the greater Philadelphia area."

Emily wanted to throw up. *Rehabilitation?* She searched her parents' faces, but they gave her nothing. She glanced out to the street. *If the next car that passes is white, this isn't happening,* she thought. *If it's red, it is.* A car swept past. Sure enough, it was red.

Edith placed her coffee cup on its saucer. "We're going to have a peer mentor come talk to you. Someone who experienced the program firsthand. She's a senior at Rosewood Senior High, and her name's Becka. She's very nice. You'll just talk. And after that, we'll discuss you joining the program properly. Okay?"

Emily looked at her parents. "I don't have time to talk to anybody," she insisted. "I have swimming in the mornings and after school, and then I have homework."

Her mother smiled tensely. "You'll make time. What about lunch tomorrow?"

Edith nodded. "I'm sure that would be fine."

Emily rubbed her throbbing head. She already hated Becka, and she hadn't even met her. "Fine," she agreed. "Tell her to meet me at Lorence chapel." There was no way Emily was talking with Little Miss Tree Tops in the cafeteria. School was going to be brutal enough tomorrow as it was.

Edith brushed her hands together and stood up. "I'll make all the arrangements."

Emily stood against the foyer wall as her parents handed Edith her coat and thanked her for coming. Edith navigated down the Fieldses' stone path to her car. When Emily's parents turned back to her, they had weary, sober looks on their faces.

"Mom, Dad . . ." Emily started.

Her mother whirled around. "That Maya girl has a few tricks up her sleeve, huh?"

Emily backed up. "Maya didn't pass that picture around."

Mrs. Fields eyed Emily carefully, then sat down on the couch and put her head in her hands. "Emily, what are we going to do *now*?"

"What do you mean, *we*?"

Her mother looked up. "Don't you see that this is a reflection on all of us?"

"*I* didn't make the announcement," Emily protested.

"It doesn't matter how it happened," her mother interrupted. "What matters is that it's out there." She stood up and regarded the couch, then picked up a decorative pillow and smacked it with her fist to fluff it up. She set it back down, picked up another, and started all over again. *Thwack.* She was punching them harder than she needed to.

"It was so shocking to see that picture of you, Emily," Mrs. Fields said. "*Horribly* shocking. And to hear that it's something you've done *more than once*, well . . ."

"I'm sorry," Emily whimpered. "But maybe it's not—"

"Have you even thought about how hard this is for the rest of us?" Mrs. Fields interrupted. "We're all . . . well, Carolyn came home crying. And your brother and sister both called me, offering to fly home."

She picked up another pillow. *Thwack, thwack.* A few feathers spewed out and floated through the air before settling on the carpet. Emily wondered what this would look like to someone passing by the window. Perhaps they'd see the feathers flying and think that something silly and happy was happening, instead of what actually was.

Emily's tongue felt leaden in her mouth. A gnawing hole at the pit of her stomach remained. "I'm sorry," she whispered.

Her mother's eyes flashed. She nodded to Emily's father. "Go get it." Her father disappeared into the living room, and Emily listened to him rooting through the drawers of their old antique bureau. Seconds later, he returned with a printout from Expedia. "This is for you," Mr. Fields said.

It was an itinerary, flying from Philadelphia to Des Moines, Iowa. With her name on it. "I don't understand."

Mr. Fields cleared his throat. "Just to make things perfectly clear, either you do Tree Tops—*successfully*—or you will go live with your aunt Helene."

Emily blinked. "Aunt Helene . . . who lives on a farm?"

"Can you think of another Aunt Helene?" he asked.

Emily felt dizzy. She looked to her mom. "You're going to send me *away*?"

"Let's hope it doesn't come to that," Mrs. Fields answered.

Tears dotted Emily's eyes. For a while, she couldn't speak. It felt as if a block of cement were sitting on her chest. "Please don't send me away," she whispered. "I'll . . . I'll do Tree Tops. Okay?"

She lowered her gaze. This felt like when she and Ali used to arm wrestle—they were matched for strength and could do it for hours, but eventually, Emily would surrender, letting her arm go limp. Maybe she was giving up too easily, but she couldn't fight this.

A small, relieved smile crept over her mother's face. She put the itinerary in her cardigan pocket. "Now, that wasn't so hard, was it?"

Before she could respond, Emily's parents left the room.

14

SPENCER'S BIG CLOSE-UP

Wednesday morning, Spencer stared at herself in her mahogany Chippendale vanity mirror. The vanity and dressing table had been in the Hastings family for two hundred years, and the watermark stain on the top had allegedly been made by Ernest Hemingway—he'd set his sweaty glass of whisky on it during one of Spencer's great-great-grandmother's cotillions.

Spencer picked up her round boar-bristle brush and began raking it through her hair until her scalp hurt. Jordana, the reporter from the *Philadelphia Sentinel,* would be showing up soon for her big interview and photo shoot. A stylist was bringing wardrobe options, and Spencer's hairdresser, Uri, was due any minute to give her a blow-out. She just finished her own makeup, going for a subtle, refined, fresh-faced look, which hopefully made her look smart, put-together—and absolutely *not* a plagiarist.

Spencer gulped and glanced at a photo she kept

wedged in the corner of the mirror. It was of her old friends on Ali's uncle's yacht in Newport, Rhode Island. They were all smashed together, wearing matching J. Crew bikinis and wide-brimmed straw hats, grinning like they were goddesses of the sea.

This will go fine, Spencer told the mirror, taking a deep breath. The article would probably end up being a tiny item in the Style section, something no one would even see. Jordana might ask her two or three questions, tops. A's note from yesterday—*I know what you did*—had only been meant to scare her. She tried to sweep it to the back of her mind.

Suddenly, her phone bleeped, and Spencer tapped the screen.

Need another warning, Spence? Ali's murderer is right in front of you. —A

Spencer's phone clattered to the floor. *Ali's murderer?* She stared at her reflection in the mirror. Then at the picture of her friends in the corner. Ali was holding the yacht's wheel, and the others were grinning behind her.

And then, something in the window caught her eye. Spencer wheeled around, but there was nothing. No one in her yard except for a lost-looking mallard duck. Nobody in the DiLaurentises' or the Cavanaughs' yards, either. Spencer turned back to the mirror and ran her cool hands down the length of her face.

"Hey."

Spencer jumped. Melissa stood behind her, leaning against Spencer's four-poster bed. Spencer whirled around, not sure if Melissa's reflection was real. She'd sneaked up on Spencer so . . . stealthily.

"Are you all right?" Melissa asked, fiddling with the ruffled collar of her green silk blouse. "You look like you've seen a ghost."

"I just got the weirdest text," Spencer blurted out.

"Really? What did it say?"

Spencer glanced at her phone on the cream-colored rug, then kicked it farther under the dressing table. "Never mind."

"Well, anyway, your reporter is here." Melissa wandered out of Spencer's room. "Mom wanted me to tell you."

Spencer stood up and walked to her door. She couldn't believe she'd almost told Melissa about A's note. But what had A meant? How could Ali's killer be right in front of her, when she was staring in the mirror?

A vision flashed in front of her eyes. *Come on,* Ali cackled nastily. *You read it in my diary, didn't you?*

I wouldn't read your diary, Spencer replied. *I don't care.*

There were a few spots and flashes, and a white rush of movement. And then, *poof,* gone. Spencer blinked furiously for a few seconds, standing dazed and alone in the middle of the upstairs hallway. It felt like a continuation of the strange, fuzzy memory from the other day. But what was it?

She strode slowly down the stairs, gripping the railing for support. Her parents and Melissa were gathered around the couch in the living room. A plump woman with frizzy black hair and black plastic cat's-eye glasses, a skinny guy with a patchy goatee and a ginormous camera around his neck, and a petite girl who had a pink streak in her hair stood near the front door.

"Spencer Hastings!" the frizzy-haired woman cried when she spied Spencer. "Our finalist!"

She threw her arms around Spencer, and Spencer's nose smushed into the woman's blazer, which smelled like the maraschino cherries Spencer used to get in her Shirley Temples at the country club. Then, she stepped back and held Spencer at arm's length. "I'm Jordana Pratt, style editor of the *Philadelphia Sentinel*," she cried. Jordana gestured to the other two strangers. "And this is Bridget, our stylist, and Matthew, our photographer. It's so nice to meet you!"

"Likewise," Spencer sputtered.

Jordana greeted Spencer's mother and father. She passed over Melissa, not even looking at her, and Melissa cleared her throat. "Um, Jordana, I believe we've met too."

Jordana narrowed her eyes and wrinkled her nose, as if a bad smell had just permeated the air. She stared at Melissa for a few seconds. "We have?"

"You interviewed me when I ran the Philadelphia Marathon a couple years ago," Melissa reminded her, standing up straighter and pushing her hair behind her ears. "At the Eames Oval, in front of the art museum?"

Jordana still looked lost. "Great, great!" she cried distractedly. "Love the marathon!" She gazed at Spencer again. Spencer noticed she was wearing a Cartier Tank Americaine watch—and not one of the cheap stainless ones, either. "So. I want to know everything about you. What you like to do for fun, your favorite foods, who you think is going to win on *The Masked Singer*, everything. You're probably going to be famous someday, you know! All Golden Orchid winners end up stars."

"Spencer doesn't watch *The Masked Singer*," Mrs. Hastings volunteered. "She's too busy with all her activities and studies."

"She got a 1490 on her PSATs this year," Mr. Hastings added proudly.

"I think the peacock is going to win. Or the bee," Melissa said. Everyone stopped and looked at her. "On *The Masked Singer*," Melissa qualified.

"Hmm, I think that was season one? They're on season six now. I'm an avid watcher." Spencer winked.

Jordana turned back to Spencer and pursed her glossy red lips. "So. Miss Finalist. We want to emphasize how fantastic and smart and wonderful you are, but we want to keep it fun, too. You were nominated for an economics essay—which is business stuff, right? I was thinking you could be dressed up as a high-powered executive. Sitting behind a big desk, in a business suit, about to tell someone they're fired. Preferably a man. Smash the glass ceiling and the patriarchy, girl."

Spencer blinked. Jordana spoke very fast and gesticulated wildly with her hands.

"The desk in my study might work," Mr. Hastings offered. "It's down the hall."

Jordana looked at Matthew. "Wanna go check it out?" Matthew nodded.

"And I have a black suit she could borrow," Melissa piped up.

Jordana pulled her phone out of her pocket and started typing. "That won't be necessary," she murmured. "We've got it covered."

Spencer took a seat on the striped chaise in the living room. Her mother plopped onto the piano bench. Melissa joined them, perching near the antique harp. "This is so exciting," Mrs. Hastings cooed, leaning over to push some hair out of Spencer's eyes.

Spencer had to admit, she loved when people fawned over her. It was such a rare occurrence. "I wonder what she's going to ask me," she mused.

"Oh, probably about your interests, your education," Mrs. Hastings singsonged. "Be sure to tell her about those educational camps I sent you to. And remember how I started teaching you French when you were eight? You were able to go straight to French II in sixth grade because of that."

Spencer giggled into her hand. "There are going to be other stories in Saturday's edition of the *Sentinel*, Mom. Not just mine."

"Maybe she'll ask you about your essay," Melissa said flatly.

Spencer looked up sharply. Melissa was calmly flipping through a *Town & Country*, her expression giving nothing away. Would Jordana ask about the essay?

Bridget waltzed back in with a rolling rack of garment bags. "Start unzipping these and see if there's anything you like," she instructed. "I just have to run out to the car and get the bag of shoes and accessories." She wrinkled her nose. "An assistant would be great right now."

Spencer ran her hands along the vinyl bags. There had to be at least twenty-five. "All these are just for my little photo shoot?"

"Didn't Jordana tell you?" Bridget widened her gray eyes. "The managing editor loved this story, especially since you're local. We're putting you on the front page!"

"Of the Style section?" Melissa seemed incredulous.

"No, of the whole paper!" Bridget cried.

"Oh my God, Spencer!" Mrs. Hastings took Spencer's hand.

"That's right!" Bridget beamed. "Get used to this. And if you win, you'll be on one wild ride. I styled 2018's winner for *Newsweek*. Her schedule was crazy."

Bridget strode back toward the front door, her jasmine

perfume punctuating the air. Spencer tried to breathe yoga fire breaths. She unzipped the first garment bag, running her hands over a dark wool blazer. She checked the tag. Calvin Klein. The next one was Armani.

Her mother and Melissa joined her in unzipping. They were quiet for a few seconds, until Melissa said, "Spence, there's something taped on this bag."

Spencer looked over. A folded piece of lined paper was affixed to a navy garment bag with duct tape. On the front of the note was a single, handwritten initial: *S.*

Spencer's legs stiffened. She pulled the note off slowly, angling her body so that Melissa and her mother couldn't see it, and then opened it up.

"What is it?" Melissa moved away from the rack.

"J-just directions for the stylist." Her words came out garbled and thick.

Mrs. Hastings continued to calmly unzip the garment bags, but Melissa held Spencer's gaze for a beat longer. When Melissa finally looked away, Spencer slowly unfolded the note again.

Dear Ms. Finalist, How'd you like it if I told your secret RIGHT NOW? I can, you know. And if you don't watch it, maybe I will. —A

15

NEVER, *EVER* TRUST SOMETHING AS OBSOLETE AS A FAX MACHINE

Wednesday afternoon at lunch, Hanna sat at a teak farm-house table that overlooked the Rosewood Day practice fields and the duck pond. Mount Kale rose up in the distance. It was a perfect afternoon. Tiffany-blue sky, no humidity, the smell of leaves and clean air all around them. The ideal setting for Hanna's perfect birthday present to Mona—now all Mona had to do was show up. Hanna hadn't been able to get a word in while they were fitted for their champagne-colored court dresses at Saks yesterday—not with Naomi and Riley around. She'd tried to call Mona to talk to her about it last night, too, but Mona had said she was in the middle of studying for a big German test. If she failed, the Sweet Seventeen was off.

But whatever. Mona was due any minute, and they'd make up for all the private Hanna-Mona time they'd missed. And yesterday's note from A about Mona not being trustworthy? *Such* a bluff. Mona might still be a little pissed about the Frenniversary misunderstanding, but there was no way she'd bail on their friendship. Anyway, Hanna's birthday surprise would make everything all better. So Mona had better speed it up before she missed the whole thing.

As Hanna waited, she scrolled through her texts. She had her phone programmed to keep messages until manually erased, so all her old Alison text conversations were still stored right in her inbox. Most of the time, Hanna didn't like going through them—it was too sad—but today, for some reason she wanted to. She found one from the first day of June, a few days before Ali went missing.

Trying to study for the health final, Ali had written. I have all this nervous energy.

Y? had been Hanna's answer.

Ali: I don't know. Maybe I'm in love. Ha ha.

Hanna: Yr in love? w/ who?

Ali: Kidding. Oh shit, Spencer's at my door. She wants to practice field hockey drills . . . AGAIN.

Tell her no, Hanna had written back. Who do U love?

You don't tell Spencer no, Ali argued. She'll, like, hurt you.

Hanna stared at the bright screen. At the time, she'd probably laughed. But now Hanna looked at the old texts with a fresh eye. A's note—saying one of Hanna's friends was hiding something—scared her. Could *Spencer* be hiding something?

All of a sudden, Hanna recalled a memory she hadn't thought of in a long time: A few days before Ali went missing, the five of them had gone on a field trip to the People's Light Playhouse to see *Romeo and Juliet*. There weren't many seventh graders who'd opted to go—the rest of the field-trippers had been high schoolers. Practically all of the Rosewood Day senior class had been there— Ali's older brother, Jason, Spencer's sister, Melissa, Ian Thomas, Katy Houghton, Ali's field hockey friend, and Preston Kahn, one of the Kahn brothers. After the play was over, Aria and Emily disappeared to the bathroom, Hanna and Ali sat on the stone wall and started eating their lunches, and Spencer sprinted over to talk to Mrs. Delancey, the English teacher, who was sitting near her students.

"She's only over there because she wants to be near the older boys," Ali muttered, glaring at Spencer.

"We could go over too, if you want," Hanna suggested.

Ali said no. "I'm mad at Spencer," she declared.

"Why?" Hanna asked.

Ali sighed. "Long, boring story."

Hanna let it drop—Ali and Spencer often got mad at each other for no reason. She started daydreaming about how the hot actor who played Tybalt had stared right at her all through his death scene. Did Tybalt think Hanna was cute . . . or fat? Or perhaps he wasn't staring at her at all—maybe he was just acting dead with his eyes open. When she looked up again, Ali was crying.

"Ali," Hanna had whispered. She'd never seen Ali cry before. "What's wrong?"

Tears ran silently down Ali's cheeks. She didn't even bother wiping them away. She stared off in the direction of Spencer and Mrs. Delancey. "Forget it."

"Shit! Look at that!" Mason Byers cried out, breaking Hanna out of her old seventh-grade thoughts. Up in the sky, a biplane cut a line through the clouds. It passed over Rosewood Day, swooped around, and then zoomed by again. Hanna jiggled up and down in her seat and swiveled around. Where the hell was Mona?

"Is that an old Curtiss?" James Freed asked.

"I don't think so," Ridley Mayfield answered. "I think it's a Travel Air D4D."

"Oh, right," James said, as if he'd known it all along.

Hanna's heart fluttered excitedly. The plane made a few long, sweeping strokes through the air, puffing out a trail of clouds that formed a perfect letter *G*. "It's writing something!" a girl near the door called out.

The plane moved on to the *E*, then the *T*, and then, after a space, the *R*. Hanna was practically bursting. This was the coolest party court gift *ever*.

Mason squinted at the plane, which was dipping and weaving in the sky. "Get . . . ready . . . to . . ." he read.

Just then, Mona slid into the seat next to her, throwing her charcoal-gray quilted Louis Vuitton bag over her chair. "Hey, Han," she said, opening her Fresh Fields bento box and sliding the paper off her wooden chopsticks. "So you'll never believe who Naomi and Riley got to play at my birthday party. It's the best gift ever."

"Forget that," Hanna squealed. "I got you something cooler."

Hanna tried to point out the plane in the sky, but Mona was riled up. "They got Lexi," she rushed on. "*Lexi!* For me! At my party! Can you believe it?"

Hanna let her spoon drop back in the yogurt container. Lexi was a female hip-hop artist from Philadelphia. A major label had signed her and she was going to be a megastar. How had Naomi and Riley managed that? "Whatever," she said quickly, and steered Mona's chin toward the clouds. "Look what *I* did for you."

Mona squinted into the sky. The plane had finished writing the message and was now doing loops over the letters. When Hanna took in the whole message, her eyes widened.

"Get ready to . . ." Mona's mouth fell open. ". . . *fart* with Mona?"

"Get ready to fart with Mona!" Mason cried. Others who saw it were repeating it, too. A freshman boy by the abstract wall mural blew into his hands to make a farting sound.

Mona stared at Hanna. She looked a little green. "What the hell, Hanna?"

"No, that's wrong!" Hanna squeaked. "It was supposed to say, 'Get ready to *party* with Mona!' P-A-R-T-Y! They messed up the letters!"

More people made fart noises. "Gross!" a girl near them screamed. "Why would she *write* that?"

"This is horrible!" Mona cried. She pulled her blazer over her head, just like celebrities did when they were avoiding the paparazzi.

"I'm calling them right now to complain," Hanna exclaimed, whipping out her phone and shakily searching for the skywriting company's number. This wasn't fair. She'd used her neatest handwriting when she'd faxed the skywriting company the request. And also? What sort of business even *used* fax machines anymore? It took her ages to hunt down a mailbox store that still had one. "I'm so sorry, Mon. I don't know how this happened."

Mona's face was shadowed under her blazer. "You're sorry, huh?" she said in a low voice. "I bet you are." She slid her blazer back around her shoulders, lurched up, and strode away as fast as her raffia Celine wedges would carry her.

"Mona!" Hanna jumped up after her. She touched Mona's arm and Mona spun around. "It was a mistake! I'd never do that to you!"

Mona took a step closer. Hanna could smell her French lavender laundry soap. "Ditching the Frenniversary is one thing, but I never thought you'd try to ruin my party," she growled, loud enough for everyone to hear. "But you want to play that way? Fine. Don't come. You're officially uninvited."

Mona stomped through the cafeteria doors, practically

pushing two nerdy-looking freshmen aside into the large stone planters. "Mona, wait!" Hanna cried weakly.

"Go to hell," Mona yelled over her shoulder.

Hanna took a few steps backward, her whole body trembling. When she looked around the courtyard, everyone was staring at her. "Oh, *snap*," Hanna heard Desdemona Lee whisper to her softball-playing friends. *"Mrow,"* a group of younger boys hissed from the moss-covered birdbaths. "Loser," an anonymous voice muttered.

The wafting smell of the cafeteria's overly sauced, mushy-crusted pizza was beginning to give Hanna that old, familiar feeling of being both hideously nauseated and crazily ravenous at the same time. She returned to her purse and rifled absentmindedly through the side pouch to find her emergency package of white cheddar Cheez-Its. She pushed one into her mouth after another, not even tasting them. When she looked up into the sky, the puffy, letter-shaped clouds announcing Mona's party had drifted.

The only letter that remained intact was the last one the plane had written: a crisp, angular letter *A*.

16

SOMEONE'S BEEN
KISSING IN THE KILN. . . .

That same Wednesday lunch period, Emily strode quickly through the art studio hallway. "Heeeyyy, Emily," crooned Cody Wallis, Rosewood Day's star tennis player.

"Hi?" Emily looked over her shoulder. She was the only person around—could Cody really be saying hi to *her*?

"Looking good, Emily Fields," murmured John Dexter, the unbelievably hot captain of Rosewood Day's crew team. Emily couldn't even muster a hello—the last time John had spoken to her was in fifth-grade gym class. They'd been playing dodgeball, and John had beaned Emily's chest to tag her out. Later, he'd come up to her and said, snickering, "Sorry I hit your boobie."

She'd never had so many people—especially guys—smile, wave, and say hi to her. This morning, Jared

Coffey, a brooding senior who rode a vintage motorcycle to school and was usually too cool to speak to anyone, had insisted on buying her a blueberry muffin out of the vending machine. And as Emily had walked from second to third period this morning, a small convoy of freshman boys followed. One filmed her on his phone—it was probably already up on YouTube. She had come to school prepared to be taunted about the photo A had passed around at the meet yesterday, so this was sort of . . . unexpected.

When a hand shot out of the pottery studio, Emily flinched and let out a small shriek. Maya's face materialized at the door. "*Psst.* Em!"

Emily stepped out of the stream of traffic. "Maya. Hey."

Maya batted her eyelashes. "Come with me."

"I can't right now." Emily checked her chunky Nike watch. She was late for her lunch with Becka—Little Miss Tree Tops. "How about after school?"

"Nah, this'll just take a second!" Maya darted inside the empty studio and around a maze of desks toward the walk-in kiln. To Emily's surprise, she pushed the kiln's heavy door open and slid inside. Maya poked her head back out and grinned. "Coming?"

Emily shrugged. Inside the kiln, everything was dark, wooden, and warm—like a sauna. Dozens of students' pots sat on the shelves. The ceramics teacher hadn't fired them yet, so they were still brick red and gooey.

"It's neat in here," Emily mused softly. She'd always liked the earthy, wet smell of raw clay. On one of the shelves was a coil pot she'd made two periods ago. She'd thought she'd done a good job, but seeing it again, she noticed that one side caved in.

Suddenly, Emily felt Maya's hands sliding up her back to her shoulders. Maya spun Emily around, and their noses touched. Maya's breath, as usual, smelled like banana gum. "I think this is the sexiest room in the school, don't you?"

"Maya," Emily warned. They had to stop . . . only, Maya's hands felt so good.

"No one will see," Maya protested. She raked her hands through Emily's dry, chlorine-damaged hair. "And besides, everyone knows about us anyway."

"Aren't you bothered by what happened yesterday?" Emily asked, pulling away. "Don't you feel . . . violated?"

Maya thought for a moment. "Not particularly. And no one really seems to care."

"That's the weird thing," Emily agreed. "I thought everyone was going to be mean today—like, teasing me or whatever. But instead . . . I'm suddenly crazily popular. People didn't even pay this much attention to me after Ali disappeared."

Maya grinned and touched Emily's chin. "See? I told you it wouldn't be so bad. Wasn't it a good idea?"

Emily stepped back. In the kiln's pale light, Maya's face shone a ghoulish green. Yesterday, she'd noticed

Maya in the natatorium stands . . . but when she'd looked after discovering the photo, she couldn't find Maya anywhere. Maya had wanted their relationship to be more open. A sick feeling washed over her. "What do you mean, *good idea?*"

Maya shrugged. "I just mean, whoever did this made things much easier for us."

"B-But it's *not* easier," Emily stammered, remembering where she was supposed to be right now. "My parents are livid about that photo. I have to go into a counseling program to prove to them I'm not gay. And if I don't, they're going to send me to Iowa to live with my aunt Helene and uncle Allen. For *good.*"

Maya frowned. "Why didn't you tell your parents the truth? That this is who you are, and it's not something you can, like, change. Even in Iowa." She shrugged. "I told my family I was bi last year. They didn't take it *that* well at first, but they got better."

Emily moved her feet back and forth against the kiln's smooth cement floor. "Your parents are different."

"Maybe." Maya stood back. "But listen. Since last year, when I was finally honest with myself and with everybody else? Ever since then, I've felt so great."

Emily's eyes instinctively fell to the snakelike scar on the inside of Maya's forearm. Maya used to cut herself—she said it was the only thing that made her feel okay. Had being honest about who she was changed that?

Emily closed her eyes and thought of her mother's angry face. And getting on a plane to live in Iowa. Never sleeping in her own bed again. Her parents hating her forever. A lump formed in her throat.

"I have to do what they say." Emily focused on a petrified piece of gum someone had stuck on a kiln shelf. "I should go." She opened the kiln door and stepped back into the classroom.

Maya followed her. "Wait!" She caught Emily's arm, and as Emily spun around, Maya's eyes searched her face. "What are you saying? Are you breaking up with me?"

Emily stared across the room. There was a sticker above the pottery teacher's desk that said, I LOVE POTS! Only, someone had crossed out the *s* and drawn a marijuana leaf over the exclamation point. "Rosewood's my home, Maya. I want to stay here. I'm sorry."

She snaked around the vats of glaze and potter's wheels. "Em!" Maya called behind her. But Emily didn't turn around.

She took the exit door that led straight out of the pottery studio to the quad, feeling like she'd just made a huge mistake. The area was empty—everyone was at lunch—but for a second, Emily could have sworn she saw a figure standing on Rosewood Day's bell tower roof. The figure had long blond hair and held binoculars to her face. It almost looked like Ali.

After Emily blinked, all she saw was the tower's

weathered bronze bell. Her eyes must have been playing tricks on her. She'd probably just seen a gnarled, twisted tree.

Or . . . had she?

Emily shuffled down the little footpath that led to Lorence chapel, which looked less like a chapel and more like the gingerbread house Emily had made for the King James Mall Christmas competition in fourth grade. The building's scalloped siding was cinnamon brown, and the elaborate trim, balusters, and gables were a creamy white. Gumdrop-colored flowers lined the window boxes. Inside, a girl was sitting in one of the front pews, facing forward in the otherwise empty chapel.

"Sorry I'm late," Emily huffed, sliding onto the bench. There was a Nativity scene placed on the altar at the front of the room, waiting to be set up. Emily shook her head. It wasn't even November yet.

"It's cool." The girl put out her hand. "Rebecca Johnson. I go by Becka."

"Emily."

Becka wore a long lacy tunic, skinny jeans, and demure pink flats. Delicate, flower-shaped earrings dangled from her ears, and her hair was held back with a lace-trimmed headband. Emily wondered if she'd end up looking as girly as Becka if she completed the Tree Tops program.

A few seconds passed. Becka took out a tube of pink lip gloss and applied a fresh coat. "So, do you want to know anything about Tree Tops?"

Not really, Emily wanted to answer. Maya was probably right—Emily would never be truly happy until she stopped feeling ashamed and denying her feelings. Although . . . she eyed Becka. *She* seemed okay.

Emily opened her Coke. "So, *you* liked girls?" She didn't entirely believe it.

Becka looked surprised. "I–I did . . . but not anymore."

"Well, when you did . . . how did you know for sure?" Emily asked, realizing she was brimming with questions.

Becka took a minuscule bite out of her sandwich. Everything about her was small and doll-like, including her hands. "It felt different, I guess. Better."

"Same here!" Emily practically shouted. "I had boyfriends when I was younger . . . but I always felt *differently* about girls. I even thought my Barbies were cute."

Becka daintily wiped her mouth with a napkin. "Barbie was never my type."

Emily smiled, as another question came to her. "Why do you think we like girls? Because I was reading that it was genetic, but does that mean that if I had a daughter, she would think her Barbies were cute, too?" She thought for a moment, before rambling on. No one was around and it felt good to ask some of the things that had been circling around in her brain. That's what this meeting was supposed to be about, right? "Although . . . my mom seems like the straightest woman on earth," Emily continued, a little manically. "Maybe it skips a generation?"

Emily stopped, realizing that Becka was staring at her with a weirded-out expression on her face. "I don't think so," she said uneasily.

"I'm sorry," Emily admitted. "I'm kind of babbling. I'm just really . . . . confused. And nervous." *And aching*, she wanted to add, dwelling for a second on how Maya's face had collapsed when Emily told her it was over.

"It's okay," Becka said quietly.

"Did you have a girlfriend before you went into Tree Tops?" Emily asked, more quietly this time.

Becka chewed on her thumbnail. "Wendy," she said almost inaudibly. "We worked together at the Body Shop at the King James Mall."

"Did you and Wendy . . . fool around?" Emily nibbled on a potato chip.

Becka glanced suspiciously at the manger figurines on the altar, like she thought that Joseph and Mary and the three wise men were listening in. "Maybe," she whispered.

"What did it feel like?"

A tiny vein near Becka's temple pulsed. "It felt *wrong*. Being . . . gay . . . it's not easy to change it, but I think you can. Tree Tops helped me figure out why I was with Wendy. I grew up with three brothers, and my counselor said I was raised in a very boy-centric world."

That was the stupidest thing Emily had ever heard. "I have a brother, but I have two sisters too. I wasn't raised in a boy-centric world. So what's wrong with me?"

"Well, maybe the root of your problem is different." Becka shrugged. "The counselors will help you figure that out. They get you to let go of a lot of feelings and memories. The idea is to replace them with new feelings and memories."

Emily frowned. "They're making you *forget* stuff?"

"Not exactly. It's more like letting go."

As much as Becka tried to sugarcoat it, Tree Tops sounded horrible. Emily didn't want to let go of Maya. Or Ali, for that matter.

Suddenly, Becka reached out and put her hand over Emily's. It was surprising. "I know this doesn't make much sense to you now, but I learned something huge in Tree Tops," Becka said. "Life is hard. If we go with these feelings that are . . . that are *wrong*, our lives are going to be even more of an uphill battle. Things are hard enough, you know? Why make it worse?"

Emily felt her lip quiver. Were all lesbians' lives an uphill battle? What about those two gay women who ran the triathlon shop two towns over? Emily had bought her New Balances from them, and they seemed so happy. And what about Maya? She used to cut herself, but now she was better.

"So is Wendy okay that you're in Tree Tops now?" Emily asked.

Becka stared at the stained-glass window behind the altar. "I think she gets it."

"Do you guys still hang out?"

Becka shrugged. "Not really. But we're still friends, I guess."

Emily ran her tongue over her teeth. "Maybe we could all hang out some time?" It might be good to see two *ex-gays* who were actually friends. Maybe she and Maya could be friends, too.

Becka cocked her head, seeming surprised. "Okay. How about Saturday night?"

"Sounds good to me," Emily answered.

They finished their lunch and Becka said goodbye. Emily started down the sloped green, falling in line with the other Rosewood Day kids heading back to class. Her brain was overloaded with information and emotions. The lesbian triathletes might be happy and Maya might be better, but maybe Becka had a point, too. What would it be like at college, then after college, then getting a job? She would have to explain her sexuality to people over and over again. Some people wouldn't accept her.

Before yesterday, the only people who knew how Emily truly felt were Maya, her ex, Ben, and Alison. Two out of the three hadn't taken it very well.

Maybe they were right.

17

BECAUSE ALL CHEESY RELATIONSHIP
MOMENTS HAPPEN IN CEMETERIES

Wednesday after school, Aria watched Sean pedal his Gary Fisher mountain bike farther in front of her, easily climbing West Rosewood's hilly country roads. "Keep up!" he teased.

"Easy for you to say!" Aria answered, pedaling furiously on Ella's old beat-up Peugeot ten-speed from college—she'd brought it with her when she moved into Sean's. "I don't run six miles every morning!"

Sean had surprised Aria after school by announcing he was ditching soccer so they could hang out. Which was a huge deal—in the 24 hours she had lived with him, Aria had learned that Sean was über-soccer boy, the same way her brother was manic about lacrosse. Every morning, Sean ran six miles, did drills, and kicked practice goals into a net set up on the Ackards' lawn until it was time to leave for school.

Aria struggled up the hill and was happy to see that there was a long descent in front of them. It was a gorgeous day, so they'd decided to take a bike ride around West Rosewood. They rode past rambling farmhouses and miles of untouched woods.

At the bottom of the hill, they passed a wrought-iron fence with an ornate entrance gate. Aria hit her brakes. "Hold on. I completely forgot about this place."

She had stopped in front of St. Basil's cemetery, Rosewood's oldest and spookiest, where she used to do gravestone rubbings. It was set on acres and acres of rolling hills and beautifully tended lawns, and some of the headstones dated back to the 1700s. Before Aria found her niche with Ali, she'd gone through a goth phase, embracing everything having to do with death, Tim Burton, Halloween, and creepy Victorian poetry. The cemetery's leafy oaks had provided the perfect shade for lounging and acting morose.

Sean stopped beside her. Aria turned to him. "Can we go in for a sec?"

He looked alarmed. "Are you *sure*?"

"I used to love coming here."

"Okay." Sean reluctantly chained his bike to a wrought-iron trash can along with Aria's and started behind her past the first line of headstones. Aria read the names and the dates that she had practically memorized a few years back. EDITH JOHNSTON, 1807–1856. BABY AGNES, 1820–1821. SARAH WHITTIER, with that Milton quote, "Death is the golden key that opens the palace of eternity." Over the hill, Aria knew, were the graves of a dog named Puff, a cat named Rover, and a parakeet named Lily.

"I love graves," Aria said as they passed a big one with an angel statue on the top. "They remind me of 'The Tell-Tale Heart.'"

"The *what*?"

Aria raised an eyebrow. "Oh, come on. You've read that short story. Edgar Allan Poe? The dead guy's buried in the floor? The narrator can still hear his heart beating?"

"Nope."

Aria put her hands on her hips, dumbstruck. How could Sean not have read that? "When we get back, I'll find my Poe book so you can."

"Okay," Sean agreed, then changed the subject. "You sleep okay last night?"

"Great." A white lie. Her Paris-hotel-like room was beautiful, but Aria had actually found it difficult to sleep. Sean's house was . . . *too* perfect. The duvet seemed *too* fluffy, the mattress *too* quilted, the room *too* quiet. It smelled too nice and clean as well.

But more than that, she'd been too worried about the movement outside her guest bedroom window, about the possible stalker sighting, *and* about A's note—saying that Ali's killer was closer than she thought. Aria had thrashed around for hours, alone, certain she'd look over and see the stalker—or Ali's killer—at the foot of her bed.

"Your stepmom got all anal on me this morning, though," Aria said, skirting around a Japanese cherry blossom tree. "I forgot to make my bed. She made me go back upstairs and do it." She snorted. "My mom hasn't done that in about a billion years."

When she looked over, Sean wasn't laughing along. "My stepmom works hard to keep the house clean. Rosewood Historic House tours come through it almost every day."

Aria bristled. She wanted to tell him that the Rosewood Historic Society had considered her house for the tour, too—some Frank Lloyd Wright protégé had designed it. Instead, she sighed. "I'm sorry. It's just . . . my mom hasn't even called me since I left a message telling her I was staying with you. I feel so . . . abandoned."

Sean stroked her arm. "I know, I know."

Aria poked her tongue into the spot at the back of her mouth where her lone wisdom tooth had been. "That's the thing," she said softly. "You don't know." Sean's family was perfect. Mr. Ackard had made them Belgian waffles this morning, and Mrs. Ackard had packed everyone's lunches—including Aria's. Even their dog, an Airedale, was well mannered.

"So explain it to me," Sean said.

Aria sighed. "It's not as easy as that."

They passed a gnarled, knotty tree. Suddenly, Aria looked down . . . and stopped short. Right in front of her was a new gravesite. The groundskeeper hadn't dug the hole for the coffin yet, but there was a taped-off, coffin-size space. The marble headstone was up, though. It read, plainly, ALISON LAUREN DILAURENTIS.

A small, gurgling noise escaped from the back of Aria's throat. The authorities were still examining Ali's remains for signs of poison and trauma, so her parents hadn't buried her yet. Aria hadn't known they were planning to bury her *here*.

She looked helplessly at Sean. He went pale. "I thought you knew."

"I had no idea," she whispered back.

The headstone said nothing but Ali's name. No *devoted daughter,* or *wonderful field hockey play*er, or *most beautiful girl in Rosewood.* There wasn't even the day, month, or year she'd died. That was probably because no one *knew* the exact date.

She shivered. "Do you think I should say something?"

Sean pursed his pink lips. "When I visit my mom's grave, sometimes I do."

"Like what?"

"I fill her in on what's going on." He looked at her sideways and blushed. "I went after Foxy. I told her about you."

Aria blushed too. She stared at the headstone but felt self-conscious. Talking to dead people wasn't her thing. *I can't believe you're dead,* Aria thought, not able to say the words out loud. *I'm standing here, looking at your grave, and it still isn't real. I hate that we don't know what happened. Is the killer still here? Is A telling the truth?*

Yesssss, Aria swore she heard a far-off voice call. It sounded like Ali's voice.

She thought about A's note. Someone had wanted something of Ali's—and had killed her for it. What? Everyone had wanted *something* of Ali's—even her best friends. Hanna had wanted Ali's personality, and seemed to have appropriated it after Ali vanished. Emily had loved Ali more than anyone—they used to call Emily "Killer," as in Ali's personal guard dog. Aria had wanted Ali's ability to flirt, her beauty, her charisma. And Spencer had always been so jealous of her.

Aria stared into the taped-off area that would be Ali's grave and asked the question that had been slowly forming in her mind: *What were you guys really fighting about?*

"This isn't working for me," Aria whispered after a moment. "Let's go."

She gave Ali's future grave a parting glance. As she turned away, Sean's fingers entwined with hers. They walked quietly for a while, but halfway to the gate, Sean stopped. "Bunny rabbit," he said, pointing at a rabbit across the clearing. He kissed Aria's lips.

Aria's mouth curled up into a smile. "I get a kiss just because you saw a rabbit?"

"Yep." Sean nudged her playfully. "It's like the game

where you punch someone when you see a VW Bug. With us, it can be kisses—and rabbits. It's our couple game."

"Couple game?" Aria snickered, thinking he was joking.

But Sean's face was serious. "You know, a game that's only for us. And it's a good thing it's rabbits, because there are *tons* of rabbits in Rosewood."

Aria was afraid to make fun of him, but really—a *couple* game? It reminded her of something Jennifer Thatcher and Jennings Silver might do. Jennifer and Jennings were a couple in her grade who had been going out since *before* Aria had left for Iceland at the end of seventh grade. They were known only as Double-J, or Dub-J, and were called that even individually. Aria could *not* be a Dub-J.

As she watched Sean walk in front of her, heading toward their bikes, the delicate hairs on the back of her neck stood up. It felt like someone was looking at her. But when she turned around, all she saw was a giant black crow standing on top of Ali's headstone.

The crow glared at her, unblinking, and then spread its massive wings and took off toward the trees.

18

A GOOD SMACK UPSIDE THE HEAD
NEVER HURT ANYONE

On Thursday morning, Dr. Evans shut her office door, settled into her leather chair, folded her hands placidly, and smiled at Spencer, who was sitting opposite her. "So. I hear you had a photo shoot and interview yesterday with the *Sentinel*."

"That's right," Spencer answered.

"And how did that go?"

"Fine." Spencer took a sip of her extra-large Starbucks vanilla latte. The interview actually *had* gone fine, even after all of Spencer's worrying—and A's threats. Jordana had barely asked her about the essay, and Matthew had told her the pictures looked exquisite.

"And how did your sister deal with you being in the spotlight?" Dr. Evans asked. When Spencer raised an eyebrow, Dr. Evans shrugged and leaned forward. "Have you ever thought she might be jealous of you?"

Spencer glanced anxiously at Dr. Evans's closed door. Melissa was sitting outside on the waiting room couch, reading *Travel + Leisure*. Yet again, she'd scheduled her session for right after Spencer's.

"Don't worry, she can't hear you," Dr. Evans assured her.

Spencer sighed. "She seemed sort of . . . pissed," she said in a low voice. "Usually, it's all about Melissa. Even when my parents just ask me a question, Melissa immediately tries to steer the conversation back to her." She stared at the undulating silver Tiffany ring on her pointer finger. "I think she hates me."

Dr. Evans tapped her notebook. "You've felt like she hates you for a long time, right? How does that make you feel?"

Spencer shrugged, hugging one of Dr. Evans's forest-green chenille pillows to her chest. "Angry, I guess. Sometimes I get so frustrated about the way things are, I just want to . . . hit her. I don't, obviously, but—"

"But it would feel good though, wouldn't it?"

Spencer nodded, staring at Dr. Evans's chrome gooseneck lamp. Once, after Melissa told Spencer she wasn't a very good actress, Spencer had come really close to punching Melissa in the face. Instead, she'd flung one of her mother's Spode Christmas plates across the dining room. It had shattered, leaving a butterfly-shaped crack in the wall.

Dr. Evans flipped a page in her notebook. "How do your

parents deal with your and your sister's . . . animosity?"

Spencer raised one shoulder. "Mostly, they don't. If you asked my mom, she'd probably say that we get along perfectly."

Dr. Evans sat back and thought for a long time. She tapped the drinking-bird toy on her desk, and the plastic bird started taking measured sips of water out of an I HEART ROSEWOOD, PA coffee mug. "This is just an early theory, but perhaps Melissa is afraid that if your parents recognize something you've done well, they'll love you instead of her."

Spencer cocked her head. "Really?"

"Maybe. You, on the other hand, think your parents don't love you at all. It's all about Melissa. You don't know how to compete with her, so that's where her boyfriends come in. But maybe it's not that you want Melissa's boyfriends exactly, but more that you want to hurt Melissa herself. Sound right?"

Spencer nodded thoughtfully. "Maybe . . ."

"You girls are both in a lot of pain," Dr. Evans said quietly, her face softening. "I don't know what started this behavior—it could have been something long ago, something you might not even remember—but you've fallen into a pattern of dealing with each other this way, and you'll continue the pattern unless you recognize what it's based on and learn how to respect each other's feelings and change. The pattern might be repeating in your other relationships, too—you might choose friends and boyfriends who treat you like Melissa does, because you're comfortable with the dynamic, and you know your role."

"What do you mean?" Spencer asked, hugging her knees. This sounded awfully psychobabblish to her.

"Are your friends sort of . . . the center of everything? They have everything you want, they push you around, you never feel good enough?"

Spencer's mouth went dry. She certainly used to have a friend like that: Ali.

She closed her eyes and saw the strange Ali memory that had been plaguing her all week. The memory was of a fight, Spencer was sure of it. Only, Spencer usually remembered all of her fights with Ali, better than she remembered the good moments of their friendship. Was it a dream?

"What are you thinking?" Dr. Evans asked.

Spencer took a breath. "About Alison."

"Ah." Dr. Evans nodded. "Do you think Alison was like Melissa?"

"I don't know. Maybe."

Dr. Evans plucked a Kleenex out of the box on her desk and blew her nose. "I saw that video of you girls on TV. You and Alison seemed angry at each other. Were you?"

Spencer took a deep breath. "Sort of."

"Can you remember why?"

She thought for a moment and gazed around the room. There was a plaque on Dr. Evans's desk that she hadn't noticed the last time she'd been here. It read "The only true knowledge in life is knowing you know nothing. —Socrates. "Those weeks before Alison went missing, she started acting . . . different. Like she hated us. None of us wanted to admit it, but I think she was planning on dropping us that summer."

"How did that make you feel? Angry?"

"Yeah. Sure." Spencer paused. "Being Ali's friend was great, but we had to make a lot of sacrifices. We went through a lot together, and some of it wasn't good. It was like, 'We go through all this for you, and you repay us by ditching us?'"

"So you felt owed something."

"Maybe," Spencer answered.

"But you feel guilty too, right?" Dr. Evans suggested.

Spencer lowered her shoulders. "Guilty? Why?"

"Because Alison's dead. Because, in some ways, you resented her. Maybe you wanted something bad to happen to her because she was hurting you."

"I don't know," Spencer whispered.

"And then your wish came true. Now you feel like Alison's disappearance is your fault—that if you hadn't felt this way about her, she wouldn't have been murdered."

Spencer's eyes clouded with tears. She couldn't respond.

"It's not your fault," Dr. Evans said forcefully, leaning forward in the chair. "We don't always love our friends every minute. Alison hurt you. Just because you had a mean thought about her doesn't mean you caused her death."

Spencer sniffed. She stared at the Socrates quote again. *The only true knowledge in life is knowing you know nothing.* "There's a memory that keeps popping into my head," she blurted out. "About Ali. We're fighting. She talks about something I read in her diary—she always thought I was reading her diary, but I never did. But I'm . . . I'm not even sure the memory is real."

Dr. Evans put her pen to her mouth. "People cope with things in different ways. For some people, if they witness or do something disturbing, their brain some-how . . . edits it out. But often the memory starts push-ing its way back in."

Spencer's mouth felt scratchy, like steel wool. "Nothing disturbing happened."

"I could try to hypnotize you to draw out the memory."

Spencer's mouth went dry. *"Hypnotize?"*

Dr. Evans was staring at her. "It might help."

Spencer chewed on a piece of hair. She pointed at the Socrates quote. "What does that mean?"

"That?" Dr. Evans's shrugged. "Think about it your-self. Draw your own conclusion." She smiled. "Now, are you ready? Lie down and get comfy."

Spencer slumped on the couch. As Dr. Evans pulled down the bamboo blinds, Spencer cringed. *This was just like what Ali did that night in the barn before she died.*

"Just relax." Dr. Evans turned off her desk lamp. "Feel yourself calming down. Try to let go of everything we talked about today. Okay?"

Spencer wasn't relaxed at all. Her knees locked and her muscles shook. Even her teeth ground together. *Now she's going to walk around and count down from one hundred. She'll touch my forehead, and I'll be in her power.*

When Spencer opened her eyes, she wasn't in Dr. Evans's office anymore. She was outside her barn. It was night. Alison was staring at her, shaking her head just like she had in the other flashes of memory Spencer had recalled during the week. Spencer suddenly knew it was the night Ali went missing. She tried to claw her way out of the memory, but her limbs felt heavy and useless.

"You try to steal everything away from me," Ali was saying with a tone and inflection that were now eerily familiar. "But you can't have this."

"Can't have what?" The wind was cold. Spencer shivered.

"Come on," Ali taunted, putting her hands on her hips. "You read about it in my diary, didn't you?"

"I wouldn't read your diary," Spencer spat. "I don't care."

"You care way too much," Ali said. She leaned forward. Her breath was minty.

"You're delusional," Spencer sputtered.

"No, I'm not," Ali snarled. "*You* are."

Rage suddenly filled Spencer. She leaned forward and shoved Ali's shoulder.

Ali looked surprised. "Friends don't shove friends."

"Well, maybe we're not friends," Spencer answered.

"Guess not," Ali said. She took a few steps away but turned back. Then she said something else. Spencer saw Ali's mouth move, then felt her own mouth move, but she couldn't hear their words. All she knew was that whatever Ali said made her angry. From somewhere far away was a sharp, splintering *crack*. Spencer's eyes snapped open.

"Spencer," Dr. Evans's voice called. "Hey. Spencer."

The first thing she saw was Dr. Evans's plaque across the room. *The only true knowledge is knowing you know nothing.* Then, Dr. Evans's face swam into view. She had an uncertain, worried look on her face. "Are you okay?" Dr. Evans asked.

Spencer blinked a few times. "I don't know." She sat up and ran the palm of her hand over her sweaty forehead. This felt like waking up from the anesthesia the time she'd had her appendix out. Everything seemed blurry and edgeless.

"Tell me what you see in the room," Dr. Evans said. "Describe everything."

Spencer looked around. "The brown leather couch, the white fluffy rug, the . . ."

What had Ali said? Why couldn't Spencer hear her? Had that really happened?

"A wire-mesh trash can," she stammered. "An Anjou pear candle . . ."

"Okay." Dr. Evans put her hand on Spencer's shoulder. "Sit here. Breathe."

Dr. Evans's window was now open, and Spencer could smell the freshly tarred asphalt on the parking lot. Two mourning doves cooed to each other. When she finally got up and told Dr. Evans she'd see her next week, she was feeling clearer. She skidded across the waiting room without acknowledging Melissa. She wanted out of here.

In the parking lot, Spencer slid into her car and sat in silence. She listed all the things she saw here, too. Her tweed bag. The farmer's market placard across the street that read, FRESH OMATOES. The T had fallen to the ground. The blue Chevy truck parked crookedly in the farmer's market lot. The cheerful red birdhouse hanging from a nearby oak. The sign on the office building door that said only service animals were permitted inside. Melissa's profile in Dr. Evans's office window.

The corners of her sister's mouth were spread into a jagged smile, and she was talking animatedly with her hands. When Spencer looked back at the farmer's market, she noticed the Chevy's front tire was flat. There was something slinking behind the truck. A cat, maybe.

Spencer sat up straighter. It wasn't a cat—it was a *person*. Staring at her.

The person's eyes didn't blink. And then, suddenly, whoever it was turned his or her head, crouched into the shadows, and disappeared.

19

IT'S BETTER THAN A
SIGN SAYING, "KICK ME"

Thursday afternoon, Hanna followed her chemistry class across the commons to the flagpole. There had been a fire drill, and now her chem teacher, Mr. Percival, was counting to make sure none of the students had run off. It was another freakishly hot October day, and as the sun beat down on the top of Hanna's head, she heard two sophomore girls whispering.

"Did you *hear* that she's a klepto?" hissed Noelle Frazier, a tall girl with cascading blond ringlets.

"I know," replied Anna Walton, a tiny brunette with enormous boobs. "She, like, organized this huge Tiffany heist. And then she went and wrecked Mr. Ackard's car."

Hanna stiffened. Normally, she wouldn't have been bothered by a couple of lame sophomore girls, but she was feeling sort of vulnerable. She pretended to be really interested in a bunch of tiny pine trees the gardeners had just planted.

"I heard she's at the police station like every day," Noelle said.

"And you know she's not invited to Mona's anymore, right?" Anna whispered. "They had this huge fight because Hanna humiliated her with that skywriting thing."

"Mona's wanted to drop her for a couple months now," Noelle said knowingly. "Hanna's become this huge loser."

That was too much. Hanna whirled around. "Where did you hear that?"

Anna and Noelle exchanged a smirk. Then they sauntered down the hill without answering.

Hanna shut her eyes and leaned against the metal flagpole, trying to ignore the fact that everyone in her chem class was now staring at her. It had been twenty-four hours since the disastrous skywriting debacle, and things had gone from bad to worse. Hanna had left at least ten apologetic messages on Mona's cell last night . . . but Mona hadn't called back. And today, she'd been hearing strange, unsavory things about herself . . . from everyone.

She thought of A's note. *And Mona? She's not your friend, either. So watch your back.*

Hanna scanned the crowd of kids on the commons. Next to the doors, two girls in cheerleading uniforms were pantomiming a cheer. Near the gum tree, a couple of boys were "blazer fighting"—whapping each other with their Rosewood Day blazers. Aria's brother, Mike, walked by playing his Nintendo Switch. Finally, she spied Mona's white-blond hair. She was heading back into the main building via one of the side doors with a bored, haughty look on her face. Hanna straightened her blazer, clenched and unclenched her fists, and made a beeline for her best friend.

When she reached Mona, she tapped her on her bony shoulder. Mona looked over. "Oh. It's you," she said in a monotone, the way she normally greeted losers not cool enough to be in her presence.

"Are you saying stuff about me?" Hanna demanded, putting her hands on her hips and keeping pace with Mona, who was striding quickly through the side door and down the art studio hallway.

Mona hitched her tangerine Dooney & Bourke tote higher on her shoulder. "Nothing that's not true."

Hanna's mouth fell open. She felt like Wile E. Coyote in one of those old Looney Toons cartoons she used to watch—he would be running and running and running and suddenly run off a cliff. Wile E. would pause, not realizing it for a second, and then rapidly plummet. "So you think I'm a loser?" she squeaked.

Mona raised one eyebrow. "Like I said, nothing that's not true."

She left Hanna standing in the middle of the hall, students swarming around her. Mona walked to the end of the corridor and stopped at a clump of girls. At first they all looked the same—expensive handbags, shiny hair, skinny fake-tanned legs—but then Hanna's eyes unblurred. Mona was standing with Naomi and Riley, and they were all whispering.

Hanna was certain she was going to cry. She fumbled through the bathroom door and closed herself into a stall next to Old Faithful, an infamous toilet that randomly spurted out plumes of water, drenching you if you were stupid enough to use it. The boys' room had a spewing toilet, too. Through the years, plumbers had tried to fix them both, but since they couldn't figure out the cause, the Old Faithfuls had become a legendary part of Rosewood Day lore. Everyone knew better than to use them.

Except . . . Mona had used Old Faithful just a few weeks after she and Hanna became friends, back when Mona was still clueless. She'd frantically texted Hanna in health class, and Hanna had rushed to the bathroom to slip Mona the extra uniform skirt and blouse she'd had in her locker. Hanna remembered balling up Mona's soaked skirt in a Fresh Fields plastic bag and sliding out of the stall so Mona could furtively change—Mona had always been funny about changing in front of other people.

How could Mona not *remember* that?

As if on cue, Old Faithful erupted. Hanna shrieked and pressed herself against the opposite stall wall as a column of blue toilet water shot into the air. A few heavy droplets hit the back of Hanna's blazer, and she curled up against the stall wall and finally started to sob. She hated that Mona no longer needed her. And that Ali had been murdered. And that her dad still hadn't called. Why was this *happening*? What had she done to deserve this?

As Old Faithful quieted down to a gurgle, the main door swung open. Hanna made tiny gasping noises, trying to keep quiet. Whoever it was walked to the sink, and Hanna peered under the door. She saw a pair of clunky, black, boyish loafers.

"Hello?" a boy's voice said. "Is . . . is someone in there?"

Hanna put her hand to her mouth. What was a *guy* doing in this bathroom?

Unless . . . *No*. She hadn't.

"Hanna?" The shoes stood in front of her stall. Hanna recognized the voice, too.

She peeked out the crack in the door. It was Lucas, the boy from Rive Gauche. She could see the edge of his nose, a long piece of white blond hair. There was a big GO ROSEWOOD SOCCER! pin on his lapel. "How did you know it was me?"

"I saw you come in here," he answered. "You know this is the boys' room, right?"

Hanna answered with an embarrassed sniff. She took off her wet blazer, shuffled out of the stall, walked to the sink, and forcefully pumped the soap dispenser. The soap had that fake almond smell Hanna hated.

Lucas's eyes cut to the Old Faithful stall. "Did that thing erupt?"

"Yes." And then Hanna couldn't control her emotions anymore. She hunched over the sink, her tears dripping into the basin.

Lucas stood there a moment, then put his hand on the middle of her back. Hanna felt it shake a little. "It's only Old Faithful. It erupts, like, every hour. You know that."

"That's not it." Hanna grabbed a scratchy paper towel and blew her nose. "My best friend hates me. And she's making everyone else hate me, too."

"What? Of course she doesn't."

"Yes, she does!" Hanna's high-pitched voice bounced off the bathroom's tiled walls. "Mona's hanging out with these girls now who we used to hate, and she's gossiping about me, all because I missed the Frenniversary and the skywriter wrote, 'Fart with Mona,' instead of, 'Party with Mona,' and she disinvited me to her birthday party, and I'm supposed to be her best friend!"

She said it all in a long sentence without breathing, despite where she was and who she was talking to. When she finished, she stared at Lucas, suddenly irritated that he was there and had heard it all.

Lucas was so tall he practically had to stoop to not hit his head on the ceiling. "I could start spreading rumors about her. Like maybe she's got a disease where she can't help but secretly eat her snot when no one's looking?"

Hanna's heart thawed. That was gross . . . but also funny . . . and sweet. "That's okay."

"Well, the offer stands." Lucas had an earnest look on his face. In the hideous green bathroom light, he was actually cute. "But hey! I know something we can do to cheer you up."

Hanna looked at him incredulously. What, did Lucas think they were friends now, because he'd seen her in the bathroom? Still, she was curious. "What?"

"Can't tell you. It's top secret. I'll come get you tomorrow morning."

Hanna shot him a warning look. "Like, *a date*?"

Lucas raised his hands in surrender. "Absolutely not. Just as . . . friends."

Hanna swallowed. She needed a friend right now. *Bad.* "All right," she said quietly, feeling too exhausted to argue. Then, with a sigh, she pushed out of the boys' Old Faithful bathroom and headed for her next class. Strangely, she felt a teensy bit better.

But as she turned the corner to the foreign languages wing, Hanna reached around to put her blazer back on and felt something sticking to the back. She pulled off a wrinkled piece of paper. *Feel sorry for me,* it said, in spiky pink handwriting.

Hanna looked around at the passing students, but no one was paying attention. How long had she been walking around with the note on her? Who could have done this? It could have been anyone. She'd been in that crowd during the fire drill. Everyone had been there.

Hanna looked down at the paper again and turned it over in her hands. On the other side was a typewritten note. Hanna got that familiar sinking feeling in her stomach.

Hanna: Remember when you saw Mona leaving the Bill Beach plastic surgery clinic? Hello, lipo!! But shh! You didn't hear it from me. —A

20

LIFE IMITATES ART

Thursday afternoon at lunch, Aria turned the corner to Rosewood Day's administrative wing. All the teachers had offices here and often tutored or advised students during their lunch periods.

Aria stopped at Ezra's closed office door. It had changed a lot since the beginning of the year. He'd installed a whiteboard, and it was chock-full of blue-inked notes from students. *Mr. Fitz—Want to talk about my Fitzgerald report. I'll stop by after school. —Kelly.* There was a *Hamlet* quote at the bottom: *O villain, villain, smiling, damned villain!* Below the marker board was a cutout of a *New Yorker* cartoon of a dog on a therapist's couch. And on the doorknob was a DO NOT DISTURB sign from a Day's Inn; Ezra had turned it to the DISTURB side: WELCOME. PLEASE SERVICE ROOM.

Aria tentatively knocked. "Come in," she heard him say from the other side. She'd expected Ezra to be with another student—from snippets she heard in class, she'd thought his lunchtime office hours were always busy—but here he was alone, with a Happy Meal box on his desk. The room smelled like McNuggets.

"Aria!" Ezra exclaimed, raising an eyebrow. "This is a surprise. Sit down."

She plopped down on Ezra's scratchy tweed couch—the same kind that was in the Rosewood Day head-master's office. She pointed at his desk. "Happy Meal?"

He smiled sheepishly. "I like the toys." He held up a car from some kids' movie. "McNugget?" He proffered the box. "I got barbecue."

She waved him away. "I don't eat meat."

"That's right." He ate a fry, his eyes locked with hers. "I forgot."

Aria felt a swoosh of something—a mix of intimacy and discomfort. Ezra looked away, probably feeling it too. She looked around on his desk. It was littered with stacks of paper, a mini zen rock garden, and about a thousand books.

"So . . ." Ezra wiped his mouth with a napkin, not noticing Aria's expression. "What can I do for you?"

Aria leaned her elbow on the couch's arm. "Well, I'm wondering if I can have an extension on the *Scarlet Letter* essay that's due tomorrow."

He set down his soda. "Really? I'm surprised. You're never late with anything."

"I know," she mumbled sheepishly. But the Ackards'

house was not conducive to studying. One, it was too quiet—Aria was used to studying while simultaneously listening to music, the TV, and Mike yammering on the phone in the next room. Two, it was hard to concentrate when she felt like someone was . . . watching her. "But it's not a big deal," she went on. "All I need is this weekend."

Ezra scratched his head. "Well . . . I haven't set a policy on extensions yet. But all right. Just this once. Next time, I'm going to have to mark you down a grade."

She pushed her hair behind her ears. "I'm not going to make a habit of it."

"Good. So, what, are you not liking the book? Or haven't you started it?"

"I finished it today. But I hated it. I hated Hester Prynne."

"Why?"

Aria fiddled with the buckle on her Urban Outfitters ivory suede flats. "She assumes her husband's lost at sea, and so she goes and has an affair," she muttered.

Ezra leaned forward on his elbow, looking amused. "But her husband isn't a very good man, either. That's what makes it complicated."

Aria stared at the books that were crammed into Ezra's cramped, wooden bookshelves. *War and Peace. Gravity's Rainbow.* An extensive collection of e. e. cummings and Rilke poetry, and not one but *two* copies of *No Exit.* There was the Edgar Allan Poe collection Sean hadn't read. All of the books looked creased and worn from reading and rereading. "But I couldn't see past what Hester did," Aria said quietly. "She *cheated*."

"But we're supposed to feel for her struggle, and how society has branded her, and how she strives to forge her own identity and not allow anyone to create one for her."

"I hated her, okay?" Aria exploded. "And I'll never forgive her!"

She covered her face with her hands. Tears spilled down her cheeks. When she shut her eyes, she pictured Byron and Meredith as the book's illicit lovers, Ella as Hester's vengeful, wronged husband. But if life really imitated art, Byron and Meredith should be suffering . . . *not* Aria. She'd tried to call her house last night, but as soon as Ella picked up and heard Aria's voice on the other end, she hung up. When Aria waved at Mike across the gym, Mike had quickly spun on his heel and marched back into the locker room. No one was on her side.

"Whoa," Ezra said quietly, after Aria let out a stifled sob. "It's okay. So you didn't like the book. It's fine."

"I'm sorry. I'm just . . ." She felt hot tears on her palms. Ezra's room had grown so quiet. There was only the whirring of the computer's hard drive. The buzz of the fluorescent lamp. The happy cries from the lower school playground—all the little kids were out for recess.

"Is there something you want to talk about?" Ezra asked.

Aria wiped her eyes with the back of her blazer sleeve. She picked at a loose button on one of the couch's seat cushions. "My father had an affair with his student three years ago," she blurted out. "He's a professor at Hollis. I knew about it the whole time, but he asked me not to tell my mom. Well, now he's back with the student . . . and my mom found out. She's furious I knew for so long . . . and now my dad's gone."

"Jesus," Ezra whispered. "This just happened?"

"A few weeks ago, yeah."

"God." Ezra stared up at the beamed ceiling for a while. "That doesn't sound very fair of your dad. *Or* your mom."

Aria shrugged. Her chin started to tremble again. "I shouldn't have kept it a secret from my mom. But what was I supposed to do?"

"It's not your fault," Ezra told her.

He got out of his chair, walked around to the front of the desk, pushed a few papers aside, and sat on the edge. "Okay. So, I've never told anyone this, but when I was in high school, I saw my mom kissing her doctor. She had cancer at the time, and since my dad was traveling, she asked me to take her to her chemotherapy treatments. Once, while I was waiting, I had to use the bathroom, and as I was walking back through the hall, I saw this exam room door open. I don't know why I looked in, but when I did . . . there they were. Kissing."

Aria gasped. "What did you do?"

"I pretended like I didn't see it. My mom had no idea that I had. She came out twenty minutes later, all straightened up and proper and in a hurry. I really wanted to bring it up, but at the same time, I couldn't." He shook his head. "Dr. Poole. I never looked at him in the same way again."

"Didn't you say your parents got divorced?" Aria asked, remembering a conversation they'd had at Ezra's house. "Did your mom go off with Dr. Poole?"

"Nah." Ezra reached over and grabbed a McNugget out of the box. "They got divorced a couple years later. Dr. Poole and the cancer were long gone."

"God," was all Aria could think to say.

"It sucks." Ezra fiddled with one of the rocks in the mini zen rock garden that sat at the edge of his desk. "I idolized my parents' marriage. It didn't seem to me like they were having problems. My whole relationship ideal was shattered."

"Mine too," Aria said glumly, running her foot against a stack of paperbacks on the floor. "My parents seemed really happy together."

"It has nothing to do with you," Ezra told her. "That's a big thing I learned. It's their thing. Unfortunately, you have to deal with it, and I think it makes you stronger."

Aria groaned and clunked her head against the couch's stiff back. "I hate when people say things like that to me. That things will make me a better person, even if the things themselves suck."

Ezra chuckled. "Actually, I do too."

Aria shut her eyes, finding this moment bittersweet.

She had been waiting for someone to talk to about all this—someone who really, truly understood. She wanted to kiss Ezra for having as messed-up a family as she did.

Or maybe, she wanted to kiss Ezra . . . because he was Ezra.

Ezra's eyes met hers. Aria could see her reflection in his inky pupils. With his hand, Ezra pushed the little Happy Meal car so that it rolled across his desk, over the edge, and onto her lap. A smile whispered across his face.

"Do you have a girlfriend in New York?" Aria blurted out.

Ezra's forehead furrowed. "A girlfriend . . ." He blinked a few times. "I *did*. But we broke up this summer."

"Oh."

"Where did *that* come from?" Ezra asked.

"Some kids were talking about it, I guess. And I . . . I wondered what she was like."

A devilish look danced in Ezra's eyes, then escaped. He opened his mouth to say something but changed his mind. "What?" Aria asked him.

"I shouldn't."

"*What?*"

"It's just . . ." He glanced at her askance. "She was nothing compared to you."

A hot feeling swished through Aria. Slowly, without taking his eyes off her, Ezra slid off the desk to stand. Aria inched toward the edge of the couch. The moment stretched on forever. And then, Ezra lunged forward, grabbed Aria at her shoulders, and pressed her to him. Her lips crashed onto his. She held the sides of his face, and he ran his hands up the length of her back. They broke away and stared at each other, then dove back in again. Ezra smelled delicious, like a mix of Pantene and mint and chai tea and something that was just . . . Ezra. Aria had never felt this way from kissing. Not with Sean, not with anyone.

Sean. His image swam into her head. Sean letting Aria lean into him while they watched the BBC version of *The Office* last night. Sean kissing her before bio class, comforting her because they were starting dissections today. Sean holding her hand at dinner with his family. Sean was her *boyfriend.*

Aria pushed Ezra away and jumped up. "I have to go." She felt sweaty, as if someone had jacked up the thermostat about fifty degrees. She quickly gathered up her things, heart thumping and cheeks blazing.

"Thanks for the extension," she blurted out, pushing clumsily through the door.

Out in the hall, she drew in a few deep breaths. Down the corridor, a figure slipped around the corner. Aria tensed. *Someone had seen.*

She noticed something on Ezra's door and widened her eyes. Someone had erased all the old white-board messages, replacing them with a new one in an unfamiliar hot pink marker.

Careful, careful! I'm always watching! —A

And then, in smaller letters, down at the bottom:

Here's a second hint: You all knew every inch of her backyard. But for one of you, it was so, so easy.

Aria pulled her blazer sleeve down and quickly wiped
the letters away. When she got to the signature, she
wiped extra hard, scrubbing and scrubbing until there
was no trace of *A* left.

21

WHAT DOES
H-O-L-Y C-R-A-P SPELL?

Thursday evening, Spencer settled into the red plushy seats at the Rosewood Country Club restaurant and looked out the bay window. On the golf course, a couple of older guys in V-neck sweaters and khakis were trying to get in a few more holes before the sun went down. Out on the deck, people were taking advantage of the last few warm days of the year, drinking gin and tonics and eating rock shrimp and bruschetta squares. Mr. and Mrs. Hastings stirred their Bombay Sapphire martinis, then looked at each other.

"I propose a toast." Mrs. Hastings pushed her blond bobbed hair behind her ears, her three-carat diamond ring glinting against the setting sun streaming through the window. Spencer's parents always toasted before they took a drink of anything—even water.

Mrs. Hastings raised her glass. "To Spencer making

the Golden Orchid finals."

Mr. Hastings clinked. "*And* to being on the front page of this Sunday's *Sentinel.*"

Spencer raised her glass and clinked it with them, but the effort was halfhearted. She didn't want to be here. She wanted to be at home, protected and safe. She couldn't stop thinking about her strange session with Dr. Evans this morning. The vision she'd seen—the forgotten fight with Ali the night she disappeared—was haunting. Why hadn't she remembered it before? Was there more to it? What if she'd *seen* Ali's killer?

"Congrats, Spencer," her mother interrupted her thoughts. "I hope you win."

"Thanks," Spencer mumbled. She worked to fold her green napkin back into an accordion, then went around the table and folded all the others, too.

"Nervous about something?" Her mother nudged her chin at the napkins.

Spencer immediately stopped. "No," she said quickly. Whenever she shut her eyes, she was right back in the Ali memory again. It was so clear now. She could smell the honeysuckle that grew in the woods that paralleled the barn, feel the early summer breeze, see the lightning bugs spatter-painting the dark sky. But it couldn't be real.

When Spencer looked up, her parents were gazing at her peculiarly. They'd probably asked her a question she'd completely missed. For the first time ever, she wished Melissa were here monopolizing the conversation.

"Are you nervous because of the doctor?" her mother whispered.

Spencer couldn't hide her smirk—she loved that her mom called Dr. Evans "the doctor" instead of "the therapist." "No. I'm fine."

"Do you think you've gotten a lot . . ." Her father seemed to search for his words, fiddling with his tie pin. ". . . accomplished, with the doctor?"

Spencer rocked her fork back and forth. *Define accomplished,* she wanted to say.

Before she could answer, the waiter appeared. It was the same waiter they'd had for years, the short little baldish guy who had a Winnie-the-Pooh voice. "Hello, Mr. and Mrs. Hastings." Pooh shook her father's hand. "And Spencer. You're looking lovely."

"Thanks," Spencer mumbled, although she was pretty sure she wasn't. She hadn't washed her hair after field hockey, and the last time she'd looked in the mirror, her eyes had a wild, scared look to them. She kept twitching, too, and looking around the restaurant to see if someone was watching her.

"How is everyone tonight?" Pooh asked. He fluffed up the napkins Spencer had just refolded and spread them on everyone's laps. "Here for a special occasion?"

"Actually, yes," Mrs. Hastings piped up. "Spencer's a finalist in the Golden Orchid competition. It's a major academic prize."

"*Mom,*" Spencer hissed. She hated how her mother

broadcast family accomplishments. Especially since Spencer had cheated.

"That's wonderful!" Pooh bellowed. "It's nice to have some *good* news, for once." He leaned in closer. "Quite a few of our guests think they've seen that stalker everyone's been talking about. Some even say they saw someone near the club last night."

"Hasn't this town been through enough?" Mr. Hastings mused.

Mrs. Hastings worriedly glanced at her husband. "You know, I swore I saw someone staring at me when I met Spencer at the doctor's on Monday."

Spencer jerked her head up, her heart racing. "Did you get a look at him?"

Mrs. Hastings shrugged. "Not really."

"Some people are saying it's a man. Others, a woman," Pooh said.

Everyone *tsk*ed in distress.

Pooh took their orders. Spencer mumbled that she wanted the ahi tuna—the same thing she'd been getting ever since she stopped ordering off the kids' menu. As the waiter trundled away, Spencer looked blearily around the dining room. It was done up in a ramshackle-Nantucket-boat theme, with dark wicker chairs and lots of life buoys and bronze figureheads. The far wall still had the ocean mural, complete with a hideous giant squid, a killer whale, and a merman that had flowing blond hair and a broken, Owen Wilson–style nose. When Spencer, Ali, and the others used to come here to eat dinner alone—a huge deal, back in sixth and seventh grades—they loved sitting next to the merman. Once, when Mona Vanderwaal and Chassey Bledsoe came in here by themselves, Ali demanded that Mona and Chassey both give the merman a big French kiss. Tears of shame had run down their cheeks as both girls stuck their tongues to the painted merman's lips.

Ali was so mean, Spencer thought. Her dream floated back. *You can't have this,* Ali had said. Why did Spencer get so angry? Spencer thought Ali was going to tell Melissa about Ian that night. Was that why? And what did Dr. Evans mean when she said that some people edit out things that happen to them? Had Spencer ever done that before?

"Mom?" Suddenly Spencer was curious. "Do you know if I ever, like, randomly forgot a whole bunch of stuff? Like . . . experienced temporary amnesia?"

Her mother held her drink in midair. "W-Why are you asking?"

The back of Spencer's neck felt clammy. Her mother had the same disturbed, *I don't want to deal with this* look she'd had the time her brother, Spencer's uncle Daniel, got too drunk at one of their parties and prattled off a few deeply protected family secrets. That was how Spencer found out her grandmother had a morphine addiction, and that her aunt Penelope had given away a child for adoption when she was seventeen. "Wait, I *have*?"

Her mom felt the plate's scalloped edge. "You were seven. You had the flu."

The cords in her mother's neck stood out, which meant she was holding her breath. And that meant she wasn't telling Spencer everything. *"Mom."*

Her mother ran her hands around the martini glass edge. "It's not important."

"Oh, tell her, Veronica," her father said gruffly. "She can handle it."

Mrs. Hastings took a deep breath. "Well, Melissa, you, and I went to the Franklin Institute—you both loved that walk-through heart exhibit. Remember?"

"Sure," Spencer said. The Franklin Institute heart exhibit spanned five thousand square feet, had veins the size of Spencer's forearm, and throbbed so loudly that when you were inside its ventricles, the beating was the only sound you could hear.

"We were walking back to our car," her mother went on, her eyes on her lap. "On our way, this man stopped us." She paused, and took Spencer's father's hand. They both looked so solemn. "He . . . he had a gun in his jacket. He wanted my wallet."

Spencer widened her eyes. *"What?"*

"He made us get down on our stomachs on the side-walk." Mrs. Hastings's mouth wobbled. "I didn't care that I gave him my wallet, but I was so scared for you girls. You kept whimpering and crying. You kept asking me if we were going to die."

Spencer twisted the end of the napkin in her lap. She didn't remember this.

"He told me to count to one hundred before we could get up again," her mother said. "After the coast was clear, we ran to our car, and I drove us home. I drove nearly thirty miles over the speed limit, I remember. It's a wonder I didn't get stopped."

She paused and sipped her drink. Someone dropped a bunch of plates in the kitchen, and most of the diners craned their necks in the direction of the shattering china, but Mrs. Hastings acted as if she hadn't even heard it. "When we got home, you had a horrible fever," she went on. "It came on suddenly. We took you to the ER. We were afraid you had meningitis—there had been a case of it a few towns over. We had to stay close to home while we waited for the test results, in case we had to rush you back to the hospital. We had to miss Melissa's national spelling bee. Remember when she was preparing for that?"

Spencer remembered. Sometimes, she and Melissa would play Bee—Melissa as the contestant, Spencer as the judge, lobbing Melissa words to spell from a long list. That was back when Melissa and Spencer used to like each other. But the way Spencer remembered it, Melissa had opted out of the competition because she had a field hockey game that same day. "Melissa went to the bee after all?" she sounded out.

"She did, but she went with Yolanda's family.

Remember her friend Yolanda? She and Melissa were in all those knowledge bowls together."

Spencer crinkled her brow. "Yolanda Hensler?"

"That's right."

"Melissa was never Yolanda's—" Spencer stopped herself. She was about to say that Melissa was never Yolanda Hensler's friend. Yolanda was the type of girl who was a sweetie-pie around adults but a bossy terror in private. Spencer knew that Yolanda had once forced Melissa to go through every knowledge bowl sample question without stopping, even though Melissa told her a zillion times that she had to pee. Melissa had ended up peeing in her pants, and it seeped all over Yolanda's Lilly Pulitzer comforter.

"Anyway, a week later, your fever broke," her mother said. "But when you woke up, you'd forgotten the whole thing ever happened. You remembered going to the Franklin Institute, and you remembered walking through the heart, but then I asked if you remembered the mean man in the city. And you said, 'What mean man?' You couldn't remember the ER, having tests run, being sick, anything. You just . . . erased it. We watched you the rest of that summer, too. We were afraid you might get sick again. Melissa and I had to miss our mother-daughter kayak camp in Colorado and that big piano recital in New York City, but I think she understood."

Spencer's heart was racing. "Why hasn't anyone ever told me this?"

Her mother looked at her dad. "The whole thing was so strange. I thought it might upset you, knowing you'd missed a whole week. You were such a worrier after that."

Spencer gripped the edge of the table. *I might have missed more than a week of my life,* she wanted to say to her parents. *What if it wasn't my only blackout?*

She shut her eyes. All she could hear was that *crack* from her memory. What if she had blacked out before Ali disappeared? What had she missed that night?

By the time Pooh set down their steaming plates, Spencer was shaking. Her mother cocked her head. "Spencer? What's wrong?" She swiveled her head to Spencer's father. "I knew we shouldn't have told her."

"Spencer?" Mr. Hastings waved his hands in front of Spencer's face. "You okay?"

Spencer's lips felt numb, as if they'd been injected with novocaine. "I'm afraid."

"Afraid?" her father repeated, leaning forward. "Of what?"

Spencer blinked. She felt like she was having the recurring dream where she knew what she wanted to say in her head, but instead of words coming out of her mouth, out came a shell. Or a worm. Or a plume of purple, chalky smoke. Then she clamped her mouth closed. She'd suddenly realized the answer she was looking for—what she feared.

Herself.

22

THERE'S NO PLACE LIKE ROSEWOOD—FROM 3,000 FEET UP

Friday morning, Hanna stepped out of Lucas's maroon Volkswagen Jetta. They were in the parking lot of Ridley Creek State Park, and the sun was barely up.

"This is my big surprise that's supposed to make me feel all better?" She looked around. Ridley Creek Park was full of undulating gardens and hiking trails. She watched as a bunch of girls in running shorts and long-sleeved T-shirts passed. Then a bunch of guys on bikes in colorful spandex shorts rode by. It made Hanna feel lazy and fat. Here it was, not even 6 a.m., and these people were virtuously burning off calories. They probably hadn't binged on a whole box of cheddar-flavored goldfish crackers last night, either.

"I can't tell you," Lucas answered. "Otherwise, it wouldn't be a surprise."

Hanna groaned. The air smelled like burning leaves,

which Hanna always found spooky. As she crunched through the parking lot gravel, she thought she heard snickering. She whipped back around, alert.

"Something wrong?" Lucas said, stopping a few paces away.

Hanna pointed at the trees. "Do you see someone?"

Lucas shaded his eyes with his hand. "You worried about that stalker?"

"Something like that."

Anxiety gnawed at her belly. When they'd driven here in semidarkness, Hanna felt like a car had been following them. A? Hanna couldn't stop thinking about the bizarre text from yesterday about Mona going to Bill Beach for plastic surgery. In some ways, it made sense—Mona never wore anything that revealed too much skin, even though she was way thinner than Hanna was. But plastic surgery—anything but a boob job, anyway—was kind of . . . embarrassing. It meant genetics were against you, and you couldn't exercise your way down to your ideal body. If Hanna spread that rumor about Mona, her popularity quotient might sink a few notches. Hanna would have done it to another girl without batting an eye . . . but to Mona? Hurting her felt different.

"I think we're okay," Lucas said, walking toward the pebbly path. "They say the stalker only spies on people in their houses."

Hanna rubbed her eyes nervously. For once, she didn't need to worry about smudging her mascara. She'd put on next to no makeup this morning. And she was wearing Juicy velour pants and a gray hoodie she often wore to run laps around the track. This was all to show they were *not* on some peculiar early morning date.

When Lucas showed up at the door, Hanna was relieved to find that he was wearing ratty jeans, a scruffy tee, and a similar gray hoodie. Then he'd flopped into a leaf pile on their way to the car and squirmed around like Hanna's miniature Doberman, Dot. It was actually kind of cute. Which was totally different from thinking that Lucas was cute, obviously.

They entered a clearing and Lucas turned around. "Ready for your surprise?"

"This better be good." Hanna rolled her eyes. "I could still be in bed."

Lucas led her through the trees. In the clearing was a rainbow-striped hot air balloon. It was limp and lying on its side, with the basket part tipped over. A couple of guys stood around it as fans blew air up into the balloon, making it ripple.

"Ta-daaa!" Lucas cried.

"Okaaay." Hanna shaded her eyes with her hand. "I'm going to watch them blow up a balloon?" She *knew* this wasn't a good idea. Lucas was so lame.

"Not quite." Lucas leaned back on his heels. "You're going *up* in it."

"What?" Hanna shrieked. "By *myself*?"

Lucas knocked her upside the head. "I'm going with

you, duh." He started walking toward the balloon. "I have a license to fly hot air balloons. I'm learning to fly a Cessna, too. But my biggest accomplishment is this." He held up a stainless steel carafe. "I made smoothies for us this morning. It was the first time I'd used the blender— the first time I've used a kitchen appliance at all, actually. Aren't you proud of me?"

Hanna smirked. Sean had always cooked for her, which always made Hanna feel more inadequate than pampered. She liked that Lucas was boyishly clueless.

"I am proud." Hanna smiled. "And sure, I'll go up in that deathtrap with you."

After the balloon got fat and taut, Hanna and Lucas climbed in the basket and Lucas shot a long plume of fire up into the envelope. In seconds, they started to rise. Hanna was surprised her stomach didn't lurch as it sometimes did on an elevator, and when she looked down, she was amazed to see that the two guys who had helped inflate the balloon were tiny specks on the grass. She saw Lucas's red Jetta in the parking lot . . . then the fishing creek, then the winding running path, then Route 352.

"There's the Hollis spire!" Hanna cried excitedly, pointing at it off in the distance.

"Cool, huh?" Lucas smiled.

"It *is*," Hanna admitted. It was so nice and quiet up here. There were no traffic sounds, no annoying birds, just the sound of wind. Best of all, A wasn't up here.

Hanna felt so free. Part of her wanted to fly away in a balloon for good, like the Wizard of Oz.

They flew over the Old Hollis neighborhood, with its Victorian houses and messy front lawns. Then the King James Mall, its parking lot nearly empty. Hanna smiled when they passed the Quaker boarding school. It had an avant-garde obelisk on the front lawn that was nicknamed William Penn's Penis.

They floated over Alison DiLaurentis's old house. From up here, it seemed so untroubled. Next to that was Spencer's house, with its windmill, stables, barn, and rock-lined pool. A few houses down was Mona's, a beautiful redbrick bordered by a grove of cherry trees with a garage off to the side of the yard. Once, right after their makeovers, they'd painted $HM + MV = BBBBBFF$ in reflective paint on the roof. They never knew what it actually looked like from above. She reached for her phone to text Mona the news.

Then she remembered. They weren't friends anymore. She sucked in a breath.

"You all right?" Lucas asked.

She looked away. "Yeah. Fine."

Lucas's eyebrows made a V. "I'm in the Supernatural Club at school. We practice mind reading. I can ESP it out of you." He shut his eyes and put his hands to his temples. "You're upset because of . . . how Mona's having a birthday party without you."

Hanna suppressed a snort. Like that was hard to

figure out. Lucas had been in the bathroom right after it happened. She unscrewed the top to the smoothie carafe. "Why are you in, like, every Rosewood Day club imaginable?" He was like a dorkier version of Spencer in that way.

Lucas opened his eyes. They were such a clear, light blue—like the cornflower crayon from the 64-Crayola box. "I like being busy all the time. If I'm not doing anything, I start thinking."

"About what?"

Lucas's Adam's apple bobbed as he swallowed. "My older brother tried to kill himself a year ago."

Hanna widened her eyes.

"He has bipolar disorder. He stopped taking his medication and . . . something went wrong in his head. He took a whole bunch of aspirin, and I found him passed out in our living room. He's at a psychiatric hospital now. They have him on all these medications and . . . he's not really the same person anymore, so . . ."

"Did he go to Rosewood Day?" Hanna asked.

"Yeah, but he's six years older than us. You probably wouldn't remember him."

"God. I'm so sorry," Hanna whispered. "That sucks."

Lucas shrugged. "A lot of people would probably just sit in their room and get stoned, but keeping busy works better for me."

Hanna crossed her arms over her chest. "My way of

staying sane is to eat a ton of cheese-based snacks and then throw them up."

She covered her mouth. She couldn't believe she just said that.

Lucas raised an eyebrow. "Cheese-based snacks, huh? Like Cheez-Its? Doritos?"

"Uh-huh." Hanna stared at the balloon basket's wooden bottom.

Lucas's fingers fidgeted. His hands were strong and well proportioned and looked like they could give really great back rubs. All of a sudden, Hanna wanted to touch them. "My cousin had that . . . problem . . . too," Lucas said softly. "She got over it."

"How?"

"She got happy. She moved away."

Hanna stared over the basket. They were flying over Cheswold, Rosewood's wealthiest housing development. Hanna had always wanted to live in a Cheswold house, and up here, the estates looked even more amazing than they did at street level. But they also looked stiff and formal and not quite real—more like an *idea* of a house instead of something you'd actually want to live in.

"I used to be happy," Hanna sighed. "I hadn't done . . . the cheese thing . . . in years. But my life's been awful lately. I *am* upset about Mona. But there's more. It's everything. Ever since I got that first note, things have gone from bad to worse."

"Rewind." Lucas leaned back. "Note?"

Hanna paused. She hadn't meant to mention A. "Just these notes I've been getting. Someone's teasing me with all this personal stuff." She peeked at Lucas, hoping he wasn't interested—most boys wouldn't be. Unfortunately, he looked worried.

"That sounds mean." Lucas furrowed his brow. "Who's sending them?"

"Don't know. At first, I thought it was Alison DiLaurentis." She paused, pushing the hair out of her eyes. "I know that's silly, but the first notes talked about this thing that only she knew."

Lucas made a disgusted face. "Alison's body was found, what, a month ago? Someone's impersonating her? That's . . . that's freaky."

Hanna waved her arms. "No, I started getting the notes before Ali's body was found, so no one knew she was dead yet. . . ." Her head started to hurt. "It's confusing and . . . don't worry about it. Forget I said anything."

Lucas looked at her uneasily. "Maybe you should call the cops."

Hanna sniffed. "Whoever it is isn't breaking any laws."

"You don't know who you're dealing with, though," Lucas said.

"It's probably some dumb kid."

Lucas paused. "Don't the cops say that if you're being harassed, like getting prank calls, it's most likely from someone you know? I saw that on a crime show once."

A chill went through Hanna. She thought of A's note—*One of your old friends is hiding something from you. Something big.* She thought again about Spencer. Once, not long after Ali vanished, Spencer's dad had taken the four of them to Wildwater Kingdom, a water park not too far from their house. As Hanna and Spencer were climbing the steps to the Devil's Drop, Hanna had asked her if she and Ali were mad at each other about something.

Spencer's face had turned the exact shade of her merlot-colored Tommy Hilfiger string bikini. "Why are you asking that?"

Hanna frowned, holding her foamy raft to her chest. "I was just curious."

Spencer stepped closer. The air became very still, and all splashing and squealing sounds seemed to evaporate. "I wasn't mad at Ali. She was mad at me. I have no clue why, okay?" Then she did a 180 and started marching back down the wooden staircase, practically knocking over other kids as she went.

Hanna curled her toes. She hadn't thought of that day in a while.

Lucas cleared his throat. "What are the notes about? The cheese thing?"

Hanna stared at the skylights on top of the Rosewood Abbey, the site of Ali's memorial. *Screw it,* she thought. She'd told Lucas about A—why not everything else? It was like that trust exercise she'd done on her sixth-grade camping trip: A girl in her bunk named Viviana Rogers had stood behind her and Hanna had to fall into her arms, having faith that she would catch Hanna instead of letting her clunk to the grass.

"Yeah, the cheese," she said quietly. "And . . . well, you may have heard some of the other things. Plenty of stuff is going around about me. Like my father. He moved out a couple years ago and now lives with his beautiful stepdaughter. She wears a size *two*."

"What size do you wear?" Lucas asked, confused.

She took a deep breath, ignoring that question. "And I got caught stealing, too—some jewelry from Tiffany, and Sean Ackard's father's car."

She looked up, surprised to see that Lucas hadn't jumped over the side of the balloon in disgust. "In seventh grade, I was a fat, ugly disaster. Even though I was friends with Alison, I still felt . . . like a nothing. Mona and I worked hard to change, and I thought we'd both become . . . *Alison*. It worked for a while, but not anymore."

Hearing her problems out loud, she sounded like such a loser. But it also felt like the time she'd gone with Mona to a spa in the country and had a colonic. The process was gross, but afterward she felt so free.

"I'm glad you're not Alison," Lucas said quietly.

Hanna rolled her eyes. "Everyone loved Alison."

"I didn't." Lucas avoided Hanna's startled look. "I know that's terrible to say, and I feel horrible about what happened to her. But she wasn't very nice to me." He blew a plume of fire into the balloon. "In seventh grade, Ali started a rumor that I was a zoophile at a soccer game."

Hanna looked up sharply. "Ali didn't start that rumor."

"She did. Actually, I started it for her. She asked if I was a zoophile at a soccer game. I said I didn't know—I had no idea what a zoophile *was*. She laughed and told everyone. It was only later that I heard the making out with my cat part."

Hanna stared at him in disbelief. "Ali wouldn't do that."

But . . . Ali *would* do that. It was Ali who had gotten everyone to call Jenna Cavanaugh Snow. She'd spread the rumor that Toby had fish gills. Everyone had taken everything Ali said as gospel.

Hanna peered over the edge of the basket. That rumor about Lucas making out with his cat had started after they found out he was going to send Hanna a heart-shaped box on Candy Day. Ali had even gone with Hanna to buy new glitter-pocketed Sevens to mark the occasion. She'd said she loved them, but she was probably lying about that, too.

"And you shouldn't say you're ugly, Hanna," Lucas said. "You're so, *so* pretty."

Hanna stuck her chin into the collar of her shirt, feeling surprisingly shy.

"You are. I can't stop looking at you." Lucas grimaced. "Yikes. I probably *way* overstepped the friends thing, huh?"

"It's okay." Heat spread over her skin. It made her feel so good to hear she was pretty. When had someone last told her that? Lucas was as different from perfect Sean as a boy could get. Lucas was tall and lanky, and not in the slightest bit cool, with his Rive Gauche job and ESP club and the sticker on the back of his car that read HAR ADONAI, which could be a band or a salon or a cult. But there was something else there, too—you just had to dig down to get to it, like how Hanna and her dad had once plundered the New Jersey beaches with their metal detector. They'd searched for hours and had found not one but two diamond earrings hiding under the sand.

"So listen," Lucas said. "I'm not invited to Mona's party, either. Do you want to get together on Saturday and have an anti-party? I have a negative-edge pool. It's heated. Or, you know, if that's not your thing, we could . . . I don't know. Play poker."

"Poker?" Hanna glanced at him askance. "*Not* strip."

"What do you take me for?" Lucas put his hand to his chest. "I'm talking Texas Hold 'Em. You'd better watch it, though. I'm good."

"All right. Sure. I'll come over and play poker." She leaned back in the balloon, realizing she was looking forward to it. She gave Lucas a coy smile. "Don't change the subject, though. Now that I've made an ass out of myself, you've got to fess up about some embarrassing stuff, too. What else are you avoiding by joining all your activities?"

Lucas leaned back. "Well, there's the fact that I'm really, *really* attracted to my cat, Mittens."

His face was dead serious. Hanna widened her eyes, caught off guard. But then Lucas grinned and started laughing, so Hanna laughed, too.

23

THE ROSEBUSHES HAVE EYES

Friday at lunch, Emily sat in the Rosewood Day green-house, where tall, leafy plants and a few species of butter-flies flourished in the humidity. Even though it was hot and smelled like dirt, a lot of people were eating lunch in here. Maybe it was to escape the drizzly weather—or maybe they just wanted to be near Rosewood Day's new It Girl, Emily Fields.

"So are you going to Mona's party?" Aria's brother, Mike, gazed expectantly at Emily. He and a few other boys on the lacrosse team had plopped down on a bench across from her and were hanging on her every word.

"I don't know," Emily replied, finishing the last of her potato chips. It was doubtful her mom would let her go to Mona's, and Emily wasn't sure if she wanted to.

"You should come hang out in my hot tub after-ward." Noel Kahn scribbled his number on a piece of lined notebook paper. He tore it off and handed it to her. "That's when the *real* party's going to start."

"Bring your girlfriend, too," Mike suggested, a hungry look in his eye. "And feel free to make out around us. We're very open-minded."

"I could even get my photo booth back out for you," Noel offered, giving Emily a wink. "Whatever turns you on."

Emily rolled her eyes. As the boys sauntered off, she leaned over her thighs and let out a frazzled breath. It was too bad she wasn't the exploitative type—she could probably make a lot of money off these sexed-up, girl-on-girl-loving Rosewood boys.

Suddenly, she felt someone's small hand curl around her wrist. "You dating a lax boy?" Maya whispered in her ear. "I saw him slip you his number."

Emily looked up. Her heart swooped. It felt like she hadn't seen Maya in weeks, and she couldn't stop thinking about her. Maya's face swam before her whenever she shut her eyes. She thought about the feel of her lips during their make-out sessions on the rock by the creek.

Not that those make-out sessions could ever happen again.

Emily pulled her hand away. "Maya. We can't."

Maya stuck out her bottom lip. She looked around. Kids were sitting on the fountains or on the wooden benches next to the flower beds or near the butterfly sanctuary, calmly talking and eating their lunches. "It's not like anyone's watching."

Emily shivered. It *felt* like someone was. This whole lunch, she'd had the most eerie feeling that there was someone right behind her, spying. The greenhouse plants were so tall and thick, they provided easy coverage for people to hide behind.

Maya unclipped her pink Swiss Army knife from her backpack and snipped off a rose from the lush bushes behind them. "Here," she said, handing it to Emily.

"Maya!" Emily dropped the rose on her lap. "You can't pick flowers in here!"

"I don't care," Maya insisted. "I want you to have it."

"Maya." Emily forcefully slapped her palms on her thighs. "You should go."

Maya scowled at her. "You're seriously doing the Tree Tops thing?" When Emily nodded, Maya groaned. "I thought you were stronger than that. And it seems so creepy."

Emily crumpled up her lunch bag. Hadn't she already gone through this? "If I don't do Tree Tops, I have to go to Iowa. And I can't—my aunt and uncle are obsessed with purity. It's . . . *weird.*"

She closed her eyes and thought of her aunt, her uncle, and her three Iowa cousins. She hadn't seen them in years, and all she could picture were five disapproving frowns. "The last time I visited, my aunt Helene told me that I should eat Cheerios *and only Cheerios* for breakfast because they suppressed sexual urges. My two male cousins went on extra-long runs through the cornfields every morning to drain their sexual energy. And my cousin Abby—she's my age—wanted to be a nun. She probably *is* one now. She carried around a notebook that she called Abby's Little Book of Evil—and she wrote down everything she thought was a sin. She recorded *thirty* sinful things about me. She even thought going *barefoot* was evil!"

Maya chuckled. "If you have really ganked-up feet, it is."

"It's not funny!" Emily cried. "And this isn't about me being strong or thinking Tree Tops is right or lying to myself. I *can't* move there."

Emily bit her lip, feeling the hot rush she always got before she was about to cry. In the past two days, if her family passed her in the halls or the kitchen, they wouldn't even look in her direction. They said nothing to her at meals. She felt weird about joining them on the couch to watch TV. And Emily's sister Carolyn seemed to have no idea how to deal with her. Since the swim meet, Carolyn had stayed away from their shared bedroom. Usually, the sisters did their homework at their desks, murmuring to each other about math problems, history essays, or random gossip they'd heard at school. Last night, Carolyn came upstairs when Emily was already in bed. She changed in the dark and climbed into her own bed without saying a word.

"My family won't love me if I'm gay," Emily explained, looking into Maya's round brown eyes. "Imagine if your family woke up and decided they hated you."

"I just want to be with you," Maya mumbled, twirling the rose between her hands.

"Well, me too," Emily answered. "But we can't."

"Let's hang out in secret," Maya suggested. "I'm going to Mona Vanderwaal's party tomorrow. Meet me there. We'll ditch and find somewhere to be alone."

Emily chewed on her thumbnail. She wished she could . . . but Becka's words haunted her. *Life is hard already. Why make it harder?* Yesterday, during her free period, Emily had typed into Google, *Are lesbians' lives hard?* Even as she typed that word—*lesbian*—her right hand pecking the *L* key and her left the *E*, *S*, and *B*, it seemed strange to think that it applied to her. She didn't like it, as a word—it made her think of rice pudding, which she despised. Every link in the list was to a blocked porn site. Then again, Emily had used the words *lesbian* and *hard* in the same search.

Emily felt someone's eyes on her. She glanced around through the whirling vines and bushes and saw Carolyn and a few other swim team girls sitting by the bougainvillea. Her sister glared right at them, a disgusted look on her face.

Emily leapt up from the bench. "Maya, go. Carolyn sees us."

She took a few steps away, pretending to be fascinated

by a planter of marigolds, but Maya didn't move. "Hurry!" Emily hissed. "Get out of here!"

She felt Maya's eyes on her. "I'm going to Mona's party tomorrow," she said in a low voice. "Are you going to be there or not?"

Emily shook her head, not meeting Maya's eye. "I'm sorry. I need to change."

Maya violently yanked up her green-and-white canvas tote. "You can't change who you are. I've told you that a thousand times."

"But maybe I can," Emily answered. "And maybe I want to."

Maya dropped Emily's rose on the bench and stomped away. Emily watched her weave through the rows of planters past the foggy windows for the exit and wanted to cry. Her life was a horrible mess. Her old, simple life—the one she'd had before this school year started—seemed like it belonged to a different girl entirely.

Suddenly, she felt someone's fingernails trace the back of her neck. A chill ran up her back, and she whirled around. It was only a tendril from another rosebush, its thorns fat and sharp, the roses plump. Then, Emily noticed something on one of the windows a few feet away. Her mouth fell open. There was writing in the condensation. *I see you.* Two wide-open, heavily lashed eyes were drawn next to the words. It was signed *A*.

Emily rushed to the writing to wipe it away with her sleeve. Had it been here all along? Why hadn't she seen it? Then, something else struck her. Because of the greenhouse's humidity, water only condensed on its inside walls, so whoever had written this had to be . . . inside.

Emily turned around, looking for some kind of tell-tale sign, but the only people glancing in her direction were Maya, Carolyn, and the lacrosse boys. Everyone else was milling around the greenhouse door, waiting for lunch period to end, and Emily couldn't help but wonder if A was among them.

24

AND IN ANOTHER
GARDEN ACROSS TOWN . . .

Friday afternoon, Spencer leaned over her mother's flower bed, pulling out the thick, stubborn weeds. Her mother usually did the gardening herself, but Spencer was doing it in an attempt to be nice—and to absolve herself of something, although she wasn't sure what.

The multicolored balloons her mother had bought a few days ago to celebrate the Golden Orchid were still tied to the patio rail. *Congratulations, Spencer!* they all said. Next to the words were pictures of blue ribbons and trophies. Spencer glanced into the balloons' shiny Mylar fabric; her warped reflection stared back. It was like looking into a funhouse mirror—her face looked long instead of round, her eyes were small instead of large, and her button nose looked wide and enormous. Maybe it was this balloon girl, not Spencer, who'd cheated to become a Golden Orchid finalist. And maybe Balloon

Girl had been the one who'd fought with Ali the night she disappeared, too.

The sprinkler system came on next door at the DiLaurentises' old house. Spencer stared up at Ali's old window. It was the last one at the back, directly across from Spencer's. She and Ali had felt so lucky their rooms faced each other. They had window signals when it was past phone curfew—one blink of the flashlight meant, *I can't sleep, can you?* Two blinks meant, *Good night.* Three meant, *We need to sneak out and talk in person.*

The memory from Dr. Evans's office floated into her head again. Spencer tried to push it down, but it bobbed right back up. *You care way too much,* Ali had said. And that far-off *crack.* Where had it come from?

"Spencer!" a voice whispered. She whirled around, heart pounding. She faced the woods that bordered the back of her house. Ian Thomas stood between two dogwoods.

"What are you doing here?" she hissed, glancing toward the edge of the yard. Melissa's barn was just a few hundred yards away.

"Watching my favorite girl." Ian's eyes grazed down her body.

"There's a stalker running around," Spencer warned him sternly, trying to suppress the hot, excited feeling in her stomach she always got when Ian looked at her. "You should be careful."

Ian scoffed. "Who's to say I'm not part of the

neighborhood watch? Maybe I'm protecting you *from* the stalker?" He pushed his palm flat up against the tree.

"Are you?" Spencer asked.

Ian shook his head. "Nah. I actually cut through here from my house. I was coming to see Melissa." He paused, shoving his hands into his jeans pockets. "What do you think of me and Melissa being back together?"

Spencer shrugged. "It's none of my business."

"It isn't?" Ian held her gaze, not even blinking. Spencer looked away, her cheeks hot. Ian wasn't making a reference to their kiss. He *couldn't* be.

She revisited that moment again. Ian's mouth had hit hers so roughly that their teeth had smacked together. Afterward, her lips had felt achy and sore. When Spencer told Ali the exciting news, Ali had cackled. "What, do you think Ian's going to go out with you?" she taunted. "Doubtful."

She eyed Ian now, calm and casual and oblivious that he'd been the cause of all that strife. She sort of wished she hadn't kissed him. It seemed like it had started a domino effect—it had led to the fight in the barn, which had led to Ali leaving, which had led to . . . what?

"So Melissa told me you're in therapy, huh?" Ian asked. "How's that going?"

Spencer stiffened. It seemed odd, Melissa talking about therapy to Ian. The sessions were supposed to be private. "Fine, I guess. Boring."

"Really? Melissa said she heard you screaming."

Spencer blinked. "Screaming?" Ian nodded. "W-What was I saying?"

"She didn't say you were saying anything. Just that you were screaming."

Spencer's skin prickled. The DiLaurentises' sprinkler system sounded like a billion little guillotines, chopping off grass-blade heads. "I have to go." She walked crookedly toward the house. "I think I need some water."

"One more sec." Ian stepped toward her. "Have you *seen* what's in your woods?"

Spencer stiffened. Ian had such a strange look on his face that Spencer wondered if maybe it was something of Ali's. One of her bones. A clue. Something to make sense of Spencer's memory.

Then Ian thrust out his open fist. Inside were six plump, pulpy blackberries. "You have the most amazing blackberry bushes back here. Want one?"

The berries had stained Ian's palm a dark, bloody purple. Spencer could see his love line and life line and all the strange etchings near his fingers.

She shook her head. "I wouldn't eat anything from those woods," she said.

After all, Ali had been killed there.

25

SPECIAL DELIVERY FOR HANNA MARIN

Friday evening, a pimply, overgelled T-Mobile sales-person inspected Hanna's phone screen. "Your phone looks okay to me," he said. "And your battery is func-tioning."

"Well, you must not be looking hard enough," Hanna replied gruffly, leaning up against the store's glass counter. "What about the service? Is T-Mobile down?"

"No." The sales boy pointed to the bars in the phone's window. "See? Five bars. Looks great."

Hanna breathed forcefully through her nose. *Something* was going on with her phone. It hadn't rung *once* all night. Mona might have ditched her, but Hanna refused to believe that everyone else would follow so quickly. And she thought A might text again, filling Hanna in with more information about Mona and her possible lipo, or explaining what it meant when A said that one of her friends had a big secret that had yet to be revealed.

"Do you just want to buy a new phone?" the sales guy asked.

"Yes," Hanna said sharply, conjuring up a voice that sounded surprisingly like her mother's. "One that works this time, please."

The sales guy retrieved a new phone from the back, pulled it out of its Styrofoam bed, and started hitting some buttons. Hanna leaned on the counter and watched the shoppers stream through the King James Mall concourse, trying not to think about what she and Mona usually did on Friday nights. First, they'd buy a Happy Friday outfit to reward themselves for making it through another week; next, they'd hit a sushi place for the salmon platter; and then—Hanna's favorite part— they'd go home and gossip on Hanna's queen-size bed, laughing and making fun of the "Am I the Asshole?" threads on Reddit. Hanna had to admit that it was hard to talk to Mona about certain things—she'd sidestepped any emotional conversations about Sean, and they were never able to talk about Ali's disappearance because Hanna didn't want to dredge up bad memories about her old friends. In fact, the more she thought about it, she wondered what she and Mona *did* talk about. Boys? Clothes? Shoes? People they hated?

"It'll be a minute," the sales guy said, frowning and looking at something on his computer monitor. "For some reason, our network isn't responding."

Ha! Hanna thought. There *was* something wrong with the network.

Someone laughed as they entered T-Mobile, and Hanna looked up. She had no time to duck when she saw Mona walking in with Eric Kahn.

Mona's light blond hair stood out against her charcoal-gray turtleneck sweater dress, black tights, and tall black boots. Hanna wished she could hide, but she didn't know where—the T-Mobile register counter was an island in the middle of the store. This stupid place didn't even have any aisles to sneak down or shelves to hide under, just four walls of cell phones and mobile devices.

Before she could do anything, Eric saw her. His eyes flashed with recognition, and he gave Hanna a nod. Hanna's limbs froze. Now she knew how a deer felt when it was face-to-face with an oncoming tractor-trailer.

Mona followed Eric's gaze. "Oh," she said flatly when her eyes met Hanna's.

Eric, who must have sensed girl trouble, shrugged and wandered to the back of the store. Hanna took a few steps toward Mona. "Hi."

Mona stared at a wall of phone headsets and car adapters. "Hey."

A long beat passed. Mona scratched the side of her nose. She had painted her nails with Chanel's limited-edition Le Vernis black lacquer—Hanna remembered the time they'd stolen two bottles from Sephora. The memory nearly brought tears to Hanna's eyes. Without Mona, Hanna felt like a great outfit without matching accessories, a screwdriver that was all orange juice and no vodka, a pair of Beats headphones without the Bluetooth. She just felt *wrong*. Hanna thought about the time in the summer after eighth grade when she'd tagged along with her mom on a work trip. Hanna's cell didn't get service there, and when she came back, there had been twenty voice mails from Mona. "It felt weird not talking to you every day, so I decided to tell you everything in messages instead," Mona had said.

Hanna let out a long, shaky breath. T-Mobile smelled overwhelmingly like carpet cleaner and sweat—she hoped it wasn't her own. "I saw that message we painted on top of your garage the other day," she blurted out. "You know, $HM + MV = BBBBBFF$? You can see it from the sky. Clear as day."

Mona seemed startled. Her expression softened. "You can?"

"Uh-huh." Hanna stared at one of T-Mobile's promo posters across the room. It was a cheesy photo of two girls giggling over something, holding their cell phones in their laps. One was auburn-haired, the other blond—like Hanna and Mona.

"This is so messed up," Hanna said quietly. "I don't even know how this started. I'm sorry I missed the Frenniversary, Mon. I didn't want to be hanging out with my old friends. I'm not getting close with them or anything."

Mona tucked her chin into her chest. "No?" Hanna could barely hear her over the mall's kiddie train, which was rumbling by right outside the T-Mobile store. There was only one pudgy, miserable-looking boy on the ride.

"Not at all," Hanna answered, after the kiddie train passed. "We're just . . . weird stuff is happening to us. I can't explain all of it right now, but if you're patient with me, I'll be able to tell you soon." She sighed. "And you know I didn't do that skywriting thing on purpose. I wouldn't do that to you."

Hanna let out a small, squeaky hiccup. She always got the hiccups before she was about to start bawling, and Mona knew it. Mona's mouth twitched, and for a second, Hanna's heart leapt. Maybe things would be okay.

Then, it was like the cool-girl software inside Mona's head rebooted. Her face snapped back to being glossy and confident. She stood up straighter and smiled icily. Hanna knew exactly what Mona was doing—she and Hanna agreed never, *ever* to cry in public. They even had a rule about it: If they even thought they were going to cry, they had to squeeze their butt cheeks together, remind themselves that they were beautiful, and smile. A few days ago, Hanna would've done the same thing, but now, she couldn't see the point. "I miss you, Mona," Hanna said. "I want things to go back to the way they were."

"Maybe," Mona answered primly. "We'll have to see."

Hanna tried to force a smile. *Maybe?* What did *maybe* mean?

When she pulled into her driveway, Hanna noticed Wilden's police cruiser next to her mother's Lexus. Inside, she found her mother and Darren Wilden snuggled up on the couch watching the news. There was a bottle of wine and two glasses on the coffee table. By the looks of Wilden's T-shirt and jeans, Hanna guessed Supercop was off duty tonight.

The news was showing the leaked video of the five of them again. Hanna leaned against the doorjamb between the living room and the kitchen and watched as Spencer threw herself at her sister's boyfriend, Ian, and Ali sat at the corner of the couch, looking bored. When the clip ended, Jessica DiLaurentis, Alison's mother, appeared on the screen. "The video is hard to watch," Mrs. DiLaurentis said. "All of this has made us go through our suffering all over again. But we want to thank everyone in Rosewood—you've all been so wonderful. The time we've spent back here for Alison's investigation has made my husband and me realize how much we've missed it."

For a brief second, the camera panned on the people behind Mrs. DiLaurentis. One of them was Officer Wilden, all gussied up in his cop uniform. "There you are!" Hanna's mother cried, squeezing Wilden's shoulder.

"You look *great* on camera."

Hanna wanted to vomit. Her mom hadn't even gotten that excited last year when Hanna had been named Snowflake Queen and had ridden on a float in the Philadelphia Mummers parade.

Wilden swiveled around, sensing Hanna's presence in the doorway. "Oh. Hi, Hanna." He moved slightly away from Ms. Marin, as if Hanna had just caught him doing something wrong.

Hanna grunted a hello, then turned and opened a kitchen cupboard and pulled down a box of peanut butter Ritz Bits.

"Han, a package came for you," her mother called, turning down the TV volume.

"Package?" Hanna repeated, her mouth full of crackers.

"Yep. It was on the doorstep when we got here. I put it in your room."

Hanna carried the box of Ritz Bits upstairs with her. There was indeed a large box propped up against her bureau, right next to her miniature Doberman Dot's Gucci dog bed. Dot stretched off the bed, his tiny nubby tail wagging. Hanna's fingers trembled as she used her nail scissors to slice open the packing tape. As she ripped open the box, a few sheets of tissue paper cascaded through the room. And then . . . a champagne-colored slip dress sat at the bottom.

Hanna gasped. Mona's court dress. All tailored and pressed and ready to wear. She rooted around the bottom of the box for a note of explanation but couldn't find one. Whatever. This could only mean one thing—she was forgiven.

The corners of Hanna's lips slowly spread into a grin. She leapt onto her bed and started jumping, making her bedsprings squeak. Dot circled around her, yapping crazily. *"Yessss,"* Hanna cried, relieved. She'd known Mona would come to her senses. She would be foolish to stay mad at Hanna for long.

She sat back down on the bed and picked up her new phone. This was short notice—she probably wouldn't be able to rebook the hair and makeup appointments she'd canceled when she thought she wasn't going to the party. Then she remembered something else: Lucas. *I'm not invited to Mona's party, either,* he'd said.

Hanna paused, drumming her hands on the phone's screen. She obviously couldn't bring him to Mona's party. Not as her *date*. Not as anything. Lucas was cute, sure, but he was definitely not party-worthy.

She sat up straighter and flipped through her red leather Coach organizer for Lucas's email address. She would write him a short, snippy email so he'd know exactly where he stood with her: nowhere. He'd be crushed, but really, Hanna couldn't please everyone now, could she?

26

SPENCER GETS IN HOT WATER . . . LITERALLY AND FIGURATIVELY

Friday evening, Spencer was soaking in the family hot tub. It was one of her favorite things to do, especially at night, when all of the stars glittered in the dark sky. Tonight the only sounds around her were the burbling of the hot tub's jets and the slobbery crunching sounds of Beatrice, one of the family's labradoodles, chewing on a rawhide bone.

Then suddenly, she heard a twig snap. Then another. Then . . . someone breathing. Spencer turned as her sister, clad in a Nova-check plaid Burberry bikini, climbed down the stairs and settled into the tub, too.

For a while, neither of them said anything. Spencer hid under a beard of bubbles, and Melissa was looking at the umbrella table next to the pool. Suddenly, Melissa inspected her sister. "So I'm a little annoyed at Dr. Evans."

"Why?"

Melissa swished her hands around in the water. "Sometimes she says all this stuff about me like she's known me for years. Does she do that to you?"

Spencer shrugged. Hadn't Melissa warned her Dr. Evans would do that?

Melissa pressed the flat of her hand against her forehead. "She told me that I choose untrustworthy men to date. That I actually go after guys I know will never commit or turn into anything long-term because I'm afraid of getting close to anyone."

Melissa reached over and drank from her big bottle of Evian, which was sitting next to the tub. Above her head, Spencer saw the silhouette of a large bird—or perhaps a bat—flap past the moon. "I was angry about it at first, but now . . . I don't know." Melissa sighed. "Maybe she's right. I've started to think about all my relationships. Some of the guys I've gone out with *have* seemed really untrustworthy, right from the start."

Her eyes needled into Spencer, and Spencer blushed.

"Wren's an obvious one," Melissa went on, as if reading Spencer's thoughts. Spencer looked away, staring at the waterfall installation that was on the other side of the pool. "She's got me wondering about Ian, too. I think he was cheating on me when we were in high school."

Spencer tensed. "Really?"

"Uh-huh." Melissa inspected her perfectly manicured pale peach nails. Her eyes were dark. "I'm almost *certain*. And I think I know who it was."

Spencer bit a hangnail on her thumb. What if Melissa had overheard Spencer and Ian in the yard earlier? Ian had alluded to their kiss. Or, worse: What if Ali *had* told Melissa what Spencer had done, years ago?

Not long before Ali vanished, Spencer's dad had taken the five of them to play paintball. Melissa had come along, too. "I'm going to tell Melissa what you did," Ali singsonged to Spencer as they put on their jumpsuits in the changing room.

"You wouldn't," Spencer hissed back.

"Oh no?" Ali teased. "Watch me."

Spencer had followed Ali and the others to the field. They all crouched behind a large bale of hay, waiting for the game to start. Then Ali leaned over and tapped Melissa on the shoulder. "Hey, Melissa. I have something to tell you."

Spencer nudged her. "Stop it."

The whistle blew. Everyone shot forward and started pelting the other team. Everyone, that was, except for Ali and Spencer. Spencer took Ali's arm and dragged her behind a nearby hay bale. She was so angry her muscles were quivering.

"Why are you doing this?" Spencer demanded.

Ali snickered, leaning against the hay. *"Why are you doing this?"* she imitated in a high falsetto. "Because it's wrong. Melissa deserves to know."

Anger gathered in Spencer's body like clouds before a huge thunderstorm. Didn't friends keep each other's secrets? They'd kept the Jenna secret for Ali, after all—*Ali* was the one who'd lit that firework, *Ali* was the one who had blinded Jenna—and they'd all vowed not to tell. Didn't Ali remember that?

Spencer didn't mean to pull the trigger of the paint-ball gun . . . it just happened. Blue paint splattered all over Ali's jumpsuit, and Ali let out a startled cry. Then she glared at Spencer and stormed away. What if she'd gone and told Melissa then, and Melissa had been waiting all this time for the right moment to drop it on Spencer? Maybe this was it.

"Any guesses who it was?" Melissa goaded, breaking Spencer out of the memory.

Spencer sank down farther into the hot tub's bubbles, her eyes stinging with chlorine. A kiss hardly qualified as cheating, and it had been so long ago. "Nope. No clue."

Melissa sighed. "Maybe Dr. Evans is full of it. What does she know, really?"

Spencer studied her sister carefully. She thought about what Dr. Evans had said about Melissa—that her sister needed validation. That she was jealous of Spencer. It was such a weird possibility to consider. And could Melissa's issues have something to do with the time they'd been mugged, Spencer had gotten sick, and Melissa had had to go to her bee with Yolanda? How many other things had her sister missed out on that summer because her parents were too busy hovering over Spencer? How many times had she been shoved to the side?

I liked when we were friends, said a voice inside Spencer's head. *I liked quizzing you with your spelling words. I hate the way things are now. I've hated it for a long time.*

"Does it really matter if Ian cheated on you in high school?" Spencer said quietly. "I mean, it was so long ago."

Melissa stared up at the dark, clear sky. All the stars had come out. "Of course it matters. It was *wrong*. And if I ever find out it's true, Ian is going to regret it for the rest of his life."

Spencer flinched. She'd never heard Melissa sound so vengeful. "And what will you do to the girl?"

Melissa turned very slowly and gave Spencer a poisonous smile. At that very moment, the backyard's timed lights snapped on. Melissa's eyes glowed. "Who says I haven't done something to her already?"

27

OLD HABITS DIE HARD

Late Saturday afternoon, Aria slumped down behind a maple in the McCreadys' yard, which was across the street from her own house. She watched as three cookie-selling Girl Scouts strode to her family's front door. *Ella's not home, but put her down for a couple boxes of Thin Mints,* she wanted to tell the girls. *They're her favorite.*

The girls waited. When no one answered, they went to the next house.

Aria knew it was weird to have biked here from Sean's, stalking her own house as if it were a velvet-rope celebrity club and she were a paparazzo, but she missed her family so badly. The Ackards were like the bizarro-Montgomerys. Mr. and Mrs. Ackard had joined the Rosewood Stalker Community Watch Board. They'd established a twenty-four-hour tip hotline, and in a few days, it would be Mr. and Mrs. Ackard's turn to make the nightly rounds. And every time any of them looked

at her, Aria felt like they could tell what she'd done with
Ezra in his office. It was as though she had a big scarlet
A on her shirt now, too.

Aria needed to clear her head and purge herself
of Ezra. Only, she couldn't stop thinking about him.
This whole bike ride had been one Ezra reminder after
another. She'd passed a chubby man eating Chicken
McNuggets and had gotten weak-kneed from the smell.
She'd seen a girl with black plastic glasses just like Ezra's
and felt chills. Even a cat on a garden wall had reminded
her of Ezra, for no good reason at all. But what was she
thinking? How could something be so wrong . . . yet so
right at the same time?

As she passed a stone house with its own water-
wheel, a Channel 7 news van whizzed by. It disappeared over the hill, the wind slid through the trees,
and the sky suddenly darkened. All at once, Aria felt as
if a hundred spiders were crawling over her. Someone
was watching.

A?

When her phone let out a whirly little ring, she nearly
fell off her bike. She hit the brakes, pulled onto the side-
walk, and reached for it in her pocket. It was Sean.

"Where are you?" he asked.

"Um . . . I went out for a bike ride," she answered,
chewing on the cuff of her beat-up red hoodie.

"Well, come home soon," Sean said. "Otherwise we'll
be late to Mona's."

Aria sighed. She'd completely forgotten about Mona Vanderwaal's party.

He sighed back at her, too. "Do you not want to go?"

Aria squeezed the bike's brakes and stared at the beautiful Gothic Revival house in front of her. The owners had decided to paint it royal purple. Aria's parents were the only people in the neighborhood who hadn't signed a petition demanding the artist-owners paint it a more conservative color, but the petition hadn't held up in court. "I'm not really friends with Mona," Aria mumbled. "Or anyone else going to that party."

"What are you talking about?" Sean sounded baffled. "They're my friends, so they're your friends. We're going to have a great time. And, I mean, other than our bike ride, I feel like I haven't seen you, really, since you moved in with me. Which is weird, if you think about it."

Suddenly, Aria's call waiting beeped. She brought her phone away from her ear and looked at the screen. *Ezra.* She clapped her hand over her mouth.

"Sean, can I put you on hold for a sec?" She tried to contain the exhilaration in her voice.

"Why?" Sean asked.

"Just . . . hang on." Aria clicked over. She cleared her throat and smoothed down her hair, as if Ezra were watching her on a video screen. "Hello?" She tried to sound cool yet seductive.

"Aria?" She swooned at Ezra's sleepy, gravelly voice.

"Ezra." Aria feigned surprise. "Hi."

A few seconds of silence passed. Aria spun her bike's pedals with her foot and watched a squirrel run across the purple house's lawn. "I can't stop thinking about you," Ezra finally admitted. "Can you meet me?"

Aria squeezed her eyes shut. She knew she shouldn't go. But she so wanted to. She swallowed hard. "Hang on."

She clicked back over to Sean. "Um, Sean?"

"Who was it?" he asked.

"It was . . . my mom," Aria fumbled.

"Really? That's great, right?"

Aria bit down hard on the inside of her cheek. She focused intently on the intricately carved pumpkins on the purple house's steps. "I have to go do something," she blurted out. "I'll call you later."

"Wait," Sean cried. "What about Mona's?"

But Aria's finger was already switching back to Ezra. "I'm back," she said breathlessly, feeling as if she'd just competed in some sort of boy triathlon. "And I'll be right over."

When Ezra opened the door to his apartment, which was in an old Victorian house in Old Hollis, he was holding a Glenlivet bottle in his right hand. "Want some Scotch?" he asked.

"Sure," Aria answered. She walked into the middle of Ezra's living room and sighed happily. She'd thought about this apartment a lot since she'd been here last. The billions of books on the shelves, the blue melted candle wax spilling over the mantel in Smurf-like lumps, and the big, useless bathtub in the middle of the room . . . it all made Aria feel so comfortable. She felt like she'd just come home.

They plopped down on Ezra's springy, mustard-yellow love seat. "Thanks for coming over," Ezra said softly. He was wearing a pale blue T-shirt with a little rip in the shoulder. Aria wanted to stick her finger through the hole.

"You're welcome," Aria said, sliding out of her checkerboard Vans slip-ons. "Should we toast?"

Ezra thought for a moment, a lock of dark hair falling over his eyes. "To coming from messed-up homes," he decided, and touched his glass to hers.

"Cheers." Aria tipped the Scotch back. It tasted like glass cleaner and smelled like kerosene, but she didn't care. She drained the Scotch fast, feeling it burn down her esophagus.

"Another?" he asked, bringing the Glenlivet bottle with him as he sat back down.

"Sure," Aria answered. Ezra got up to get more ice cubes and glanced at the tiny muted TV in the corner. There was a GEICO commercial on. It was funny to see that little gecko gesticulating wildly without any sound.

Ezra returned and poured Aria another drink. With every sip of the Scotch, Aria's tough exterior melted away. They talked for a while about Ezra's parents—his mom lived in New York City now, his dad in Wayne, a town not too far away. Aria began to talk about her family again. "You know what my favorite memory of my parents is?" she said, hoping she wasn't slurring. The bitter Scotch was doing a number on her motor skills. "My thirteenth birthday at Ikea."

Ezra raised an eyebrow. "You're kidding. Ikea's a nightmare."

"It sounds weird, right? But my parents knew someone who was really high up who ran the Ikea store near here, and we rented it out after-hours. It was so much fun—Byron and Ella went there early and planned this whole big scavenger hunt all around the Ikea bedrooms and kitchens and offices. They were so giddy about it. We all had Swedish furniture names for the party—Byron's was Ektorp, I think, and Ella's was Klippan. They seemed so . . . together."

Tears dotted Aria's eyes. Her birthday was in April; Aria had found Bryon with Meredith in May, and then Ali had vanished in June. It seemed like that party had been the last perfect, uncomplicated night of her life. Everyone had been so happy, even Ali—especially Ali. At one point in a cavern of Ikea shower curtains, Ali had grabbed Aria's hands and whispered, "I'm so happy, Aria! I'm *so* happy!"

"Why?" Aria had asked.

Ali grinned and wiggled. "I'll tell you soon. It's a surprise."

But she'd never had the chance.

Aria traced her finger around the top of the Scotch

glass. The news had just come on the TV. They were talking about Ali—again. *Murder investigation,* the banner at the bottom of the screen said. Ali's seventh-grade school picture was in the left-hand corner: Ali flashing her brilliant smile, the diamond hoops glinting in her ears, her blond hair wavy and lustrous, her Rosewood Day blazer perfectly fitted and lint-free. It was so odd that Ali would be a seventh grader forever.

"So," Ezra said. "Have you spoken to your dad?"

Aria turned away from the TV. "Not really. He wanted to talk to me, although he probably doesn't now. Not after the Scarlet *A* thing."

Ezra frowned. "Scarlet *A* thing?"

Aria picked at a loose thread in her favorite APC jeans from Paris. This was *not* something she could explain to someone who had a degree in English literature. But Ezra was learning forward, his beautiful lips parted in expectation. So she took another sip of Scotch and told him all about Meredith, Hollis, and the dripping red *A*.

To her horror, Ezra burst out laughing. "You're *kidding* me. You really did that?"

"Yes," Aria snapped. "I shouldn't have told you."

"No, no, it's great. I love it." Ezra impetuously grabbed Aria's hands. His palms were warm and big and slightly sweaty. He met her eyes . . . then kissed her. First lightly, then Aria leaned in and kissed him harder. They stopped for a moment, and Aria slumped back on the couch.

"You okay?" Ezra asked softly.

Aria had no idea if she was okay. She'd never felt so much in her life. She couldn't quite figure out what to do with her mouth. "I don't—"

"I know we shouldn't be doing this," Ezra interrupted. "You're my student. I'm your teacher. But . . ." He sighed, pushing back a lock of hair. "But . . . I wish that maybe . . . somehow . . . this could work."

How badly had she wanted Ezra to say these things weeks ago? Aria felt perfect with him—more alive, more *herself*. But then Sean's face appeared in Aria's mind. She saw him leaning over to kiss her the other day in the cemetery when he saw a rabbit. And she saw A's note: *Careful, careful! I'm always watching.*

She glanced at the television again. The familiar video clip came on for the billionth time. Aria could read Spencer's lips: *Want to read her texts?* The girls crowded around the phone. Ali swam into the picture. For a moment, Ali looked squarely into the camera, her eyes round and blue. It seemed like she was staring out of the TV screen into Ezra's living room . . . straight at Aria.

Ezra turned his head and noticed what was on. "Shit," he said. "I'm sorry." He rooted around in the pile of magazines and Thai takeout menus on his coffee table and finally found the remote. He switched one channel up, which was QVC. Lisa Rinna was talking up an oversized silk blouse the color of a mushroom.

Ezra pointed at the screen. "I'll buy that for you, if you want."

Aria giggled. "No thanks." She put her hand on Ezra's and took a deep breath. "So, what you said . . . about making this work. I . . . I think I want it to work with you, too."

He brightened and Aria could see her reflection in his glasses. The old grandfather clock near Ezra's dining room table chimed out the hour. "R-really?" he murmured.

"Yes. But . . . but I also want to do it right." She swallowed hard. "I have a boyfriend right now. So . . . I have to take care of that, you know?"

"Sure," Ezra said. "I understand."

They stared at each other for at least a minute more. Aria could have reached over, torn his glasses off, and kissed him a billion times. "I think I should go now," she said wistfully.

"Okay," Ezra answered, his eyes not leaving hers. But when she slid off the couch and tried to put on her shoes, he pulled at the edge of her T-shirt. Even though she'd wanted to leave, she just . . . couldn't.

"Come here," Ezra whispered, and Aria fell back into him. Ezra reached out his arms and caught her.

28

SOME OF HER LETTERS
ALSO SPELL *JAIL*

A little before eight on Saturday night, Spencer was lying on her bed, watching her palm-leaf ceiling fan go around and around. The fan cost more than a decent-running car, but Spencer had begged her mom to buy it because it looked identical to the fan in her private cabana the time her family stayed at the Caves in Jamaica. Now, however, it looked so . . . Spencer at thirteen.

She got out of bed and slid her feet into her black Chanel sling-backs. She knew she should muster up some enthusiasm for Mona's party. She would have last year—then again, everything had been different last year. All day, she'd been having strange visions—fighting with Ali outside the barn, Ali's mouth moving but Spencer not hearing the words, Spencer taking a step toward her, a *crack*. It was as if the memory, pent up for all these years, wanted to be the star.

She swiped more toasted-almond-colored gloss on her lips, straightened her kimono-sleeve black dress, and clomped downstairs. When she reached the kitchen, she was surprised to see that her mother, father, and Melissa were sitting at the table around an empty Scrabble board. The two dogs snuggled at their feet. Her father wasn't wearing his standard uniform of either a suit or cycling clothes, but a soft white T-shirt and jeans. Her mom was in yoga pants. The room smelled like steamed milk from the Miele espresso maker.

"Hey." Spencer couldn't remember the last time she'd seen her parents home on a Saturday night. They were all about being seen—whether it was at a restaurant opening or at the symphony or at one of the dinner parties the partners at her father's firm were always having.

"Spencer! There you are!" Mrs. Hastings cried. "Guess what we just got?" With a flourish, she presented a printout she had been holding behind her back. It had the *Philadelphia Sentinel*'s gothic-script logo on the top. Underneath was the headline, *Future Chairwoman of the Board!* Spencer stared at the photo of herself sitting at her father's desk. The battleship-gray Calvin Klein suit with the raspberry silk camisole underneath had been a good choice.

"Jordana just emailed us the link," her mother chirped. "Sunday's front page won't be ready until tomorrow morning, of course, but your story is already up online!"

"Wow," Spencer said shakily, too unfocused to actually read the story. So this was really happening. How far was this going to go? What if she actually *won*?

"We're going to open a bottle of champagne to celebrate," Mr. Hastings said. "You can even have some, Spence. Special occasion and all."

"And maybe you want to play Scrabble?" Mrs. Hastings asked.

"Mom, she's all dressed up for a party," Melissa urged. "She doesn't want to sit here and drink champagne and play Scrabble."

"Nonsense," Mrs. Hastings said. "It's not even eight yet. Parties don't start this early, do they?"

Spencer felt trapped. They were all staring at her. "I . . . I guess not," she said.

She dragged a chair back, sat down, and kicked off her shoes. Her father got a bottle of Moët out of the fridge, popped the cork, and took out four Riedel glasses from the cabinet. He poured a whole glass for himself, Spencer's mother, and Melissa, and a half glass for Spencer. Melissa put a Scrabble rack in front of her.

Spencer plunged her hand into the velvet bag and selected letters. Her father selected his letters next. Spencer was amazed he knew how to do it—she'd never seen him play a game, not even on vacation. "When do you hear what the judges' final decision is?" he asked, taking a sip of his champagne.

Spencer shrugged. "I don't know." She glanced at

Melissa, who gave her a brief, indecipherable smile. Spencer hadn't talked to Melissa since their hot-tub session last night, and she felt a little strange around her sister. Apprehensive, almost.

"I had a chance to read it yesterday," Mr. Hastings continued, folding his hands. "I love how you updated the concept for modern times."

"So who goes first?" Spencer asked shrilly. There was no way they were talking about the *content* of the essay. Not around Melissa.

"Didn't 2012's Golden Orchid winner win a Pulitzer last year?" Mrs. Hastings asked.

"No, it was a National Book Award," Melissa said.

Please stop talking about the Golden Orchid, Spencer thought. Then, she realized: For once, they were talking about *her*—not Melissa.

Spencer looked at her tiles. She had *I, A, S, J, L, R,* and *H.* She rearranged the letters and almost choked on her tongue. LIAR SJH. SJH, as in Spencer Jill Hastings.

Outside, the sky was raven-colored. A dog howled. Spencer grabbed her champagne flute and drained its contents in three seconds flat. "Someone's not driving for at least an hour," her father mock-scolded.

Spencer tried to laugh, sitting on her hands so her dad wouldn't see that they were shaking.

Mrs. Hastings spelled WORM with her tiles. "Your turn, Spence," she said.

As Spencer picked up her *L* tile, Melissa's phone lit

up. A fake cello vibrated out of the cell's speaker, playing the theme to *Jaws. Duh-DUH. Duh-DUH.* Spencer could see the screen from here: new text message.

Melissa glanced at the screen, angling it away from Spencer's view. She frowned. "Huh?" she said aloud.

"What is it?" Mrs. Hastings asked, raising her eyes from her tiles.

Melissa scratched her head. *"The great Scottish economist Adam Smith's invisible-hand concept can be summed up very easily, whether it's describing the markets of the nineteenth century or those of the twenty-first: You might think people are doing things to help you, but in reality, everyone is only out for himself.* Weird! Why would someone send me part of an essay I wrote when I was in *high school?*"

Spencer opened her mouth to speak, but only a dry exhalation came out.

Mr. Hastings put down his glass. "That's Spencer's Golden Orchid essay."

Melissa examined the screen. "No, it's not, it's my . . ." She looked at Spencer. *"No."*

Spencer shrank down in her chair. "Melissa, it was a mistake."

Melissa's mouth was open so wide, Spencer saw all the way to the back of her throat. "You bitch!"

"Things got out of hand!" Spencer cried. "The situation slipped away from me!"

Mr. Hastings frowned, confused. "What's going on?"

Melissa's face contorted, the corners of her eyes turning down and her lips curling up sinisterly. "First you steal my boyfriend. And then my *paper*? Who do you think you are?"

"I said I was sorry!" Spencer cried at the same time.

"Wait. It's . . . Melissa's paper?" Mrs. Hastings said, growing pale.

"There must be some mistake," Mr. Hastings insisted.

Melissa put her hands on her hips. "Should I tell them? Or would you like to?"

Spencer jumped up. "Tell on me like you always do." She ran down the hall toward the stairs. "You've gotten so good at it by now."

Melissa followed. "They need to know what a liar you are."

"They need to know what a bitch *you* are," Spencer shot back.

Melissa's lips spread into a smile. "You're so lame, Spencer. Everyone thinks so. Including Mom and Dad."

Spencer scrambled up the stairs backward. "They do not!"

"Yes, they do!" Melissa taunted. "And it's the truth, isn't it? You're a boyfriend-stealing, plagiarizing, pathetic little bitch!"

"I'm so sick of you!" Spencer screamed. "Why don't you just *die*?"

"Girls!" Mr. Hastings cried.

But it was as if the sisters were in a force-field bubble all their own. Melissa didn't break her stare from Spencer.

And Spencer started shaking. It was true. She *was* pathetic. She *was* worthless.

"Rot in hell!" Spencer screamed. She took two stairs at a time.

Melissa was right behind her. "That's right, little baby who means nothing, run away!"

"Shut *up*!"

"Little baby who steals my boyfriends! Who isn't even smart enough to write her own papers! What were you going to say on TV if you won, Spencer? *Yes, I wrote every word of it myself. I'm such a smart, smart girl!* What, did you cheat on the PSATs, too?"

It felt like fingernails scraping against Spencer's heart. "Stop it!" she rasped, nearly tripping over an empty J. Crew box her mother had left on the steps.

Melissa grabbed Spencer's arm and swung her around. She put her face right up to Spencer's. Her breath smelled like espresso. "Little baby wants everything of mine, but you know what? You can't have what I have. You never will."

All the anger that Spencer had held in for years broke free and flooded her body, making her feel hot, then wet, then shaky. Her insides were so bathed in fury they were starting to prune. She braced herself against the railing, grabbed Melissa by the shoulders and started to shake her as if she were a Magic Eight Ball. Then she shoved her. "I said, *stop* it!"

Melissa stumbled, grabbing the railing for support. A

frightened look danced over her face.

A crack started to form in Spencer's brain. But instead of Melissa she saw Ali. They both wore the same smug, *I'm everything and you're nothing* expression. *You try to steal everything away from me. But you can't have this.* Spencer smelled the dewy humidity and saw the lightning bugs and felt Ali's breath close to her face. And then, a strange force invaded Spencer's body. She let out an agonized grunt from somewhere deep inside her and shot forward. She saw herself reaching out and pushing Ali—or was it Melissa?—with all her strength. Both Melissa and Ali fell backward. Their heads both made skull-shattering cracks as they fell against something. Spencer's vision cleared and she saw Melissa tumbling down, down, down the stairs, falling into a heap at the bottom.

"Melissa!" Mrs. Hastings cried.

And then, everything went black.

29

THERE'S A FULL MOON AT THE HOLLIS PLANETARIUM

Hanna staggered to the planetarium gates a little after nine. It was the weirdest thing, but it was kind of hard to walk in the court dress. Or sit down. Or, well, breathe.

Okay, so the whole thing was too damn tight. It had taken Hanna forever to wriggle into the thing and then even longer to zip up the back. She had even considered borrowing her mom's Spanx girdle, but that would have meant taking the dress off and going through the zipper torture again. The process had taken so long, in fact, she'd hardly had time to do anything else before coming here, like touch up her makeup, tally the calories she'd eaten today, or import her old phone numbers into her new phone.

Now the dress fabric seemed to have shrunk even more. It cut into her skin and clung so tightly to her hips that she had no idea how she would pull it up to pee. Every time she moved, she could hear tiny threads tearing. There were certain spots, too, like around the belly, the side of her boobs, and across her butt, that . . . bulged.

She *had* eaten a lot of Cheez-Its over the past few days . . . and she'd tried really hard not to throw any of them up. Could she have gained weight that fast? What if something was suddenly wrong with her metabolism? What if she had turned into one of those girls who gained weight by simply *looking* at food?

But she had to wear this dress. Maybe the fabric would loosen the more she wore it, like leather. The party would probably be dark, too, so no one would notice. Hanna tottered up the planetarium's steps, feeling a bit like a stiff, champagne-colored penguin.

She heard the pumping bass from inside the building and steeled herself. She hadn't felt this nervous about a party since Ali's seventh-grade Halloween bash, when she'd still felt like she was teetering on the edge of dorkdom. Not long after Hanna had arrived, Mona and her geeky friends Chassey Bledsoe and Phi Templeton had shown up as three Hobbits from *The Lord of the Rings*. Ali had taken one look at them and turned them away. "You look like you're covered in fleas," she'd said, laughing in their faces.

The day after Ali's party, when Hanna had gone with her mom to the grocery store, she'd seen Mona and her dad in the checkout line. There, on the lapel of Mona's denim jacket, was the crystal-studded jack-o'-lantern pin that had been in Ali's party gift bag. Mona was wearing it proudly, as if she belonged.

Hanna felt a twinge of guilt about ditching Lucas—he hadn't emailed her back after she canceled on him—but what choice did she have? Mona had all but forgiven her in T-Mobile and then sent her the dress. Best friends always came first, especially best friends like Mona.

She carefully pushed through the large metal front door. Immediately, the music washed over her like a wave. She saw bluish ice sculptures in the main hall, and farther back, a giant trapeze. Glittering planets hung from the ceiling, and an enormous video screen loomed over the stage. A larger-than-life Noel Kahn gazed through a telescope on the Jumbotron.

"Oh my God," Hanna heard behind her. She turned around. Naomi and Riley stood by the bar. They wore matching emerald sheaths and carried tiny satin clutches. Riley smirked behind her hand, giving Hanna the once-over. Naomi let out a loud guffaw. Hanna would have nervously pulled in her stomach if the dress hadn't already unnaturally been doing it for her.

"Nice *dress*, Hanna," Riley said smoothly. With her blazing red hair and shiny bright green dress, she looked like an inverted carrot.

"Yeah, it looks really good on you," Naomi simpered.

Hanna stood up straighter and strode away. She skirted around a black-suited waitress carrying a tray of mini crab cakes and tried not to look at them, worried she really might gain a pound. Then she watched as the image on the Jumbotron changed. Nicole Hudson and Kelly Hamilton, Riley and Naomi's bitchy underlings, appeared on the screen. They also wore slinky green sheaths and carried the same delicate satin bags. "Happy birthday, Mona, from your party court posse!" they cried, blowing kisses.

Hanna frowned. *Party court?* No. The court dress wasn't green—it was champagne. Right?

Suddenly, a crowd of dancing kids parted. A beautiful blond girl strode right up to Hanna. It was *Mona*. She wore the exact same champagne-colored gown as Hanna—the one they'd both been fitted for at Saks. Except hers didn't pull across the stomach or the ass. The zipper didn't look puckered and strained, and there were no bulges. Instead, it accentuated Mona's thin waist and showed off her long, lithe legs.

Mona's eyes boggled. "What are *you* doing here?" She looked Hanna up and down, her mouth wobbling into a smile. "And where the *hell* did you get that dress?"

"You sent it to me," Hanna answered.

Mona stared at her in disbelief. She pointed at Riley. "*That's* the court dress. I changed it. I wanted to be the only one wearing champagne—not all of us." She looked Hanna up and down. "And certainly not any whales."

Everyone tittered, even the waitresses and the bartender. Hanna stepped back, confused. The room was quieter for a moment—the DJ was between songs. Mona wrinkled her nose and Hanna suddenly felt like a drawstring had pulled her throat closed. It all made horrible, sickening sense.

Of course Mona hadn't sent the dress. *A had.*

"Please leave." Mona crossed her arms over her chest and stared pointedly at Hanna's various bulges. "I disinvited you, remember?"

Hanna walked toward Mona, wanting to explain, but she stepped down unsteadily on her gold Jimmy Choo heel. She felt her ankle twist, her legs go out from under her, and her knees hit the ground. Worse, Hanna heard a loud, undeniable *riiiiiiip.* Suddenly, her butt felt a lot less constricted. As she twisted around to assess the damage, her side seam gave way, too. The whole side of the dress burst open from Hanna's ribs to her hip, exposing the thin, lacy straps of her Eberjey bra and thong.

"Oh my God!" Riley cried. Everyone howled with laughter. Hanna tried to cover herself up, but she didn't know where to start. Mona just stood there and let it happen, beautiful and queenlike in her perfect-fitting gown. It was hard for Hanna to imagine that only days ago, they'd loved each other as only best friends could.

Mona placed her hands on her hips and looked over at the others. "Come on, girls," she sniffed. "This train wreck isn't worth our time."

Hanna's eyes filled with tears. Kids started to trample away, and someone tripped over Hanna, spilling warm beer on her legs. *This train wreck isn't worth our time.* Hanna heard the words echo in her head. Then she thought of something.

Remember when you saw Mona leaving the Bill Beach plastic surgery clinic? Hello, lipo!!

Hanna propped herself up against the cool marble floor. "Hey, Mona."

Mona turned and stared at her.

Hanna took a deep breath. "You look a lot skinnier since I saw you leaving Bill Beach. For *lipo*."

Mona cocked her head. But she didn't look horrified or embarrassed—just confused. She let out a snort and rolled her eyes. "Whatever, Hanna. You're so pathetic."

Mona tossed her hair over her shoulder and wove toward the stage. A wall of kids quickly separated them. Hanna sat up, covering the tear on her side with one hand and the tear on her ass with the other. And then, she saw it: her face, magnified a billion times on the Jumbotron screen. There was a long, panning shot of her dress. The fat under her arms bulged. The lines of her thong showed through the tight fabric. The Hanna on the screen took a step toward Mona and toppled over. The camera captured her dress splitting apart.

Hanna screamed and covered her eyes. Everyone's laughter felt like needles tattooing her skin. Then she felt a hand on her back. "Hanna."

Hanna peeped through her hands. *"Lucas?"*

He was wearing dark trousers, an Atlantic Records

T-shirt, and a pinstriped jacket. His longish blond hair looked thick and wild. The look on his face said he'd seen everything.

He took off his jacket and handed it to her. "Here. Put this on. Let's get you out of here."

Mona was climbing onstage. The crowd quivered with anticipation. On any normal party night, Hanna would have been front and center, ready to grind to the music. But instead, she grabbed Lucas's arm.

30

CHANGE IS GOOD . . .
EXCEPT WHEN IT'S NOT

On Saturday evening, Emily laced up her rental ice skates until she could barely feel the circulation in her feet. "I can't believe we have to wear three pairs of socks," she complained to Becka, who was next to her on the bench, lacing up the pair of white skates she'd brought from home.

"I know," Becka agreed, adjusting her lace headband. "But it keeps your feet from getting cold."

Emily tied her skate laces in a bow. It had to be about fifty degrees in the rink, but she was only in a Rosewood Swimming short-sleeve T-shirt. She felt so numb, cold didn't affect her. On the way here, Emily told Becka that her first Tree Tops session was Monday. Becka seemed startled, then happy. Emily didn't say much else the rest of the ride over. All she was thinking about was how she'd rather be with Maya.

Maya. Whenever Emily shut her eyes, she saw Maya's angry face in the greenhouse. Emily's cell phone had been quiet all day. Part of her wanted Maya to call, to try to get Emily back. And then of course, part of her didn't. She tried to look at the positives—now that her parents saw that she was really making a commitment to Tree Tops, they had been kinder to her. At Saturday swim practice, Coach Lauren had told her that the U of A swim coach still wanted to meet with her. All the swim team boys were still hitting on her and inviting Emily to hot-tub parties, but it was better than them making fun of her. And as they were driving home from practice, Carolyn had said, "I like this song," when an old Gwen Stefani song came on Emily's playlist. It was a start.

Emily stared at the ice rink. After The Jenna Thing, she and Ali used to come here practically every weekend, and nothing about the place had changed since then. There were still the same blue benches that everyone sat on to lace up their boots, the machine that dispensed hot chocolate that tasted like aspirin, the giant plastic polar bear that greeted everyone at the main entrance. The whole thing was so eerily nostalgic, Emily almost expected to see Ali out on the ice practicing her backward crossovers. The rink was practically empty tonight, though—there were clusters of kids, but no one Emily's age. Most likely, they were all at Mona's party—in a parallel world, Emily would have been there too.

"Becka?"

Emily and Becka looked up. A tall girl with short dark curly hair, a button nose, and hazel eyes stared at them. She had on a pink A-line dress, white cable-knit tights, a delicate pearl bracelet, and hot pink lip gloss. A pair of white ice skates with rainbow laces dangled from her wrists.

"Wendy!" Becka cried, standing up. She went to hug Wendy but then seemed to correct herself and stood back. "You're . . . you're here!"

Wendy had a big smile on her face. "Wow, Becks. You look . . . great."

Becka smiled sheepishly. "So do you." She inspected Wendy almost in disbelief, as if Wendy had been resurrected from the dead. "You cut your hair."

Wendy touched it self-consciously. "Is it too short?"

"No!" Becka said quickly. "It's really cute."

Both of them kept smiling and giggling. Emily coughed, and Becka looked over. "Oh! This is Emily. My new Tree Tops friend."

Emily shook Wendy's hand. Wendy's short fingernails were painted seashell pink, and there was a Pokémon appliqué on her thumb.

Wendy sat down and started lacing up her skates. "Do you guys skate a lot?" Emily asked. "You both have your own skates."

"We used to," Wendy said, glancing at Becka. "We took lessons together. Well . . . sort of."

Becka giggled and Emily glanced at her, confused. "What?"

"Nothing," Becka answered. "Just . . . remember the skate rental room, Wendy?"

"Oh my God." Wendy clapped a hand over her mouth. "The look on that guy's face!"

Oh-*kaaay*. Emily coughed again, and Becka immediately stopped laughing, as if she realized where she was—or, perhaps, *who* she was.

When Wendy finished lacing up, they all stepped onto the rink. Wendy and Becka immediately twirled around and began skating backward. Emily, who only knew how to skate forward in a somewhat jerky fashion, felt bumbling and oafish next to them.

No one said anything for a while. Emily listened to the slicing noises their skates made in the ice. "So, are you still seeing Jeremy?" Wendy asked Becka.

Becka chewed on the end of her wool mitten. "Not really."

"Who's Jeremy?" Emily asked, skirting around a blond girl in a Brownie uniform.

"A guy I met at Tree Tops," Becka answered. She glanced at Wendy uncomfortably. "We went out for a month or two. It didn't really work out."

Wendy shrugged and pushed a lock of hair behind her ear. "Yeah, I was going out with a girl from history class, but it didn't go anywhere either. And I have a blind date next week, but I'm not sure if I'll go."

Emily suddenly realized that Wendy had said *she*. Before she could ask, Becka cleared her throat. Her jaw was tense. "I might go on a blind date, too," she said, louder than usual. "With another boy from Tree Tops."

"Well, good luck with that," Wendy said stiffly, spinning to skate forward again. Only, she didn't take her eyes off Becka, and Becka didn't take her eyes off Wendy. Becka skated up next to Wendy, and it seemed like she purposefully bumped hands.

The lights dimmed. A disco ball descended from the ceiling and colored lights swirled around the rink. Everyone except for a few couples tottered off the ice. "Couples skate," said an Isaac Hayes imposter over the loudspeaker. "Grab the one you love."

The three of them collapsed on a nearby bench as "Unchained Melody" belted out of the speakers. Ali had once remarked that she was tired of sitting out of couples skate. "Why don't we just skate together, Em?" she suggested, offering Emily her hand. Emily would never forget what it felt like to wrap her arms around Ali. To smell the sweet, Granny Smith apple scent of Ali's neck. To squeeze Ali's hands when Ali lost her balance, to accidentally brush her arm against Ali's bare skin.

Emily wondered if she'd remember that event differently next week. Would Tree Tops wipe those feelings from her mind, the way the Zamboni machine smoothed away all the nicks and skate-marks from the ice?

"I'll be back," Emily murmured, stumbling clumsily on the blades of her skates to the bathroom. Inside, she ran her hands under scalding hot water and stared at herself in the streaky mirror. *Doing Tree Tops was the right decision*, she told her reflection. It was the *only* decision. After Tree Tops, she would probably date boys just like Becka did. Right?

When she walked back to the rink, she noticed that Becka and Wendy had left the bench. Emily plopped down, figuring they'd gone to get a snack, and stared at the darkened rink. She saw couples with their hands intertwined. Others were attempting to kiss while skating. One couple hadn't even made it to the ice—they were going at it by one of the entrances. The girl plunged her hands into the guy's curly dark hair.

The slow song abruptly ended and the fluorescent lights snapped back on. Emily's eyes widened at the couple by the door. The girl wore a familiar lace headband. Both were wearing white ice skates. The guy's had rainbow laces. And . . . he was in a pink A-line dress.

Becka and Wendy saw Emily at the same time. Becka's mouth went round, and Wendy looked away. Emily could feel herself shaking.

Becka walked over and stood next to Emily. She exhaled a puff of frosty air. "I guess I should explain, huh?"

The ice smelled cold, like snow. Someone had left a single, child-size red mitten on the next bench over. On the rink, a child swooped by and cried, "I'm an airplane!" Emily stared at Becka. Her chest felt tight.

"I thought Tree Tops worked," Emily said quietly.

Becka ran her hands through her long hair. "I thought it did, too. But after seeing Wendy . . . well, I guess you got the picture." She pulled her Fair Isle sweater's cuffs down over her hands. "Maybe you can't really change."

A hot feeling spread in Emily's stomach. Thinking that Tree Tops could change something so fundamental about her had scared her. It seemed so against the principles of . . . of being human, maybe. But it couldn't. Maya and Becka were right—you *couldn't* change who you were.

Maya. Emily clapped her hand over her mouth. She needed to talk to Maya, right now. "Um, Becka," she said quietly. "Can I ask you a favor?"

Becka's eyes softened. "Sure."

Emily skated for the exit. "I need you to drive me to a party. Right now. There's someone I have to see."

31

THEY FOUGHT THE LAW
AND THE LAW WON

Aria aimed her phone's camera lens at Spencer as she adjusted the rhinestone crown perched atop her head. "Hey, guys," Spencer whispered, sauntering over to a phone that was lying facedown on the Hastingses' leather couch. "Want to read her texts?"

"I do," Hanna whispered.

Emily stood up from her perch on the leather couch's arm. "I don't know. . . ."

"C'mon. Don't you want to know who texted her?" Spencer demanded. Spencer, Hanna, and Emily gathered around Ali's cell phone. Aria moved closer, too. She wanted to get all of this on film. All of Ali's secrets. She zoomed in to get a good shot of the cell phone's screen when suddenly she heard a voice from the hall.

"Were you looking at my phone?" Ali shrieked, marching into the room.

"Of course not!" Hanna cried. Ali eyed her cell on the couch, but then turned her attention to Melissa and Ian, who had just come into the kitchen.

"Hey, girls," Ian said, stepping into the family room. He glanced at Spencer. "Cute crown."

Spencer, Ian, and Ali gathered on the couch, and Spencer began playing talk-show host. Suddenly, a second Ali walked right up to the camera. Her skin looked gray. Her irises were black and her neon red lipstick was applied clownishly, in wriggly lines around her mouth.

"Aria," Ali's doppelganger commanded, staring straight into the camera. "*Look.* The answer is right in front of you."

Aria furrowed her brow. The rest of the scene was rolling forward as usual—Spencer was asking Ian about base-jumping. Melissa was growing more pissed off as she put away their takeout bags. The other Ali—the normal-looking one on the couch—seemed bored. "What do you mean?" Aria whispered to the Ali closer to her.

"It's right in front of you," Ali urged. "Look!"

"Okay, okay," Aria said hastily. She searched the room again. Spencer was leaning into Ian, hanging on his every word. Hanna and Emily were perched against the credenza, seeming relaxed and chill. What was Aria supposed to be looking for?

"I don't understand," she whimpered.

"But it's there!" Ali screamed. "It's. Right. There!"

"I don't know what to do!" Aria argued helplessly.

"Just *look!*"

Aria sprang up in bed. The room was dark. Sweat poured down her face. Her throat hurt. When she looked over, she saw Ezra lying on his side next to her, and jumped.

"It's okay," Ezra said quickly, wrapping his arms around her. "It was just a dream. You're safe."

Aria blinked and looked around. She wasn't in the Hastingses' living room but under the covers of Ezra's futon. The bedroom, which was right off the living room, smelled like mothballs and old-lady perfume, the way all Old Hollis houses smelled. A light, peaceful breeze rippled the blinds, and a William Shakespeare bobble-head nodded on the bureau. Ezra's arms were around her shoulders. His bare feet rubbed her ankles.

"Bad dream?" Ezra asked. "You were screaming."

Aria paused. Was her dream trying to tell her something? "I'm cool," she decided. "It was just one of those weird nightmares."

"You scared me," Ezra said, squeezing her tight.

Aria waited until her breathing returned to normal, listening to the wooden, fish-shaped wind chimes knocking together right outside Ezra's window. Then she noticed that Ezra's glasses were askew. "Did you fall asleep in your glasses?"

Ezra put his hand to the bridge of his nose. "I guess," he said sheepishly. "I fall asleep in them a lot."

Aria leaned forward and kissed him. "You're such a weirdo."

"Not as weird as you, screamer," Ezra teased, pulling her on top of him. "I'm going to get you." He started to tickle her waist.

"No!" Aria shrieked, trying to wriggle away from him. "Stop!"

"Uh-uh!" Ezra bellowed. But his tickling hastily turned into caressing and kissing. Aria shut her eyes and let his hands flutter over her. Then, Ezra flopped back on the pillow. "I wish we could just go away and live somewhere else."

"I know Iceland really well," Aria suggested. "Or what about Costa Rica? We could have a monkey. Or maybe Capri. We could hang out in the Blue Grotto."

"I always wanted to go to Capri," Ezra said softly. "We could live on the beach and write poems."

"As long as our pet monkeys can write poems with us," Aria bargained.

"Of course," Ezra said, kissing her nose. "We can have as many monkeys as you want." He got a far-off look on his face, as if he were actually considering it. Aria felt her insides swell. She'd never felt so happy. This felt . . . right. They would make it work. She would figure out the rest of her life—Sean, A, her parents—tomorrow.

Aria snuggled into Ezra. She started dozing off again, thinking about dancing monkeys and sandy beaches when suddenly, there was pounding at the front door. Before Aria and Ezra could react, the door split open and two policemen burst inside. Aria screamed. Ezra sat up and straightened his boxers, which had pictures of fried eggs, sausages, and pancakes all over them. The words *Tasty Breakfast!* were scrolled around the waistband. Aria hid under the covers—she was wearing an oversize Hollis University T-shirt of Ezra's that barely covered her thighs.

The cops stomped through Ezra's living room and into his bedroom. They shined their flashlights first over Ezra, then on Aria. She wrapped the sheets around her tighter, scanning the floor for her clothes and undies. They were gone.

"Are you Ezra Fitz?" demanded the cop, a burly, Popeye-armed man with slick black hair.

"Uh . . . yeah," Ezra stammered.

"And you teach at Rosewood Day School?" Popeye asked. "Is this the girl? Your *student*?"

"What the hell is going on?" Ezra shrieked.

"You're under arrest." Popeye unhooked silver handcuffs from his belt. The other cop, who was shorter and fatter and had shiny skin that Aria could only describe as ham-colored, yanked Ezra out of bed. The threadbare, grayish sheets went with him, exposing Aria's bare legs. She screamed and dropped to the other side of the bed to hide. She found a pair of plaid pajama pants balled up behind the radiator. She stuffed her legs into them as fast as she could.

"You have the right to remain silent," Ham-face began. "Anything you say can and will be used against you in a court of law."

"Wait!" Ezra screamed.

But the cops didn't listen. Ham-face spun Ezra around and snapped the cuffs on his wrists. He glanced disgustedly at Ezra's futon. Ezra's jeans and T-shirt were snarled up near the headboard. Aria suddenly noticed that the lacy black bra she'd had custom-fitted in Belgium was snagged on one of the bedposts. She quickly ripped it down.

They shoved Ezra through the living room and out his own door, which hung precariously on one hinge. Aria ran after them, not even bothering to put on her checkerboard Vans, which waited in the second ballet position on the floor near the television. "You can't do this!" she shouted.

"We'll deal with you next, little girl," Popeye growled.

She hesitated in the dingy, dimly lit front hall. The cops restrained Ezra. Ham-face kept stepping on his knobby bare feet. It made Aria love him even more.

As they bumbled out the door and onto the front porch, Aria realized someone else was in the hall with her. Her mouth fell open.

"Sean," Aria sputtered. "What . . . what are you doing here?"

Sean was crumpled up against the gray mailbox unit, staring at Aria with dread and disappointment. "What are you doing here?" he demanded, staring pointedly at Ezra's oversize pajama pants, which were threatening to fall down to her ankles. She quickly yanked them back up.

"I was going to explain," Aria mumbled.

"Oh yeah?" Sean challenged, putting his hands on his hips. He looked sharper tonight, meaner. Not the soft Sean she knew. "How long have you been with him?"

Aria silently stared at an Acme market coupon circular that had fallen on the floor.

"I've packed up all your stuff," Sean went on, not even waiting for her answer. "It's on the porch. There's no way you're coming back to my house."

"But . . . Sean . . ." Aria said weakly. "Where will I go?"

"That's not my problem," he snapped, storming out the front door.

Aria felt woozy. Through the open door, she could see the cops guiding Ezra down his front walk and pushing him into a Rosewood Police cruiser. After they slammed the back door, Ezra glanced toward his house again. He looked at Aria, then Sean, then back again. There was a betrayed look on his face.

A light switched on in Aria's head. She followed Sean to the porch and grabbed his arm. "*You* called the police, didn't you?"

Sean crossed his arms over his chest and looked away.

She felt dizzy and sick, and clutched the porch's rusty blue-gray glider for balance.

"Well, once I got this . . ." Sean whipped out his cell phone and brought it close to Aria's face. On the screen was a picture of Aria and Ezra kissing in Ezra's office. Sean hit the side arrow. There was another photo of them kissing, just from a different angle. "I figured I should let the authorities know a teacher was with a student." His lips curled around the word *student,* as if it was disgusting to him. "And on school property," he added.

"I didn't mean to hurt you," Aria whispered. And then, she noticed the text message that accompanied the last photo. Her heart sank a few thousand feet deeper.

Dear Sean, I think someone's girlfriend has a LOT of explaining to do. —A

32

NOT-SO-SECRET LOVERS

"And they were all over each other!" Emily took a huge sip of the sangria Maya had gotten for them from the planetarium bar. "All this time, I was afraid they could, like, change you, but it turns out that it's fake! My sponsor's back with her girlfriend and everything!"

Maya gave Emily a dubious look, poking her in the ribs. "You seriously thought they could change you?"

Emily leaned back. "I guess that *is* stupid, isn't it?"

"*Yes.*" Maya smiled. "But I'm glad it doesn't work too."

About an hour ago, Becka and Wendy had dropped Emily off at Mona's party and she had torn through the rooms, searching for Maya, terrified that she had left—or worse, that she was with someone else. She'd found Maya by herself near the DJ booth, wearing a black-and-white striped dress and patent-leather Mary Janes. Her hair was up in white butterfly clips.

They had escaped outside to a little patch of grass

in the planetarium's garden. They could see the party still raging through the two-story, frosted-glass windows, but they couldn't hear it. Shady trees, telescopes, and bushes pruned into the shapes of planets filled the garden. A few of the partygoers had spilled out and were sitting on the other side of the patio, smoking and laughing, and there was a couple making out by the giant, Saturn-shaped topiary, but Emily and Maya were pretty much sequestered. They hadn't kissed or anything, but were merely staring up at the sky. It had to be almost midnight, which was normally Emily's curfew, but she'd called her mom to say that she would be staying the night at Becka's. Becka had agreed to corroborate the story, if need be.

"Look," Emily said, pointing at the stars. "That section of stars up there, don't they look like they could form an *E* if you drew lines between them?"

"Where?" Maya squinted.

Emily positioned Maya's chin correctly. "There are stars next to them that form an *M*." She smiled in the darkness. "*E* and *M*. Emily and Maya. It's, like, a sign."

"You and your signs," Maya sighed. They were comfortably quiet for a second.

"I was furious at you," Maya said softly. "Breaking up with me in the kiln like that. Refusing to even look at me in the greenhouse."

Emily squeezed her hand and stared at the constellations. A tiny jet streaked past, a thousand feet up. "I'm sorry," she said. "I know I haven't exactly been fair."

Now Maya eyed Emily carefully. Glittery bronzer illuminated her forehead, cheeks, and nose. She looked more beautiful than Emily had ever seen her. "Can I hold your hand?" she whispered.

Emily gazed at her own rough, square hand. It had held pencils and paintbrushes and pieces of chalk. Gripped the starting blocks before a swimming race. Clutched a balloon on the swim team's homecoming float last year. It had held her boyfriend Ben's hand . . . and it had even held Maya's, but it seemed like this time it was more official. It was real.

She knew there were people around. But Maya was right—everyone already knew. The hard part was over, and she'd survived. She'd been miserable with Ben, and she hadn't been kidding anybody with Toby. Maybe she should be out there with this. As soon as Becka had said it, Emily knew she was right: She *couldn't* change who she was. The idea was terrifying but thrilling.

Emily touched Maya's hand. First lightly, then harder. "I love you, Em," Maya said, squeezing back. "I love you so much."

"I love you, too," Emily repeated, almost automatically. And she realized—she did. More than anyone else, more than Ali, even. Emily had kissed Ali, and for a split second, Ali had kissed her back. But then Ali had pulled back, disgusted. She'd quickly started talking about some boy she was really into, a boy whose name she wouldn't tell Emily because Emily might "really freak." Now Emily wondered if there even *had* been a boy, or if Ali had said it to undo the tiny moment when she had kissed Emily for real. To say, *I'm not like you. No frickin' way.*

All this time, Emily had fantasized about what things would have been like if Ali hadn't disappeared, and if that summer and their friendship had proceeded as planned. Now she knew: It wouldn't have gone on. If Ali hadn't disappeared, she would have drifted farther and farther away from Emily. But maybe Emily would still have found her way to Maya.

"You okay?" Maya asked, noting Emily's silence.

"Yeah." They sat quietly for a few minutes, holding hands. Then Maya lifted her head, frowning at something inside the planetarium. Emily followed her eyes to a shadowy figure, staring straight at them. The figure knocked on the glass, making Emily jump.

"Who is that?" Emily murmured.

"Whoever it is," Maya said, squinting, "they're coming outside."

Every hair on Emily's body stood up. *A?* She scooted backward. Then she heard an all-too-familiar voice. "Emily Catherine Fields! Get over here!"

Maya's mouth dropped open. "Oh my God."

Emily's mother stepped under the courtyard spotlights. Her hair was uncombed, she wore no makeup, she had on a ratty T-shirt, and her sneaker lace was untied. She looked ridiculous among the throng of done-up partygoers. A few kids gaped at her.

Emily clumsily struggled off the grass. "W-What are you doing here?"

Mrs. Fields grabbed Emily's arm. "I *cannot* believe you. I get a call fifteen minutes ago saying you're with *her*. And I don't believe them! Silly me! I don't believe them! I say they're lying!"

"Mom, I can explain!"

Mrs. Fields paused and sniffed the air around Emily's face. Her eyes widened. "You've been drinking!" she screamed, enraged. "What has *happened* to you, Emily?" She glanced down at Maya, who was sitting very still on the grass, as if Mrs. Fields had put her in suspended animation. "You're *not* my daughter anymore."

"Mom!" Emily screamed. It felt like her mother had thrust a curling iron into her eye. That statement sounded so . . . legal and binding. So final.

Mrs. Fields dragged her to the little gate that led from the courtyard to a back alley that led to the street. "I'm calling Helene when we get home."

"No!" Emily broke free, then faced her mother halfway hunched over, the way a sumo wrestler squares off when he's about to fight. "How can you say I'm not your daughter?" she screeched. "How can you send me away?"

Mrs. Fields reached for Emily's arm again, but Emily's sneakers caught on an uneven divot in the grass. She fell backward, hitting the ground on her tailbone, experiencing a white, blinding flash of pain.

When she opened her eyes, her mother was above her. "Get up. Let's go."

"No!" Emily bellowed. She tried to get up, but her mother's nails pierced her arm. Emily struggled but knew it was hopeless. She glanced once more at Maya, who still hadn't moved. Maya's eyes were huge and watery, and she looked tiny and alone. *I might never see her again*, Emily thought. *This might be it.*

"What's so wrong with it?" she screamed at her mother. "What's so wrong with being different? How can you *hate* me for that?"

Her mother's nostrils flared. She balled up her fists and opened her mouth, ready to scream something back. And then, suddenly, she seemed to deflate. She turned away and made a small noise at the back of her throat. All at once, she looked so spent. And scared. And ashamed. Without any makeup on and in her pajamas, she seemed vulnerable. There was a redness around her eyes, as if she had been crying for a long time. "Please. Let's just go."

Emily didn't know what else to do but get up. She followed her mother down the dark, deserted alley and into a parking lot, where Emily saw their familiar Volvo. The parking lot attendant met her mother's eyes and gave Emily a judging sneer, as if Mrs. Fields had explained why she was parking here and retrieving Emily from the party.

Emily threw herself in the front seat. Her eyes landed

on the Dial-a-Horoscope laminated wheel that was in the car's seat pocket. The wheel foretold every sign's horoscopes for all the twelve months of this year, so Emily pulled it out, spun the wheel to Taurus, her sign, and looked at October's predictions. *Your love relationships will become more fulfilling and satisfying. Your relationships may have caused difficulties with others in the past, but all will be smooth sailing from now on.*

Ha, Emily thought. She hurled the horoscope card out the window. She didn't believe in horoscopes anymore. Or tarot cards. Or signs or signals or anything else that said things happened for a reason. What was the reason *this* was happening?

A chill went through her. *I get a call fifteen minutes ago saying you're with her.*

She dug through her bag, her heart pounding. Her phone had one new message. It had been in her inbox for nearly two hours.

Em, I see you! And if you don't stop it, I'm calling you-know-who. —A

Emily put her hands over her eyes. Why didn't A just kill her instead?

33

SOMEONE SLIPS UP. BIG TIME.

First, Lucas gave Hanna a shrunken Rosewood Day sweatshirt and a pair of red gym shorts from his car. "An Eagle Scout is always prepared for anything," he proclaimed.

Second, he led Hanna to the Hollis College Reading Room so she could change. It was a few streets over from the planetarium. The reading room was simply that—a big room in a nineteenth-century house completely devoted to chilling out and reading. It smelled like pipe smoke and old leather bookbindings and was filled with all sorts of books, maps, globes, encyclopedias, magazines, newspapers, chessboards, leather couches, and cozy love seats for two. Technically, it was only open to college students and faculty, but it was easy enough to jimmy your way in the side door.

Hanna went into the tiny bathroom, removed her ripped dress, and threw it into the little chrome trash can, stuffing it in so it would fit. She slumped out of the bathroom, threw herself on the couch next to Lucas, and just . . . lost it. Sobs that had been pent up inside of her for weeks—maybe even years—exploded out of her. "No one will like me anymore," she said chokingly, between sobs. "And I've lost Mona forever."

Lucas rubbed her hair. "It's all right. She doesn't deserve you anyway."

Hanna cried until her eyes swelled and her throat stung. Finally, she pressed her head into Lucas's chest, which was more solid than it looked. They lay there in silence for a while. Lucas ran his fingers through her hair.

"What made you come to her party?" she asked after a while. "I thought you weren't invited."

"I was invited." Lucas lowered his eyes. "But . . . I wasn't going to go. I didn't want you to feel bad, and I wanted to spend the night with you."

Little sparkles of giddiness snapped through her stomach. "I'm so sorry," she said quietly. "Bagging our poker game at the last minute like that, for Mona's stupid party."

"It's okay," Lucas said. "It doesn't matter."

Hanna stared at Lucas. He had such soft blue eyes and adorably pink cheeks. It *did* matter to her, a lot. She was so consumed with doing the perfect thing all the time—wearing the perfect outfit, picking out the perfect ringtone, keeping her body in perfect shape, having the perfect best friend and the perfect boyfriend—but what was all that perfection for? Maybe Lucas was perfect, just in a different way. He *cared* about her.

Hanna didn't quite know how it had happened, but they'd settled in on one of the cracked-leather love seats, and she was on Lucas's lap. Strangely, she didn't feel self-conscious that she was breaking Lucas's legs. Last summer, to prepare for her trip with Sean's family to Cape Cod, Hanna had eaten nothing but grapefruit and cayenne pepper, and she hadn't let Sean touch her when she was wearing her bathing suit, afraid he'd find her Jell-O-ish. With Lucas, she didn't worry.

Her face moved closer to Lucas's. His face moved closer to hers. She felt his lips touch her chin, then the side of her mouth, then her mouth itself. Her heart pounded. His lips whispered across hers. He pulled her toward him. Hanna's heart was beating so fast and excitedly, she was afraid it would burst. Lucas cradled Hanna's head in his hands and kissed her ears. Hanna giggled.

"What?" Lucas said, pulling away.

"Nothing," Hanna answered, grinning. "I don't know. This is fun."

It *was* fun—nothing like the serious, important make-out sessions she'd had with Sean, where she felt like a panel of judges was scoring each and every kiss. Lucas was sloppy, wet, and overly joyful, like a boy Labrador. Every so often, he'd grab her and squeeze. At one point, he started tickling her, making Hanna squeal and roll off the couch right onto the floor.

Eventually, they were lying on one of the couches,

Lucas on top of her, his hands drifting up and down her bare stomach. He took off his shirt and pressed his chest against hers. After a while, they stopped and lay there, saying nothing. Hanna's eyes grazed across all the books, chess sets, and busts of famous authors. Then, suddenly, she sat up.

Someone was looking in the window.

"Lucas!" She pointed to a dark shape moving toward the side door.

"Don't panic," Lucas said, easing off the couch and creeping toward the window. The bushes shook. A lock began to turn. Hanna clamped down on Lucas's arm.

A was here.

"Lucas . . ."

"Shhh." Another click. Somewhere, a lock was turning. Someone was coming in. Lucas cocked his head to listen. Now there were footsteps coming from the back hall. Hanna took a step backward. The floor creaked. The footsteps came closer.

"Hello?" Lucas grabbed his shirt and pulled it on backward. "Who's there?"

No one answered. There were more creaks. A shadow slithered across the wall.

Hanna looked around and grabbed the largest thing she could find—a *Farmer's Almanac* from 1972. Suddenly, a light flicked on. Hanna screamed and raised the almanac over her head. Standing before them was an older man with a beard. He wore small, wire-framed glasses and a corduroy jacket and held his hands over his head in surrender.

"I'm with the history department!" the old man sputtered. "I couldn't sleep. I came here to read. . . ." He looked at Hanna strangely. Hanna realized the neck of Lucas's sweatshirt was pulled to the side, exposing her bare shoulder.

Hanna's heart started to slow down. She put the book back on the table. "Sorry," she said. "I thought—"

"We'd better go anyway." Lucas sidestepped the old man and pulled Hanna out the side door. When they were next to the house's iron front gate, he burst into giggles.

"Did you see that guy's face?" he hooted. "He was terrified!"

Hanna tried to laugh along, but she felt too shaken. "We should go," she whispered, her voice trembling. "I want to go home."

Lucas walked Hanna to the valet at Mona's party. She gave the valet the ticket for her Prius, and when he brought it back, she made Lucas look all through it to make sure no one was hiding in the backseat. When she was safely inside with the door locked, Lucas tapped his hand against the window and mouthed that he'd call her tomorrow. Hanna watched him walk away, feeling both excited and horribly distracted.

She started down the planetarium's spiral drive. Every twenty feet or so was a banner advertising the new exhibit. THE BIG BANG, they all said. They showed a picture of the universe exploding.

When Hanna's cell phone beeped, she jumped so

violently, she nearly broke out of the seat belt. She pulled over into the bus lane and whipped her phone out of her bag with trembling fingers. She had a new text.

Oops, guess it wasn't lipo! Don't believe everything you hear! —A

Hanna looked up. The street outside the planetarium was quiet. All the old houses were closed up tight, and there wasn't a single person on the street. A breeze kicked up, making the flag on the porch of an old Victorian house flap and a jack-o'-lantern-shaped leaf bag on its front lawn flutter.

Hanna looked back down at the text. This was odd. A's latest text wasn't from *caller unknown*, as it usually was, but an actual number. And it was a 610 number—Rosewood's area code.

The number seemed familiar, although Hanna never memorized anyone's number—she'd gotten a cell in seventh grade and had since relied on speed dial. There was something about this number, though. . . .

Hanna covered her mouth with her hand. "Oh my God," she whispered. She thought about it another moment. Could it *seriously* be?

Suddenly, she knew exactly who A was.

34

IT'S RIGHT THERE IN FRONT OF YOU

"Another coffee?" A waitress who smelled like grilled cheese and had a very large mole on her chin hovered over Aria, waving a coffee carafe around.

Aria glanced at her nearly empty mug. Her parents would probably say this coffee was loaded with carcinogens, but what did they know? "Sure," she answered.

This was what it had come to. Aria sitting in a booth at the diner near Ezra's house in Old Hollis with all of her worldly goods—her laptop, her bike, her clothes, her books—around her. She had nowhere to go. Not Sean's, not Ezra's, not even her own family's. The diner was the only place open right now, unless you counted the twenty-four-hour Taco Bell, which was a total stoner hangout.

She stared at her phone, weighing her options. Finally, she dialed her home number. The phone rang six times and then voice mail picked up. "Thanks for calling the Montgomerys," Ella's cheery voice rang out. "We're not home right now. . . ."

Please. Where on earth would Ella be after midnight on a Saturday? "Mom, I know you're there," Aria said. She sighed. "Listen. I need to come home tonight. I broke up with my boyfriend. I have nowhere else to stay. I'm sitting at a diner, homeless."

She paused, waiting for Ella to call back. She didn't. Maybe she'd seen Aria's name on the caller ID and hit ignore. So this time, she texted. I'm in danger, she wrote. I can't explain how, exactly, but I'm . . . I'm afraid something's going to happen to me.

She hit send. Nothing. Aria let her phone clatter to the Formica tabletop. She could call back, but what would be the point? She could almost hear her mother's voice: *I can't even look at you right now.*

She lifted her head, considering something. Slowly, Aria picked up her phone again and scrolled through her texts. Byron's text with his number was still there. Taking a deep breath, she dialed. Byron's sleepy voice answered.

"It's Aria," she said quietly.

"Aria?" Byron echoed. He sounded stunned. "It's, like, two in the morning."

"I know." The diner's jukebox switched records. The waitress married two ketchup bottles. The last remaining people besides Aria got up from their booth, waved goodbye to the waitress, and pushed through the front door. The diner's bells jingled.

Byron broke the silence. "Well, it's nice to hear from you."

Aria curled her knees into her chest. She wanted to tell him that he'd messed up everything, making her keep his secret, but she felt too drained to fight. And also . . . part of her really missed Byron. Byron was her dad, the only dad she knew. He had warded off a snake that had slithered into Aria's path during a hiking trip to the Grand Canyon. He'd gone down to talk to Aria's fifth-grade art teacher, Mr. Cunningham, when he gave Aria an F on her self-portrait because she had drawn herself with green scales and a forked tongue. "Your teacher simply doesn't understand postmodern expressionism," Byron had said, grabbing his coat to go do battle. Byron used to pick her up, throw her over his shoulder, carry her to bed, and tuck her in. Aria missed that. She *needed* that. She wanted to tell him she was in danger. And she wanted him to say, "I'll protect you." He would, wouldn't he?

But then she heard someone's voice in the background. "Everything okay, Byron?"

Aria bristled. *Meredith.*

"Be there in a sec," Byron called.

Aria fumed. A *sec*? That was all he planned to devote to this conversation? Byron's voice returned to the phone. "Aria? So . . . what's up?"

"Never mind," Aria said icily. "Go back to bed, or whatever you were doing."

"Aria–" Byron started.

"Seriously, go," Aria said stiffly. "Forget I called."

She hit end and put her head on the table. She tried to breathe in and out, thinking calm thoughts, like about the ocean, or riding a bicycle, or the mindlessness of knitting a scarf.

A few minutes later, she looked around the diner and realized she was the only person there. The ripped, faded counter stools were all vacant, the booths all cleaned off and empty. Two carafes of coffee sat on warmers behind the counter, and the cash register's screen still glowed WELCOME, but the waitresses and cooks had all vanished. It was like one of those horror movies where somehow, all at once, the main character looks up to find everyone dead.

Ali's killer is closer than you think.

Why didn't A just *tell* her who the killer was? She was sick of playing Scooby-Doo. Aria thought of her dream again, of how that pale, ghostly Ali had stepped in front of the camera. "Look closer!" she'd screamed. "It's right in front of you! It's right there!" But *what* was right there? What had Aria missed?

The waitress with the mole trundled out from behind the counter and eyed Aria. "Want a piece of pie? The apple's edible. On the house."

"Th-That's okay," Aria stuttered.

The waitress leaned an ample hip against one of the counter's pink stools. She had the kind of curly black hair that always looked wet. "You heard about the stalker?"

"Uh-huh," Aria answered.

"You know what I heard?" the waitress said. "It's a *rich* kid." When Aria didn't respond, she went back to washing an already clean table.

Aria blinked a few times. *Look closer,* Ali had said. She reached into her messenger bag and opened her laptop. It took a while to boot up, and then it took even longer for Aria to find the file folder that held her old videos. It had been so long since she'd searched for them. When she finally unearthed it, she realized that none of the video files were labeled very accurately. They were titled things like "Us Five, #1," or "Ali and Me, #6," and the dates were from when they'd last been viewed, not when they were made. She had no idea how to find the video that had been leaked to the press . . . besides going through all of them.

She clicked randomly on a video titled "Meow!" Aria, Ali, and the others were in Ali's bedroom. They were struggling to dress up Ali's Himalayan cat, Charlotte, in a hand-knit sweater, giggling as they stuffed her legs through the armholes.

She watched another movie called "Fight #5," but it wasn't what she thought it would be—she, Ali, and the others were making chocolate-chip cookies and got in a food fight, flinging cookie dough around Hanna's kitchen. In another, they were playing foosball on the table in Spencer's basement.

When Aria clicked on a new video file that was simply

called "DQ," she noticed something.

By the looks of Ali's haircut and all their new warm-weather clothes, the video was from a month or so before Ali had gone missing. Aria had zoomed in on a shot of Hanna downing a monster-size Dairy Queen Blizzard in record time. In the background, she heard Ali start making retching noises. Hanna paused, and her face quickly drained of color. Ali giggled in the background. No one else seemed to notice.

A strange sensation slithered over Aria. She'd heard the rumors that Hanna had a bulimia problem. It seemed like something that A—and Ali—would know.

She clicked on another. They were flipping through the channels at Emily's house. Ali stopped on a news-cast of a Gay Pride parade that had taken place in Philly earlier that day. She turned pointedly to Emily and grinned. "That looks fun, doesn't it, Em?" Emily turned red and pulled her sweatshirt hood around her head. None of the others batted an eye.

And another. This one was only sixteen seconds long. The five of them were lounging around Spencer's pool. They all wore massive Gucci sunglasses—or, in Emily's and Aria's cases, knockoffs. Ali sat up and pushed her glasses down her nose. "Hey, Aria," she said abruptly. "What does your dad do if, like, he gets sexy students in his class?"

The clip ended. Aria remembered that day—it had been shortly after the time she and Ali had discovered Byron and Meredith kissing in Byron's car, and Ali had begun dropping hints that she was going to tell the others.

Ali really *did* know all their secrets, and she'd been dangling them over their heads. It had all been right in front of them, and they hadn't realized it. Ali had known everything. About all of them. And now, A did, too.

Except . . . what was Spencer's secret?

Aria clicked on another video. Finally, she saw the familiar scene. There was Spencer, sitting on her couch with that crown on her head. "Want to read her texts?" She pointed at Ali's phone, which was lying between the couch cushions.

Spencer opened Ali's phone. "It's locked."

"Do you know her password?" Aria heard her own voice ask.

"Try her birthday," Hanna whispered.

"Were you looking at my phone?" Ali screamed.

The phone clattered to the ground. Just then, Spencer's older sister, Melissa, and her boyfriend, Ian, walked up to Aria, who was using her phone as a camera. Both of them smiled into the screen. "Hey, guys," Melissa said. "What's up?"

Spencer batted her eyes. Ali looked bored. Aria zoomed in on her face and panned down to the phone on the couch.

"Oh, this is the clip I've seen on the news," said a voice behind Aria. The waitress was leaning against the counter, filing her nails with a Tweety Bird nail file.

Aria paused the clip and whirled around. "I'm sorry?"

The waitress blushed. "Oops. When it's dead like this, I turn into my evil eavesdropping twin. I didn't mean to look at your computer. That poor boy, though."

Aria squinted at her. She noticed for the first time that the waitress's name tag said ALISON. Spelled the same way and everything. "What poor boy?" she asked.

Alison pointed at the screen. "No one ever talks about the boyfriend. He must have been so heartbroken."

Aria stared at the screen, baffled. She pointed at Ian's frozen image. "That's not her boyfriend. He's with the girl who's in the kitchen. She's not onscreen."

"No?" Alison shrugged and started wiping the counter again. "The way they're sitting . . . I just assumed."

Aria didn't know what to say. She set the video back to the beginning, confused. She and her friends tried to hack Ali's phone, Ali came back, Melissa and Ian smiled, cinematic shot of Ali's phone, *finis*.

She restarted the movie one more time, this time at half-speed. Spencer slowly readjusted her crown. Ali's cell phone dragged across the screen. Ali came back, every expression languid and contorted. Instead of scurrying past, Melissa plodded. Suddenly, she noticed something in the corner of the screen: the edge of a small, slender hand. Ali's hand. Then came another hand. It was larger and masculine. She slowed down the frame speed. Every so often, the big hand and the little hand bumped each other. Their pinkies intertwined.

Aria gasped.

The camera swung up. It showed Ian, who was looking at something in the distance. Off to the right was Spencer, looking longingly at Ian, not realizing he and Ali were touching. The whole thing happened in a blink. But now that she saw it, it was all so obvious.

Someone wanted something of Ali's. Her killer is closer than you think.

Aria felt sick. They all knew Spencer liked Ian. She talked about him constantly: how her sister didn't deserve him, how he was so funny, how cute he was when he ate dinner at their house. And all of them had wondered if Ali was keeping a big secret—it could have been *this.* Ali must have told Spencer. And Spencer couldn't deal.

Aria put more pieces together. Ali had run out of Spencer's barn . . . and turned up not that far away, in a hole in her own backyard. Spencer knew that the workers were going to fill the hole with concrete the very next day. A's note had said: *You all knew every inch of her backyard. But for one of you, it was so, so easy.*

Aria sat motionless for a few seconds, then picked up her own phone and dialed Emily's number. The phone rang six times before Emily answered. "Hello?" Emily's voice sounded like she'd been crying.

"Did I wake you up?" Aria asked.

"I haven't gone to sleep yet."

Aria frowned. "Are you okay?"

"No," Emily's voice cracked. Aria heard a sniffle. "My parents are sending me away. I'm leaving Rosewood in the morning. Because of A."

Aria leaned back. "*What?* Why?"

"It's not even worth getting into." Emily sounded defeated.

"You have to meet me," Aria said. "Right now."

"Didn't you hear what I said? I'm punished. I'm *beyond* punished."

"You have to." Aria turned into the booth, trying to hide what she was about to say from the diner staff as best she could. "I think I know who killed Ali."

Silence. "No, you don't," Emily said.

"I do. We have to call Hanna."

There was scratching at Emily's end of the phone. After a short pause, her voice came back. "Aria," she whispered, "I'm getting another call. It's *Hanna.*"

A shiver went through Aria. "Put her on three-way."

There was a click, and Aria heard Hanna's voice. "You guys," Hanna was saying. She sounded out of breath and the connection was rumbly, like Hanna was talking through a fan. "You're not going to believe this. A messed up. I mean, I think A messed up. I got this note from this number and I suddenly *knew* whose number it was, and . . ."

In the background, Aria heard a horn honk. "Meet me at our spot," Hanna said. "The Rosewood Day swings."

"Okay," Aria breathed. "Emily, can you come pick me up at the Hollis Diner?"

"Sure," Emily whispered.

"Good," Hanna said. "Hurry."

35

WORDS WHISPERED FROM THE PAST

Spencer shut her eyes. When she opened them, she was standing outside the barn in her backyard. She looked around. Had she been *transported* here? Had she run out here and not remembered?

Suddenly, the barn door swung open and Ali stormed out. "Fine," Ali said over her shoulder, arms swinging confidently. "See ya." She walked right past Spencer, as if Spencer were a ghost.

It was the night Ali went missing again. Spencer started breathing faster. As much as she didn't want to be here, she knew that she needed to see all of this—to remember as much as she could.

"Fine!" she heard herself scream from inside the barn. As Ali stormed down the path, Spencer, younger and smaller, flew to the porch. "Ali!" the thirteen-year-old Spencer screamed, looking around.

Then, it was like the seventeen-year-old Spencer and

the thirteen-year-old Spencer merged into one. She could suddenly feel all the emotions of her younger self. There was fear: What had she done, telling Ali to leave? There was paranoia: None of them had ever challenged Ali. And Ali was angry with her. What was she going to do?

"Ali!" Spencer screamed. The tiny, pagoda-shaped lanterns on the footpath back to the main house provided only a whisper of light. It seemed like things were moving in the woods. Years ago, Melissa had told Spencer that evil trolls lived in the trees. The trolls hated Spencer and wanted to hack off her hair.

Spencer walked to where the path split: She could either go toward her house, or toward the woods that bounded her property. She wished she'd brought a flashlight. A bat swooped out of the trees. As it flew away, Spencer noticed someone far down the path near the woods, hunched over and looking at her cell phone. Ali.

"What are you doing?" Spencer called out.

Ali narrowed her eyes. "I'm going somewhere way cooler than hanging out with you guys."

Spencer stiffened. "Fine," she said proudly. "Go."

Ali sank onto one hip. The crickets chirped at least twenty times before she spoke again. "You try to steal everything away from me. But you can't have this."

"Can't have what?" Spencer shivered in her tissue-thin T-shirt.

Ali laughed nastily. "*You* know."

Spencer blinked. "No . . . I don't."

"Come on. You read about it in my diary, didn't you?"

"I wouldn't read your stupid diary," Spencer spat. "I don't care."

"Right." Ali took a step toward Spencer. "You care way too *much*."

"You're delusional," Spencer sputtered.

"No, I'm not." Ali was right next to her now. "*You* are."

Anger boiled up inside Spencer, and she shoved Ali on the shoulder. It was forceful enough to make Ali stagger back, losing her footing on the path's rocks, which were slippery with dew. The older Spencer winced. She felt like she was a pawn, being dragged along for the ride. A look of surprise crossed Ali's face, but it quickly turned to mocking. "Friends don't shove friends."

"Well, maybe we're not friends," Spencer said.

"Guess not," Ali said. Her eyes danced. The look on her face indicated she had something really juicy to say. There was a long pause before she spoke, as if she was considering her words very, very carefully. *Hang on,* Spencer urged herself. *REMEMBER.*

"You think kissing Ian was so special," Ali growled. "But you know what he told me? That you didn't even know how."

Spencer searched Ali's face. "Ian . . . wait. Ian told you that? When?"

"When we were on our date."

Spencer stared at her.

Ali rolled her eyes. "You're so lame, acting like you don't know we're together. But of course you do, Spence. That's why you liked him, isn't it? Because *I'm* with him? Because your sister's with him?" She shrugged. "The only reason he kissed you the other night was because I asked him to. He didn't want to, but I begged."

Spencer's eyes boggled. *"Why?"*

Ali shrugged. "I wanted to see if he would do *anything* for me." Her face went into a mock pout. "Oh, Spence. Did you really believe he *liked* you?"

Spencer took a step back. Lightning bugs strobed in the sky. There was a poisonous smile on Ali's face. *Don't do it,* Spencer screamed to herself. *Please! It doesn't matter! Don't!*

But it happened anyway. Spencer reached out and pushed Ali as hard as she could. Ali slid backward, her eyes widening in alarm. She fell straight into the stone wall that surrounded the Hastings property. There was a terrible *crack*. Spencer covered her eyes and turned away. The air smelled metallic, like blood. An owl screeched in the trees.

When she took her hands away from her eyes, she was back in her bedroom again, curled up and screaming.

Spencer sat up and checked the clock. It was 2:30 a.m. Her head throbbed. The lights were all still on, she was lying on top of her covers, and she was still wearing her black party dress and Elsa Peretti silver bean necklace. She hadn't washed her face or brushed her hair one hundred times, her typical before-bed rituals. She ran her hands over her arms and legs. There was a purplish bruise on her thigh. She touched it and it ached.

She clapped a hand over her mouth. That memory. She instantly knew all of it was true. Ali was with *Ian*. And she had forgotten all of it. That was the part of the night that was missing.

She walked to her door, but the handle wouldn't turn. Her heart started to pound. "Hello?" she called tentatively. "Is someone there? I'm locked in."

No one answered.

Spencer felt her pulse start to speed up. Something felt really, really wrong. Part of the night surged back to her. The Scrabble game. LIAR SJH. A sending Melissa the Golden Orchid essay. And . . . and then what? She cupped her hands over the crown of her head, as if trying to jostle the memory free. *And then what?*

All at once, she couldn't control her breathing. She started to hyperventilate, sinking to her knees on the ivory carpet. *Calm down,* she told herself, curling into a ball and trying to breathe easily in and out. But it felt like her lungs were filled with Styrofoam peanuts. She felt like she was drowning. "Help!" she cried weakly.

"Spencer?" Her father's voice emerged from the other side of the door. "What's going on?"

Spencer jumped up and ran to the door. "Daddy? I'm locked in! Let me out!"

"Spencer, you're in there for your own good. You scared us."

"Scared you?" Spencer asked. "H-How?" She stared at her reflection in the mirror on the back of her bedroom door. Yes, it was still her. She hadn't woken up in someone else's life.

"We've taken Melissa to the hospital," her father said.

Spencer suddenly lost equilibrium. *Melissa? Hospital? Why?* She shut her eyes and saw a flash of Melissa falling away from her, down the stairs. Or was that Ali falling? Spencer's hands shook. She couldn't *remember*. "Is Melissa all right?"

"We hope so. Stay there," her father said from outside the door, sounding wary. Perhaps he was afraid of her—perhaps that was why he wasn't coming in.

She sat on her bed, stunned, for a long time. How could she not have remembered this? How could she not remember hurting Melissa? What if she did lots of horrible things and, in the next second, erased them?

Ali's murderer is right in front of you, A had said. Just when Spencer was looking in the mirror. Could it be?

Her cell phone, which was sitting on her desk, began to ring. Spencer stood up slowly and looked at the screen on her phone. *Hanna.*

Spencer opened her phone. She pressed her ear to the receiver.

"Spencer?" Hanna jumped right in. "I know something. You have to meet me."

Spencer's stomach tightened and her mind whirled. *Ali's killer is right in front of you.* She killed Ali. She *didn't* kill Ali. It was like pulling petals off a flower: *He loves me, he loves me not.* Perhaps she could meet Hanna and . . . and what? Confess?

No. It couldn't be true. Ali had turned up in a hole in her backyard . . . not on the path against the stone wall. Spencer couldn't have carried Ali to her backyard. She wasn't strong enough, right? She wanted to tell someone about this. Hanna. And Emily. Aria, too. They would tell her she was imagining things, that she *couldn't* have killed Ali.

"Okay," Spencer croaked. "Where?"

"At the Rosewood Day Elementary swings. Our place. Get there as fast as you can."

Spencer looked around. She could hoist up her window and shimmy down the face of her house—it would be practically as easy as climbing the rock wall at her gym.

"All right," she whispered. "I'll be right there."

36

IT WILL ALL BE OVER

Hanna's hands were shaking so badly, she could barely drive. The road to the Rosewood Day Elementary School swings seemed darker and spookier than usual. She swerved, thinking she saw something darting out in front of her car, but when she glanced in her rearview mirror, there was nothing. Barely any cars passed her going the other direction, but all of a sudden, as she was cresting a hill not far from Rosewood Day, a car pulled out behind her. Its headlights felt hot against the back of Hanna's head.

Calm down, she thought. *It's not following you.*

Her brain whirled. She *knew* who A was. But . . . how? How was it possible that A knew so much about Hanna . . . things A couldn't possibly know? Perhaps the text had been a mistake. Perhaps A had gotten hold of someone else's cell phone to throw Hanna off the trail.

Hanna was too shocked to think about it carefully. The only thought that cycled in a continuous loop in her brain was: *This makes no sense. This makes no sense.*

She glanced in her rearview mirror. The car was *still there.* She took a deep breath and eyed her phone, considering calling someone. Officer Wilden? Would he come down here on such short notice? He was a cop—he'd have to. She reached for her phone, when the car behind her flashed its brights. Should she pull over? Should she stop?

Hanna's finger was poised over her cell, ready to dial 911. And then, suddenly, the car veered around Hanna and passed her on the left. It was a nondescript car—maybe a Toyota—and Hanna couldn't see the driver inside. The car moved back into her lane, then sped off into the distance. Within seconds, its taillights vanished.

The Rosewood Day Elementary playground's parking lot was wide and deep, separated by a bunch of little landscaped islands, which were full of nearly bare trees, spiny grass, and piles of crisp leaves that gave off that signature leaf-pile smell. Beyond the lot were the jungle gym and climbing dome. They were illuminated by a single fluorescent light, which made them look like skeletons. Hanna slid into a space at the southeast corner of the lot—it was the closest to the park information booth and a police call box. Just being near something that said *Police* made her feel better. The others weren't here yet, so she watched the entrance for any cars.

It was nearly 3 a.m. Hanna shivered in Lucas's sweatshirt. She felt goose bumps form on her bare legs. She'd read once that at 3 a.m., people were in their deepest stages of REM sleep—it was the closest they would come every day to being dead. Which meant that right now, she couldn't rely on too many of Rosewood's inhabitants to help her. They were all corpses. And it was so quiet, she could hear the car's engine winding down and her slow, please-stay-calm breathing. Hanna opened her car door and stood outside it on the yellow line that marked her parking space. It was like her magic circle. Inside it, she was safe.

They'll be here soon, she told herself. In a few minutes, this would all be over. Not that Hanna had any idea what was going to *happen.* She wasn't sure. She hadn't thought that far ahead.

A light appeared at the school's entrance and Hanna's heart lifted. An SUV's headlights slid across the trees and turned slowly into the parking lot. Hanna squinted. Was that them? "Hello?" she called softly.

The SUV hugged the north end of the parking lot, passing the high school art building and the student lot and the hockey fields. Hanna started waving her arms. It had to be Emily and Aria. But the car's windows were tinted.

"Hello?" she yelled again. She got no answer. Then

she saw another car turn into the lot and drive slowly toward her. Aria's head was hanging out the passenger window. Sweet, refreshing relief flooded Hanna's body. She waved and started toward them. First she walked, then she jogged. Then sprinted.

She was in the middle of the lot when Aria called, "Hanna, look out!" Hanna turned her head to the left and her mouth fell open, at first not understanding. The SUV was headed straight for her.

The tires squealed. She smelled burnt rubber. Hanna froze, not sure what to do. "Wait!" she heard herself say, staring into the SUV's tinted window. The car kept coming, faster and faster. *Move,* she told her limbs, but they seemed hardened and dried out, like cacti.

"Hanna!" Emily cried. "Oh my God!"

It only took a second. Hanna didn't even realize she'd been hit until she was in the air, and she didn't realize she was in the air until she was on the pavement. Something in her cracked. And then pain. She wanted to cry out, but she couldn't. Sound was amplified—the car's engine roared, her friends' screams were like sirens, even her heart pumping blood sounded wet in her ears.

Hanna rolled her neck to the side. Her tiny, champagne-colored clutch had landed a few feet away; its contents had sprung out like candy from a burst piñata. The car had run over everything, too: her mascara, her car keys, her mini bottle of Chloé perfume. Her brand-new iPhone was crushed.

"Hanna!" Aria screamed. It sounded like she was coming closer. But Hanna wasn't able to turn her head to look. And then it all faded away.

37

IT WAS NECESSARY

"Oh my God!" Aria screamed. She and Emily crouched down at Hanna's contorted body and started yelling. "Hanna! Oh my God! *Hanna!*"

"She's not breathing," Emily wailed. "Aria, she's not *breathing!*"

"Do you have your cell?" Aria asked. "Call 911."

Emily reached shakily for her phone, but it slid out of her hands and skidded across the parking lot, coming to a stop by Hanna's exploded evening bag. Emily had begun panicking when she picked Aria up and Aria told her everything—about A's cryptic notes, about her dreams, about Ali and Ian, and about how Spencer must have killed Ali.

At first, Emily had refused to believe it, but then a feeling of horror and realization washed over her. She explained that not long before Ali went missing, Ali had confessed that she was seeing someone.

"And she must have told Spencer," Aria had answered.

"Maybe that's what they'd been fighting about all those months before the end of school."

"911, what's your emergency?" Aria heard a voice say on Emily's speakerphone.

"A car just hit my friend!" Emily wailed. "I'm in the Rosewood Day School parking lot! We don't know what to do!"

As Emily cried out the details, Aria put her mouth against Hanna's lips and tried to give her mouth-to-mouth like she'd learned in lifeguarding class in Iceland. But she didn't know if she was doing it correctly. "C'mon, Hanna, breathe," she wailed, pinching Hanna's nose.

"Just stay on the line until the ambulance gets there," Aria could hear the 911 dispatcher's voice say through Emily's phone. Emily leaned down and reached out to touch Hanna's faded Rosewood Day sweatshirt. Then she pulled back, as if she was afraid. "Oh my God, please don't die. . . ." She glanced at Aria. "Who could have done this?"

Aria looked around. The swings swayed back and forth in the breeze. The flags on the flagpole fluttered. The woods adjacent to the playground were black and thick. Suddenly, Aria saw a figure standing next to one of the trees. She had dirty-blond hair and wore a short black dress. Something in her face looked wild and unhinged. She was staring right at Aria, and Aria took a step back across the pavement. *Spencer.*

"Look!" Aria hissed, pointing to the trees. But just

as Emily raised her head, Spencer disappeared into the shadows.

The buzzing startled her. It took Aria a moment to realize it was her cell phone. Then Emily's Call Waiting lit up. One new text message, Emily's screen said. Aria and Emily exchanged a familiar, uneasy look. Slowly, Aria brought her phone out of her bag and looked at the screen. Emily leaned over to look, too.

"Oh no," Emily whispered.

The wind abruptly stopped. The trees stood still like statues. Sirens wailed in the distance.

"Please, no," Emily wailed. The text was only four chilling words long.

She knew too much. —A

ACKNOWLEDGMENTS

Perfect was the toughest *Pretty Little Liars* book to date, because there were so many pieces that had to fit in exactly the right places to make everything work. So I want to thank all of the careful readers, plotters, chart-makers, word arrangers, and other brilliant people who helped in the process: Josh Bank and Les Morgenstern, who saw *Perfect* through its early stages, spending days with me hashing out how exactly Spencer should go mad. I'm very grateful to have you guys on my side. The wonderful people at HarperCollins, Elise Howard and Farrin Jacobs, who puzzled over many drafts, catching all kinds of things I constantly missed. Alloy's Lanie Davis, who drew brilliant charts, was on-call whenever, wherever, and remained an unflagging fan. And, last but not least, my patient, incredibly competent and wonderfully innovative editors—Sara Shandler at Alloy and Kristin Marang at HarperCollins—whose hard work helped to really snap this book into focus. I appreciate all of you for knowing these characters so well, loving this series as much as I do, and really believing in its success. We truly are Team *Pretty Little Liars*, and I propose we start a bowling team, or perhaps a synchronized swimming team, or perhaps we could all just wear matching Lacoste polo shirts.

Many thanks and much love to Nikki Chaiken for professional advice on early drafts about Spencer and Dr. Evans. Love to my wonderful husband, Joel, for his research on what sort of plane would be used to write messages in the sky and the physics of what happens to cars when they crash into each other, and who continues to read all the drafts of this book—amazing! Love also to my wonderful friends and readers, including my fabulous parents, Shep and Mindy (no swanky bar that serves red wine would be complete without either of you), my sweet and loyal cousin Colleen (no swanky bar would be complete without you, either), and my good friend Andrew Zaeh, who texted me as soon as he stepped off a plane to tell me that someone was reading *Pretty Little Liars*, 20,000 feet up. And thanks to all who have reached out so far with your thoughts and questions about the series. It's great to hear you're out there. You guys are part of Team Pretty Little Liars, too.

And thanks to the zany girl this book is dedicated to—my sister, Ali! Because she's nothing like the Alison in this book, because we can still go on for hours about the magical, fictitious world of pelicans, owls, and square-headed creatures we made up when we were six, because she doesn't get mad when I accidentally wear her $380 Rock and Republics, and because tattoos look very nice on the back of her neck—even though I think she should've gone with a certain man's face and a huge eagle tattooed there instead. Ali is quality with a capital _Q_, and the best sister anyone could ask for.

Oooops! So I made one teensy tiny slip-up. It happens.
I've got a busy life, things to do, people to torture. Like four
pretty little ex-best friends.

Yeah, yeah. I know you're upset about Hanna. Wah.
Get over it. I'm already planning my outfit for her funeral:
appropriately somber with a touch of flash. Don't you think
little Hannakins would want us to mourn in style? But
maybe I'm getting ahead of myself—Hanna *does* have a
history of rising from the dead. . . .

Meanwhile, Aria just can't catch a break. Her soul-
mate's in jail. Sean hates her. She's homeless. What's a girl
to do? Looks like it's time for a life makeover—new house,
new friends, maybe even a new name. But watch out,
Aria—even if your new BFF is blind to your real identity,
I've got 20/20 vision. And you know I can't keep a secret.

I wonder how CONVICT is going to look next to CLASS
VP on Spencer's college apps? Seems like Little Miss
Golden Orchid is about to trade her kelly-green Lacoste
polo for a scratchy orange jumpsuit. Then again, Spence

wouldn't have that perfect GPA if she didn't have a few tricks up her sleeve—like, say, finding someone *else* to blame for Ali's murder. But know what? She just might be right.

What about Emily, off to live with her wholesome, Cheerios-eating cousins in Iowa? Hey, maybe it won't be so bad—she'll be a girl-loving needle in a big old sexually repressed haystack, far, far away from my prying eyes. As if! She's gonna go haywire when she realizes she can't hide from me. *Yeee-haw!*

And finally, with Hanna out of commission, it's time for me to take on a new victim. Who, you ask? Well, nosypants, I'm still deciding. It's not like it'll be hard: *Everyone* in this town has something to hide. In fact, there's something even juicier than the identity of moi bubbling beneath Rosewood's glistening surface. Something so shocking, you wouldn't believe me if I told you. So I won't even bother. HA. You know, I kind of love being me. . . .

Buckle up, girlies. *Nothing* is as it seems.

Mwah!

—A

READ ON FOR A PREVIEW OF
PRETTY LITTLE LIARS BOOK FOUR.

FROM

EVER WISH YOU COULD GO back in time and undo your mistakes? If only you hadn't drawn that clown face on the doll your best friend got for her eighth birthday, she wouldn't have dropped you for the new girl from Boston. And back in ninth grade, you would never have skipped soccer practice to hit the beach if you'd known Coach would bench you for the rest of the season. If only you hadn't made those bad choices, maybe your ex-BFF would have given you that extra front-row ticket to Marc Jacobs's fashion show. Or maybe you'd be playing goalie for the women's national soccer team by now, with a Nike modeling contract and a beach house in Nice. You could be jet-setting around the Mediterranean instead of sitting in geography class, trying to find it on a map.

In Rosewood, fantasies about reversing fate are as common as girls receiving Tiffany heart pendants for their thirteenth birthdays. And four former best friends would do anything to travel back in time and make things right. But what if they really could go back? Would they be able to keep their fifth best friend alive . . . or is her tragedy part of their destiny?

Sometimes the past holds more questions than answers. And in Rosewood, nothing is *ever* what it seems.

"She's going to be so psyched when I tell her," Spencer Hastings said to her best friends Hanna Marin, Emily Fields, and Aria Montgomery. She straightened her sea-green eyelet T-shirt and pressed Alison DiLaurentis's doorbell.

"Why do *you* get to tell her?" Hanna asked as she hopped from the porch step to the sidewalk and back again. Ever since Alison, their fifth best friend, had told Hanna that only fidgety girls stayed thin, Hanna had been making a lot of extra movements.

"Maybe we should all tell her at the same time," Aria suggested, scratching the temporary dragonfly tattoo she'd pasted on her collarbone.

"That would be fun." Emily pushed her blunt-cut, reddish-blond hair behind her ears. "We could do a choreographed dance and say, 'Ta-da!' at the end."

"No way." Spencer squared her shoulders. "It's my barn—*I* get to tell her." She rang the DiLaurentises' doorbell again.

As they waited, the girls listened to the buzz of the landscapers pruning Spencer's hedges next door and the *thwock-thwock* of the Fairfield twins playing tennis on their backyard court two houses down. The air smelled like lilacs, mown grass, and Neutrogena sunscreen. It was a typical idyllic Rosewood moment—everything about the town was pretty, and that included its sounds, smells, and inhabitants. The girls had lived in Rosewood nearly all their lives, and they felt lucky to be part of such a special place.

They loved Rosewood summers best of all. Tomorrow morning, after they completed their last seventh-grade final at Rosewood Day, the school they all attended, they would take part in the school's annual graduation-pin ceremony. One by one Principal Appleton would call each student's name, from kindergarten through eleventh grade, and each student would receive a twenty-four-karat gold pin. After that, they would be released for ten glorious weeks of tanning, cookouts, boating trips, and shopping excursions to Philly and New York. They couldn't *wait*.

But the graduation ceremony wasn't the true rite of passage for Ali, Aria, Spencer, Emily, and Hanna. Summer wouldn't really start for them until tomorrow night, at their end-of-seventh-grade slumber party. And the girls had a surprise for Ali that was going to make this summer's kickoff extra special.

When the DiLaurentises' front door was finally flung open, Mrs. DiLaurentis stood before them, wearing a short pale pink wrap dress that showed off her long, muscular, tanned calves. "Hello, girls," she said coolly.

"Is Ali here?" Spencer asked.

"She's upstairs, I think." Mrs. DiLaurentis stepped out of the way. "Go on up."

Spencer led the group through the hall, her white pleated field hockey skirt swinging, her dirty-blond braid bouncing against the middle of her back. The girls loved Ali's house—it smelled like vanilla and fabric softener, just like Ali. Lush photographs of past DiLaurentis trips to Paris, Lisbon, and Lake Como lined the walls. There were plenty of photos of Ali and her brother, Jason, from grade school on. The girls especially loved Ali's second-grade school picture. Ali's vibrant pink cardigan made her whole face glow. Back then, Ali's family had lived in Connecticut, and Ali's old private school hadn't required her to wear stuffy blue blazers for yearbook pictures like Rosewood Day did. Even as an eight-year-old, Ali was irresistibly cute—she had clear blue eyes, a heart-shaped face, adorable dimples, and a naughty-yet-charming expression, which made it impossible to stay mad at her.

Spencer touched the bottom-right corner of their favorite photo, the one of the five of them camping in the Poconos the previous July. They were all standing next to a giant canoe, drenched in murky lake water, grinning from ear to ear, as happy as five twelve-year-old best friends could be. Aria put her hand on top of Spencer's, Emily put her hand on top of Aria's, and Hanna piled her hand on last. They closed their eyes for a split second, hummed, and broke away. The girls had started the photo-touching habit when the picture first went up, a memento of their first summer of best-friendship. They couldn't believe that Ali, *the* girl of Rosewood Day, had chosen the four of them as her inner circle. It was a little like being joined at the hip with an A-list celebrity.

But admitting that would be . . . well, lame. Especially now.

As they passed the living room, they noticed two graduation robes hanging on the knob of a French door. The white one was Ali's, and the more official-looking navy one was Jason's, who would be going on to Yale in the fall. The girls clasped their hands, excited to put on their own graduation gowns and berets, which Rosewood Day graduates had worn ever since the school had opened in 1897. Just then, they noticed a movement in the living room. Jason was sitting in the leather love seat, staring blankly at CNN.

"Heeyyy, Jason," Spencer called, waving. "Are you *so* psyched for tomorrow?"

Jason glanced at them. He was the hot boy version of Ali, with buttery blond hair and stunning blue eyes. He smirked and went back to the TV without saying a word.

"Oh-kaay," the girls all murmured in unison. Jason had his hilarious side—he was the one who had invented the "not it" game with his friends. The girls had borrowed and reinvented the game for their own uses, which mostly meant making fun of nerdier girls in their presence. But Jason definitely got into funks, too. Ali called them his Elliott Smith moods, after the morose singer-songwriter he liked. Only, Jason certainly didn't have any reason to be upset now—by this time tomorrow, he'd be on a plane to Costa Rica to teach adventure kayaking all summer. Boo-hoo.

"Whatever." Aria shrugged. The four girls turned and bounced up the stairs to Ali's room. As they reached the landing, they noticed that Ali's door was closed. Spencer frowned. Emily cocked her head. Inside the room, Ali let out a giggle.

Hanna gently pushed the door open. Ali had her back to them. Her hair was up in a high ponytail, and she'd tied her striped silk halter top in a perfect bow at her neck. She stared down at the open notebook in her lap, completely entranced.

Spencer cleared her throat, and Ali whirled around, startled. "Guys, hi!" she cried. "What's up?"

"Not much." Hanna pointed at the notebook in Ali's lap. "What's that?"

Ali closed the notebook fast. "Oh. Nothing."

The girls felt a presence behind them. Mrs. DiLaurentis pushed past, waltzing into Ali's bedroom. "We need to talk," she said to Ali, her voice clipped and taut.

"But, Mom . . ." Ali protested.

"Now."

The girls glanced at one another. That was Mrs. DiLaurentis's you're-in-trouble voice. They didn't hear it often.

Ali's mother faced the girls. "Why don't you girls wait on the deck?"

"It'll just take a second," Ali said quickly, shooting them an apologetic smile. "I'll be right down."

Hanna paused, confused. Spencer squinted, trying to see what book Ali was holding. Mrs. DiLaurentis raised an eyebrow. "C'mon, girls. Go."

The four of them swallowed hard and filed back down the stairs. Once on Ali's wraparound porch, they arranged themselves in their usual places around the family's enormous square patio table—Spencer at one end, and Aria, Emily, and Hanna at the sides. Ali would sit at the table's head, next to her father's deck-mounted stone birdbath. For a moment, the four girls watched as a couple of cardinals frolicked in the bath's cold, clear water. When a blue jay tried to join them, the cardinals squawked and quickly sent him away. Birds, it seemed, were just as cliquey as girls.

"That was weird upstairs," Aria whispered.

"Do you think Ali's in trouble?" Hanna whispered. "What if she's grounded and can't come to the sleepover?"

"Why would she be in trouble? She hasn't done anything wrong," whispered Emily, who always stuck up for Ali—the girls called her Killer, as in Ali's personal guard dog.

"Not that *we* know of," Spencer muttered under her breath.

Just then, Mrs. DiLaurentis burst out of the French patio doors and across the lawn. "I want to make sure you have the dimensions right," she screamed to the workers who were perched lazily on an enormous bulldozer at the back of the property. The DiLaurentises were building a twenty-person gazebo for summer parties, and Ali had mentioned that her mom was being very type A about the whole process, even though they were only at the hole-digging stage. Mrs. DiLaurentis marched up to the workers and started chastising them. Her diamond wedding ring glinted in the sun as she waved her arms around frenetically. The girls exchanged glances—it looked like Ali's lecture hadn't taken very long.

"Guys?"

Ali stood at the edge of the porch. She had changed out of her halter into a faded navy blue Abercrombie tee. There was a baffled look on her face. "Uh . . . hi?"

Spencer stood up. "What did she bust you for?"

Ali blinked. Her eyes darted back and forth.

"Were you getting in trouble *without* us?" Aria cried, trying to make it sound like she was teasing. "And why'd you change? That halter you had on was so cute."

Ali still looked flustered . . . and kind of upset. Emily stood up halfway. "Do you want us to . . . go?" Her voice dripped with uncertainty. All the others looked at Ali nervously—was *that* what she wanted?

Ali twisted her blue string bracelet around her wrist three full rotations. She stepped onto the patio and sat down in her rightful seat. "Of course I don't want you to go. My mom was mad at me because I . . . I threw my hockey clothes in with her delicates again." She gave them a sheepish shrug and rolled her eyes.

Emily stuck out her bottom lip. A small beat went by. "She got mad at you for *that*?"

Ali raised her eyebrows. "You know my mom, Em. She's more anal than Spencer." She snickered.

Spencer faux-glared at Ali while Emily ran her thumb along one of the grooves in the teak patio table.

"But don't worry, girls, I'm not grounded or anything." Ali pressed her palms together. "Our sleepover extravaganza can proceed as planned!"

The four of them sighed with relief, and the odd, uneasy mood began to evaporate. Only, each of them had a weird feeling Ali wasn't telling them everything—it certainly wouldn't be the first time. One minute, Ali would be their best friend, and the next, she'd drift away from them, making covert phone calls and sending secret texts. Weren't they supposed to share everything? The other girls had certainly shared enough of themselves— they'd slipped secrets to Ali that no one, absolutely *no one* else, knew. And, of course, there was the big secret that they all shared about Jenna Cavanaugh—the one they'd sworn to take to the grave.

"Speaking of our sleepover extravaganza, I have huge news," Spencer said, breaking them out of their thoughts. "Guess where we're having it?"

"Where?" Ali leaned forward on her elbows, slowly morphing back into her old self.

"Melissa's barn!" Spencer cried. Melissa was Spencer's older sister, and Mr. and Mrs. Hastings had renovated the family's backyard barn and allowed Melissa to use it as her own personal pied-à-terre during her junior and senior years of high school. Spencer would get the same privilege, once she was old enough.

"Sweet!" Ali whooped. "How?"

"She's flying out to Prague tomorrow night after graduation," Spencer answered. "My parents said we could use it, so long as we clean it up before she gets back."

"Nice." Ali leaned back and laced her hands together. Suddenly, her eyes focused on something a bit to the left of the workers. Melissa herself was traipsing through the Hastingses' bordering yard, her posture rigid and proper. Her white graduation gown swung from a hanger in her hand, and she'd slung the school's royal blue valedictorian mantle over her shoulders.

Spencer let out a groan. "She's being so obnoxious about the whole valedictorian thing," she whispered. "She even told me I should feel grateful that Andrew Campbell will probably be valedictorian instead of me when we're all seniors—the honor is '*such* a huge responsibility.'" Spencer and her sister hated each other, and Spencer had a new story about Melissa's bitchiness nearly every day.

Ali stood up. "Hey! Melissa!" She started waving.

Melissa stopped and turned around. "Oh. Hey, guys." She smiled cautiously.

"Excited to go to Prague?" Ali singsonged, giving Melissa her brightest smile.

Melissa tilted her head slightly. "Of course."

"Is *Ian* going?" Ian was Melissa's gorgeous boyfriend. Just thinking about him made the girls swoon.

Spencer dug her nails into Ali's arm. *"Ali."* But Ali pulled her arm away.

Melissa shaded her eyes in the harsh sunlight. The royal blue mantle flapped in the wind. "No. He's not."

"Oh!" Ali simpered. "Are you sure that's a good idea—leaving him alone for two weeks? He might get another girlfriend!"

"Alison," Spencer said through her teeth. "Stop it. *Now.*"

"Spencer?" Emily whispered. "What's going on?"

"Nothing," Spencer said quickly. Aria, Emily, and Hanna looked at one another again. This had been happening lately—Ali would say something, one of them would freak, and the rest of them would have no clue what was going on.

But this clearly wasn't nothing. Melissa straightened the mantle around her neck, squared her shoulders, and turned. She looked long and hard at the giant hole at the edge of the DiLaurentises' yard, then walked into the barn, slamming the door behind her so hard that it made the twig-braided wreath on the back of the door thump up and down.

"Something's certainly up *her* butt," Ali said. "I was just kidding, after all." Spencer made a little whimpering noise at the back of her throat, and Ali started giggling. She had a faint smile on her face. It was the same smile Ali gave them whenever she dangled a secret over one of their heads, taunting that she could tell the others if she wanted to.

"Anyway, who cares?" Ali gazed at each of them, her eyes bright. "You know what, girls?" She drummed her fingers excitedly on the table. "I think this is going to be the Summer of Ali. The Summer of *All* of Us. I can just feel it. Can't you?"

A stunned moment passed. It seemed like a humid cloud hung above them, fogging up their thoughts. But slowly, the clouds faded and an idea formed in each of their minds. Maybe Ali was right. This *could* be the best summer of their lives. They could turn their friendship around and make it as strong as it had been last summer. They could forget all the scary, scandalous things that had happened and just start over.

"I can feel it, too," Hanna said loudly.

"Definitely," Aria and Emily said at the same time.

"Sure," Spencer said softly.

They all grabbed hands and squeezed hard.

It rained that night, a hard, pounding rain that made puddles in driveways, watered gardens, and created little mini pools on top of the Hastingses' swimming pool cover. When the rain stopped in the middle of the night, Aria, Emily, Spencer, and Hanna awakened and sat up in bed at almost the exact same moment. A foreboding feeling had settled over each of them. They didn't know if it was from something they'd just dreamed about, or excitement about the next day. Or maybe it was due to something else entirely . . . something far deeper.

They each looked out their windows onto Rosewood's tranquil, empty streets. The clouds had shifted and all the stars had come out. The pavement shone from the rain. Hanna stared at her driveway—only her mother's car was there now. Her father had moved out. Emily looked at her backyard and the forest beyond it. She'd never braved those woods—she'd heard ghosts lived in them. Aria listened to the sounds emanating from her parents' bedroom, wondering if they'd woken up, too—or perhaps they were fighting again and hadn't fallen asleep yet. Spencer gazed at the DiLaurentises' back porch, then across their yard to the huge hole the workers had dug for the gazebo's foundation. The rain had turned some of the dug-up dirt to mud. Spencer thought about all the things in her life that made her angry. Then she thought about all the things in her life she wanted to have—and all the things she wanted to change.

Spencer reached under her bed, found her red flashlight, and shone it into Ali's window. One flash, two flashes, three flashes. This was her secret code to Ali that she wanted to sneak out and talk in person. She thought she saw Ali's blond head sitting up in bed too, but Ali didn't flash back.

All four of them fell back onto their pillows, telling themselves that the feeling was nothing and they needed their sleep. In twenty-four short hours, they'd be at the end of their seventh-grade sleepover, the first night of summer. The summer that would change everything.

How right they were.